THE TOYMAKER'S CURSE

GLASS AND STEELE, #11

C.J. ARCHER

CHAPTER 1

LONDON, WINTER 1891

"That Mason woman needs a thorough talking to," Aunt Letitia said in her most imperial voice. "And you, India, must be the one to do it."

I looked up from the deck of cards I'd been shuffling and shook my head. "I won't interfere unless Cyclops wants me to." I eyed him where he sprawled in an armchair by the fireplace, his long legs outstretched and a thin instruction book on the topic of policing loosely clasped in one hand. I thought him asleep until his eye cracked open.

"Nobody can change Mrs. Mason's opinion of me except me," he said.

"Maybe not even you," Duke muttered from where he sprawled in an almost identical manner to Cyclops in the armchair positioned on the opposite side of the fireplace.

I glared at him.

He shrugged an apology. "I'm just saying she might be one of those people who never see reason because they're blinded by their prejudice."

"Mrs. Mason isn't like that," I said. "She can't be or she wouldn't have brought up such a kind, considerate and open-minded daughter as Catherine."

1

Cyclops brightened at my response after deflating upon hearing Duke's statement. "I reckon you're right, India."

"She usually is," Matt said from behind the newspaper he'd been reading, proving he'd been listening to our conversation despite appearances suggesting otherwise.

The only one missing from our quiet evening was Willie, which probably explained why the evening was quiet. She'd joined Lord Farnsworth for a night of card playing at a gambling den. They might never frequent that venue again after tonight, however. Lord Farnsworth had lost a wager on Christmas Day to Willie and had to wear a dress. No doubt he'd be too embarrassed to face the other gamblers again.

Cyclops, suppressing a yawn, set the book on the occasional table nearest his chair. "I'm going to bed."

"You don't want to hear how Willie's night with Farnsworth went?" Duke asked.

"Not enough to stay up. I've had to work all day, unlike some who've lazed about here, drinking tea and eating cake."

Duke opened his mouth to protest but quickly shut it again. He couldn't argue the point. He'd done very little today, whereas Cyclops had been performing drills as part of his police training. He was two days into the three-week course and had come home tired both nights from the drills and lectures.

Once Cyclops departed, Aunt Letitia asked for the cards. "Matthew, Duke, we need you for a game of whist." She indicated the spare chairs.

Duke dutifully joined us but Matt murmured a distracted, "In a moment."

"What has you so engrossed over there?" I asked.

"Electricity." He folded the newspaper and indicated the article about the newly opened City and South London Railway, the first deep underground railway and the first to use trains powered by electricity. "One day every home in the country will be powered by electricity, not just the street-lights, some trains, and a few public spaces."

"But it's so expensive."

"To convert the whole house, yes, and it'll be some years before it's affordable to everyone, but I think it's worth investing in now. I'll speak to my man of business tomorrow. Duke, do you want to invest in an electric lighting company?"

Duke shook his head. "I ain't got nothing to invest. Cyclops might. He's better at saving than me."

"And he has a future wife and family to think about," I added with a smile for Aunt Letitia.

She, however, was staring at Matt with something akin to horror. "You are *not* going to install electricity in this house, Matthew."

"One day," he said. "It's inevitable."

"It's much too dangerous!"

"Actually it's safer than gas if installed properly."

"If every home gets electricity we'll be overshadowed by wires." She dubiously eyed the ceiling rose above us. "Not to mention the illness caused by leaking electricity."

"There's no proof of that, Aunt."

She didn't look convinced but dealt the cards anyway and mercifully didn't mention electricity again. Nor did Matt, wisely.

We played for a mere half hour before Willie returned home with Lord Farnsworth in tow. The dandy was dressed in an ill-fitting gown of russet silk with brown fur sewn into a diamond pattern on the skirt and trimmed with more fur at the collar and cuff. It was the most hideous dress I'd ever seen and I burst out laughing at the sight of it.

Lord Farnsworth sashayed into the sitting room with all the elegance of a debutante showing off the swish of her hemline. "It is rather ghastly, isn't it?" he said as he looked down at the dress.

"It wouldn't be so bad on a woman," Duke told him.

Willie snorted. "You think all women look good."

"That's because all women do. In a dress," he added with a pointed glance at her buckskin trousers.

Willie poked her tongue out at him and strode to the drinks trolley where she poured two glasses of brandy.

"I think you make a very pretty woman, my lord," Aunt Letitia said. "Doesn't he, Willemina?"

Willie handed one of the tumblers to Lord Farnsworth. "He would if he wore a wig and shaved. I reckon he's been growing the fluff on his face just for tonight so no one would mistake him for a woman."

"It's called a beard, Willie." Lord Farnsworth sat in one of the armchairs by the fire and flattened a hand over the silk skirt. "And I grew it because I felt like growing it." He rubbed a hand over the patchy red-gold hairs that couldn't quite be called a proper beard yet. "I think it makes me look even more handsome."

"It certainly does," Aunt Letitia said. "Very handsome indeed."

"He can't be pretty *and* handsome." Willie threw herself into the other armchair, somehow managing not to spill a drop from her glass. "Anyway, I reckon the beard was a nice touch. You should have seen everyone's faces and heard their lewd comments." She chuckled into her tumbler. "He even got a proposition, and I reckon it was a real one, too. The fellow was blind drunk and thought Farnsworth was the bearded lady escaped from the fair."

Lord Farnsworth sank into the armchair, his legs spread wide beneath the skirts. "He was just having a lark."

"He kept trying to look down your bodice."

Aunt Letitia clicked her tongue. "That's enough of that talk, Willemina. You're not in America anymore. We don't talk like that here in England."

"Not in drawing rooms, but the English are just as vulgar

as we Americans if you go to the right places. Maybe even more so."

"Last time I looked, this was a drawing room, so stop it. Lord Farnsworth has had a rather trying evening, thanks to you. It's time you let him enjoy some peace and quiet." Her tight smile softened as she turned to Lord Farnsworth. "Perhaps you'd like to change into more suitable clothing then join us for a game of whist. Duke will give up his seat, won't you, Duke? And perhaps India can give hers up for Willemina."

Duke dutifully rose, but I merely eyed Aunt Letitia with a narrowed gaze. This wasn't the first time she'd tried to keep Lord Farnsworth and Willie in close proximity to one another.

"I ain't playing whist," Willie declared. "Not unless there's money on the table."

"You know we don't gamble with real money in this household," Aunt Letitia said.

"I'll decline too, dear Miss Glass," Lord Farnsworth said. "This place by the fire will do me well for a while." To prove his point, he stretched out his legs and sighed with contentment.

"If you want to change clothes, I can send for Bristow," Matt told him.

Lord Farnsworth held up a hand. "Thanks, but I didn't bring a change and your clothing won't fit. You've got an inch or two on me."

Willie barked a laugh only to wince when Duke smacked her shoulder to shut her up.

Aunt Letitia looked pained at the spectacle they were making of themselves in front of a nobleman. No matter how ridiculous Lord Farnsworth acted, he was still an earl, and she'd always think him above the rest of us, including her own brother, a baron. "Duke, come back and rejoin us. Let his lordship and Willemina have some privacy."

It was Willie's turn to narrow her gaze at Aunt Letitia.

Duke sat again, seemingly unaware that Aunt Letitia was trying to get him out of the way so that Lord Farnsworth and Willie could form a deeper understanding. It was such a ridiculous notion that I almost allowed a bubble of laughter to escape. I managed to limit it to a smile, however, and only Willie noticed.

She gave me a knowing smile in response. Curiously, she did not seem appalled or amused. Surely she wasn't giving it serious consideration?

I spent the next hour watching them to see if Aunt Letitia's plan had merit and there was something more than friendship between Lord Farnsworth and Willie. I was so determined to spot even the smallest sign of flirting that I forgot to concentrate.

"You're a terrible whist partner, India," Duke said as we lost another game.

Matt gathered up the cards and glanced over his shoulder. "She's distracted by Farnsworth in a dress."

Lord Farnsworth, who'd been nodding off by the fire, roused with a snuffle upon hearing his name. "I say, is that the time? I'd better head off. I need my beauty sleep if I'm to look my best for my future wife."

We all stared at him, even Willie. This was news to her too.

"You're getting married?" I asked.

"Possibly. If I like her. I'm not one of these fellows who can wed a lady if she looks like a horse and has the character of a donkey." He chuckled. "No matter if she's the daughter of a duke and as rich as the queen."

"Is she either of those?"

"No. Her father is a moderately wealthy viscount. The girl will be making an excellent match if she manages to catch me." He rocked back on his heels. He was either quite pleased with himself or a little drunk.

"What if *she* doesn't like *you*?" Willie asked.

"Of course she'll like me. Everybody does. I'm quite

6

possibly the most liked peer in all the realm. And I'm handsome, of course."

"What woman could resist?" Duke asked with a large dose of sarcasm in his tone.

Lord Farnsworth pointed his finger at Duke. "Precisely."

Matt rolled his eyes, threw his hands in the air, and pushed up from the chair. "I'll walk you out."

Lord Farnsworth gave his leave and they left together.

"Such a shame he's getting married," Aunt Letitia said on a sigh.

"Why?" Duke asked. "A gentleman with a large fortune's got to get married and have heirs. You know it better than anyone."

"Yes, but I hoped he'd consider marrying a particular woman of our acquaintance. If I'd known he was so close to choosing a wife, I'd have written up a list of her good traits to present to him." She winked at Willie who was staring at her, mouth ajar. "I'm sure we can find some if we all put our minds to it."

Willie set her tumbler down on the table with a thud. "All right, Letty, that's enough. Seems like I've got to make it clear. I ain't interested in Farnsworth like that, and I wouldn't marry him even if I didn't have a nickel to my name."

"Which you don't," Duke pointed out. "You owe me money. Anyway, she wasn't talking about you. She was talking about Charity Glass."

Willie screwed up her nose. "She'd make an even worse wife than me!"

"It'd be about even."

"*Did* you mean Charity?" Willie asked Aunt Letitia. "Or me?"

Aunt Letitia passed the deck of cards to me and rose. "I think I'll retire. Goodnight, all."

"Letty?" Willie said as Aunt Letitia left the room. Once she'd gone, Willie clicked her tongue and picked up the glass again. "I'd make him a better wife than Charity Glass, ain't no mistaking it."

Duke and I shared a glance. He shrugged, and I saw his point. In the race to be the worst wife, it would be a tie between Charity and Willie.

Lord Farnsworth and Willie got along, however, which was a necessity for a successful marriage. He also seemed patient, which was a necessity when dealing with Willie, something Duke lacked. A marriage between Willie and Lord Farnsworth wouldn't be a complete disaster, I decided. The thought took me by surprise.

It would make Willie the wife of an earl. She'd outrank almost everyone, including Matt and his family. I giggled at the thought of Lady Rycroft begging for an invitation to a luncheon hosted by the incomparable Lady Farnsworth.

"What's so amusing?" Matt asked as he strolled in.

"Willie marrying Farnsworth."

He pulled a face. "I don't know which one I should pity more in that relationship."

"You ain't funny, Matt," Willie snapped. "I reckon we'd make a good match. We'd go gambling together, and host wild parties. All of London would talk about us."

"I'm not sure that's a good reason to marry someone."

"We ain't getting married, though. It's just talk. Seems like he's got a girl in mind anyway." Was that a hint of disappointment in her voice?

Perhaps it was just disappointment that she might lose her gambling partner. Cyclops and Duke seemed less inclined to go out with her lately. Cyclops was settling down, and Duke spent many evenings with Widow Rotherhide, whom he'd met during our investigation into the theft of a magical gold coronet.

"What'd you want to speak to Farnsworth about in private?" Duke asked Matt.

Matt poured himself a small glass of brandy at the

drinks trolley then refilled Willie's glass. "I asked him to introduce me to a gentleman who frequents his club. The gentleman is a good friend of the home secretary's, and I'm hoping he can find out why Sir Charles Whittaker was knighted."

We had learned that Sir Charles's knighthood was given to him in secret with no reason given. Usually such things went through a committee, but his nomination did not. Matt and I had come to the conclusion that Sir Charles could be a spy for the government, and both he and the government wanted to keep that fact a secret. Obtaining evidence to support the theory was proving difficult, however.

"I'll meet Farnsworth at the club tomorrow night," Matt went on.

Willie retired to her room, and Duke bade us goodnight a few minutes later. Matt and I snuggled on the sofa until the fire died down to glowing embers then he kissed the top of my head and unseated me from his lap.

He rose and extended his hand to me. "We'll find out more soon enough," he said.

I accepted his hand and stood. "I do hope so. I'm wildly curious about her."

He frowned. "Her?"

"Lord Farnsworth's prospective wife. Oh. You were referring to Sir Charles again, weren't you?"

"Just something slightly more important than the future Lady Farnsworth."

"Of course it is. Although it's not necessarily more interesting."

* * *

THE FOLLOWING AFTERNOON, after returning from a walk with Aunt Letitia, I was met by a frantic visitor upon our arrival at the Park Street house. Louisa—Lady Hollingbroke—was

9

about to step into her carriage when she spotted us approaching along the pavement.

"India, thank goodness you've returned." She gave Aunt Letitia a cursory greeting out of politeness but her entire attention focused on me. "Please, come with me. We must hurry."

"What is it, Louisa? What's happened?"

"My dear, you'll do yourself harm with your fretting," Aunt Letitia cut in before Louisa could respond. "Do come inside and have tea. The problem will seem less important after a soothing cup."

Louisa ignored her and clasped my hand. "Come, India, before Oscar does something he'll regret."

"Why? What's he about to do?"

"Confront Sir Charles Whittaker."

"Oh dear," Aunt Letitia muttered.

I gasped. "Is this about Sir Charles setting a thug upon him in the lane on the day Lord Coyle married Hope?"

"That, and the fact he blames Sir Charles for costing him his job at the paper," Louisa said. "There's no time to explain. You must come. I tried to talk him out of it, but he won't listen to me. I do think he'll listen to you, however. He respects your opinion."

I doubted I could stop Oscar if he was angry enough. The situation might require a more physical solution. "Wait here," I ordered as I gathered my skirts. "I'll ask Matt to accompany us, and perhaps Duke."

"You ought to fetch Willemina," Aunt Letitia said from behind me. "And her gun."

"When did you get so bloodthirsty?"

"You must admit it can be quite an efficient way to resolve a confrontation."

"We will not be shooting anyone."

"I think it's a good idea," Louisa called out from the pavement as Bristow opened the front door for me. "Oscar was rather furious, and I don't trust either he or Sir Charles to back away without a fight."

Even so, I would not invite Willie or her gun along. Adding her to an already volatile situation seemed about as smart as lighting a match in a room filled with gas.

CHAPTER 2

*W*e did not find Oscar and Sir Charles engaged in fisticuffs when we arrived at the modest Hammersmith row house where Sir Charles rented rooms, but we could hear their shouts from the pavement. The landlady was eager to let us in when we explained we were there to resolve the conflict peacefully. The poor woman was as white as a sheet.

Matt took the stairs three at a time, and when Louisa and I caught up to him in Sir Charles's parlor, he'd already positioned himself between the men, arms outstretched to keep them apart. They each glared past him at the other, although only Oscar's hands were clenched into fists.

Sir Charles looked more relieved than angry as he smoothed a hand over hair slicked with Makassar Oil. Not that his hair had been disheveled. Sir Charles's appearance was as sleek and sophisticated as ever. "Thank you, Glass, but there's no need for you to be here. Barratt and I were about to have a civilized conversation."

"It didn't look civilized to me." Matt lowered his arms, keeping a wary eye on Oscar. "Barratt, can I count on you to be a gentleman and talk your differences through?"

"A gentleman?" Oscar scoffed. He uncurled his fists and put his hands in the air, however. "Very well, I'll lower my voice. But I've come here for answers, and I won't be leaving until I get them."

"I already told you, I don't know what you're talking about." Sir Charles spoke mildly, as if he were addressing a friend with a minor complaint. "Come now, let's be chums again, Barratt. We have similar interests, after all. It would be a shame to attend Collectors' Club meetings and have to avoid one another."

"You had me dismissed from the *Gazette*," Oscar snarled.

"I'm flattered that you think I have such influence, but I do not."

"You set upon me in a lane," Oscar snarled.

"I didn't."

"You shot at me outside the *Gazette's* office!"

"What?" Sir Charles blurted out. It was the first sign that his feathers were ruffled.

"India and Glass were there. Don't try to deny it."

"I certainly did not shoot at you!"

Oscar bared his teeth and took a step closer to Sir Charles. Matt shoved him back and Oscar stood there, his chest rising and falling with ragged breaths as his gaze drilled into Sir Charles. Sir Charles glared right back, his feathers once again smooth. He was not a man who let emotions unsettle him, even when confronted by a determined member of the press.

"You *are* responsible for the beating," Matt said to Sir Charles. "We know it."

We didn't, but Matt's lie worked. Sir Charles gave a slight nod of his head.

Again, Oscar stepped toward him; again, Matt had to hold him back.

"That fellow went too far," Sir Charles admitted. "I never intended for you to get injured. All I wanted to do was frighten you into giving up on that damned book."

Oscar gave a thin smile. "Congratulations. Your plan succeeded."

I tried to gauge if he was sincere or not, but it was impossible to tell. Louisa's face gave nothing away either. She moved up alongside Oscar and clung to his arm. It was a show of solidarity for a couple I was never quite sure were solid enough to make a good marriage. As a lady, she was marrying far beneath her station, but that didn't mean it was a love match. She wanted Oscar for his magical bloodline. He agreed to marry her because her money could fund the publication of his book. Now that he'd decided not to write it, he no longer needed to marry her.

Considering they were standing side by side, it suggested he wasn't giving up on the book at all and was lying to us. I wasn't surprised.

"Why don't you want the book written?" Louisa asked Sir Charles.

"The book's publication could see magic brought into the open. I stand with Coyle and don't wish my collection to be devalued if magicians infuse their magic into everything, which is precisely what will happen if the general public learn of its benefits."

I kept my gaze directed forward, despite wanting to look around for the objects Sir Charles claimed were magical. I'd touched them in the past and felt no magical warmth in them. If he did own any magical objects, he kept them hidden. Or he had none and lied about it.

"Selfish, greedy little man," Louisa spat. "You choose money over allowing magicians to live a free life."

Sir Charles bristled. To my surprise, so did Matt. It was he who spoke while Sir Charles searched for a response.

"They won't be free. Not if the book is published. Magicians will be reviled and feared by their artless competitors and that will lead to their persecution. History shows us what the majority do to the minorities they fear."

"Magic is common knowledge now, Mr. Glass," Louisa said. "It's too late to suppress that knowledge now."

"It's not too late. Thanks to your fiancé's articles, some suspect, that's true, but not all. If the book is published…" His gaze shifted to Oscar. "If the world knew about magicians, I'm afraid they'd suffer persecution."

Sir Charles cleared his throat. "Agreed. Now, if you don't mind, I have to return to work. I'm late enough as it is."

"Not yet," Matt said. "Were you being honest when you claimed you didn't shoot at Barratt?"

"Of course. I did not shoot at him, nor did I get him dismissed from the paper." He turned to Oscar. "You have my word as a gentleman."

Oscar's lip lifted in a sneer.

Louisa tugged her fiancé toward the door, and I followed them.

"Am I still invited to your meeting tonight?" Sir Charles asked.

Louisa glanced back at him over her shoulder. "Of course. You are a club member."

Outside on the pavement, Oscar extricated himself from Louisa, who'd continued to cling to his arm. "I don't think he should be invited," he said. "Can't you ban him?"

"That's not how it works, Oscar. He's a member. It's not up to me."

"You can ban him from your house."

She gave him an arched look.

"I'm sure either he or Coyle had me dismissed from the paper. My editor is a good fellow. He likes me. He wouldn't get rid of me unless someone forced his hand."

Matt opened the door of our waiting carriage and extended his hand to assist me inside. "Coyle is the most likely suspect. He has the greater influence."

"I'll confront him tonight," Oscar growled.

"You'll do no such thing," his fiancée shot back. "Besides, you don't need to work. I can support us both."

"When are you getting married?" I asked as I smoothed the blanket over my lap.

"Soon," Louisa said from the pavement.

Oscar looked away.

Matt offered to drive them home but both declined. He gave our coachman, Woodall, instructions before climbing in and sitting beside me.

"India, will you come to the meeting tonight?" Louisa asked before Matt closed the door. "You too, Mr. Glass, of course."

"Thank you for including me, but I have a prior engagement tonight." Matt's wry tone wasn't lost on me, but Louisa didn't flinch.

"Do come, India. You'll be most welcome, as always. The members of the club adore you, and there'll be a special guest tonight too."

"I'll come," I said.

"Wonderful. We begin at eight."

Louisa and Oscar stepped back and our coach rolled off. I took Matt's hand. "Before you comment, you should know that I only agreed to attend so that I can spy on Sir Charles. I might learn something about him by observing him more closely."

"I wasn't going to comment." He leaned back to look at me better. "Did you think I'd forbid you?"

"You wouldn't dare. But I thought you might question my judgement."

"Never. Your judgement is perfectly sound."

I tilted my head to the side. "But...?"

"But I think you should take Duke or Cyclops with you, just in case."

"Not Willie?"

"I want you protected, not thrust into the path of scandal or danger."

* * *

WILLIE WOULD NOT BE LEFT out, however. Since Duke and Cyclops were both coming with me, she was determined to accompany us.

"You ain't going to miss out on anything," Duke told her. "It'll just be the usual toffs boasting about the usual magical things they've bought."

Willie accepted her Stetson from Bristow. "I ain't got nothing better to do, seeing as Farnsworth's with Matt at his club. Besides, Louisa always has nice food."

"She has a French chef," I told her.

Bristow gasped.

We all stared at him. "Is something the matter?" I asked.

He checked over his shoulder then leaned closer. "Don't let Mrs. Potter hear you mention French chefs. She doesn't like them."

"All of them?"

"One in particular, a Monsieur Claud, a chef-for-hire who caters for parties at the finest houses. Apparently she disparaged his pastry and he heard about it, and now they're having an ongoing war."

"A war over pastry. How extraordinary."

"Ain't no contest," Cyclops said. "Mrs. Potter makes the best pastry."

"You haven't tried the French chef's yet," Duke said.

"I don't need to."

I patted Cyclops's arm. "Mrs. Potter will be pleased to hear you say that."

He sighed. "I'm going to miss her cooking when Catherine and I set up our own house."

It was the first time I'd heard him admit that he and Catherine would have a life together soon. I was shocked into speechlessness but immensely pleased. They both deserved happiness.

I spent the journey to Louisa's townhouse with a smile on my face. I was even looking forward to the evening, particularly once Willie told me that Lord Farnsworth had informed her that the guest of honor tonight was a toymaker magician. Most magicians performed magic on a natural element, such as metal, wood, cotton, silk, or even the human body. My magic worked with crafted objects—watches and clocks—that could contain more than one element. I infused my magic into the watch, not its metal components. A toymaker magician would work the same way.

It was an important difference between the magics, and one that had me curious about the nature of magic. While all magicians were craftsmen—even Gabe Seaford, the doctor magician—our magic didn't manifest in the same manner.

Before he left the house, Matt had asked me not to tell the toymaker magician my name. After Amelia Moreton, the fireworks magician, tried to force me to infuse my extension spell with her friend's magic, Matt worried that other magicians would try to do the same. Despite keeping Amelia's threats out of the newspapers, word would have got out among certain magicians that I could extend the length of other magicians' magic. The Pandora's box had been opened and we could not close it again, but I liked to think common sense would prevail and no one else would go to the extremes Amelia had.

Matt wasn't quite as trusting.

Louisa didn't bat an eyelid at my inviting extra guests to her soiree, but others narrowed their gaze at first and widened them again upon seeing Willie. With her thumbs hooked into her belt loops, the men's clothing and disheveled hair, she was quite the curiosity among the elegant ladies in their evening gowns. Those who'd met her before gave forced smiles as she passed, while others changed direction to avoid crossing her path altogether. Only Mrs. Delancey surged towards her like a steam engine encased in purple silk with velvet trim.

Willie didn't see her coming until it was too late. She groaned when Mrs. Delancey reached us, not even trying to cover it up. "I ain't signing no temperance agreement," Willie told her. "You can shove it—"

"Willie!" I drew in a breath and hoped to draw in some patience along with it. "What she's trying to say is, she prefers to have a drink now and again rather than completely abstain," I told Mrs. Delancey.

Willie peered past Mrs. Delancey. "Speaking of which, have refreshments been served yet?"

Mrs. Delancey moved to block Willie's view of the adjoining refreshment room. Willie stepped the other way and Mrs. Delancey responded. It looked like an odd dance performed between unwilling partners.

"You can't supervise me all night," Willie said.

Mrs. Delancey patted her arm. "I know, dear. That's why I've convinced Louisa to serve alcoholic beverages to the men only. The women will have tea."

Willie stamped her hands on her hips. "That ain't fair."

Duke chuckled. "It's her house; she can do what she wants."

"How did you convince her?" I asked Mrs. Delancey.

"By telling her the story of Miss Johnson's visit to my home just before Christmas and how she threw up in my magical vase after drinking too much the night before." Mrs. Delancey gave Willie a smug look. "She suspected you might bring Miss Johnson tonight and agreed it was best to keep the brandy away from her so it doesn't happen again."

"I ate a bad oyster that time," Willie muttered. "I can hold my liquor." She marched off toward a group of men that included Oscar. Perhaps she hoped to blend in with them and be offered a glass of brandy by an unobservant footman.

Mrs. Delancey looped her arm through mine as if we were intimate friends. "What a delight to see you here, India. Have you met Mr. Trentham yet?"

I followed her gaze to where Fabian Charbonneau was chatting to a portly middle-aged man with a bushy moustache and a thick crop of curly gray hair. He gazed up at the French iron magician with what could only be described as adoring eyes. "Is he the toymaker magician?"

"He is indeed. I'm looking forward to hearing him speak. He brought a large trunk with him that I suspect is filled with all sorts of magical wonders. I do hope he's prepared to sell some things. Mr. Delancey has given me free reign to purchase any item I wish, no matter the cost. He couldn't come tonight, alas, but it appears all the usual members are here, except Lord Farnsworth."

"Mr. Trentham and Fabian seem deep in conversation."

"They've been inseparable ever since Louisa introduced them. Would you like to meet him?"

"Perhaps later." I searched the room for Sir Charles and spotted him talking to Lord Coyle. They stood to one side of the room by a large potted fern.

"Speaking of Mr. Charbonneau," Mrs. Delancey said. "Do tell me you've reconsidered and will resume creating new spells with him. You two can achieve so much together."

"Dear me, it seems Willie has managed to get a drink already."

I took the opportunity that Mrs. Delancey's distraction provided and slipped away. I unfolded my fan and placed it in front of my face. With a shake of my head at Cyclops and Duke, I distanced myself from my conspicuous companions and hid behind the potted fern.

Lord Coyle's tone was cross, but I couldn't make out his words. From my position, I couldn't see either of their faces. It was possible Lord Coyle wasn't cross with Sir Charles at all, but simply irritable thanks to his new wife banning him from smoking cigars.

As if my thoughts summoned her, Hope appeared by my side. She was dressed in a dark green gown with black lace ruffles down the skirt and at the elbows. The low neckline showed off her décolletage and the emerald and jet necklace nestled there. "India, what are you doing hiding back here? Why, it's almost as if you're trying to eavesdrop on my husband and Sir Charles."

Lord Coyle and Sir Charles broke off their conversation. Sir Charles bowed to me as I emerged from my hiding place, but Coyle merely grunted.

"Glass not here?" Lord Coyle asked as he peered around the room.

"He had another engagement," I said.

"I see you have your other bulldogs with you instead."

"I know you're not familiar with the concept, my lord, but they're my friends. I wanted them to come."

His eyes narrowed so much they almost disappeared beneath the folds of his protuberant eyelids. "You're bold tonight, India."

The corners of Hope's mouth turned down. "Indeed. You become more and more American every day."

I laughed. "That isn't the disparagement you think it is."

Hope's gaze turned hard and became even harder when her husband laughed too. "I like this boldness in you, India," he said. "You should leave your husband home more often."

"Perhaps we all should." Hope marched off and was soon swallowed up by the gathering.

Sir Charles cleared his throat and he too made his excuses, although more politely. I was left alone with Lord Coyle, but instead of feeling trapped, I did feel emboldened. It was most likely because, for the first time since meeting him, I had the upper hand. He owed me a favor. Matt had sold him the magic flying carpet we'd used to fly to Brighton to capture Amelia Moreton. The cost of the sale had been Lord Coyle's information. We were yet to collect our debt.

But it was a debt we shouldn't even be owed. Matt hadn't sold him the actual flying carpet, but a fake one that held no magic. Being artless, Lord Coyle couldn't tell the difference.

"Your wife despises you already?" I asked cheerfully. "That was fast. It took me more than two weeks to decide I didn't like you."

"She is simply upset that I haven't given her free access to my fortune."

"Isn't that a new necklace she's wearing?"

"It's a family heirloom. She wants more."

"In my experience, she always does." I went to walk off.

"I have some news for you," he called after me.

"I don't want to hear it." Even so, I hesitated.

He leaned on his walking stick. "This is free and won't be covered by my debt for the rug." His jowls trembled with his smile. "Do you remember Hendry?"

"The paper magician who murdered a man and tried to kill me?"

"The very same. He's getting married."

I blinked slowly. Mr. Hendry preferred men to women. For him to marry, he must have good reason, and I suspected that reason was because he owed his freedom to Lord Coyle, who'd saved him from being hanged for murder. It seemed Lord Coyle had collected *that* debt by forcing him to wed.

It also seemed his lordship was going to great lengths to ensure the continuation of the paper magic line; a lineage that would end with Mr. Hendry if he didn't have children.

"Is his new wife a magician?" I asked.

"You're an intelligent woman, India. What do you think?"

"I think she is."

He simply smiled, or attempted to. Lord Coyle's smiles

tended to look more like grimaces. "Let's hope the happy couple enjoy a long and fruitful life together."

"In peace, without the interference of others." I strode off and joined Cyclops who stood alone, trying to look inconspicuous near another potted palm on the opposite side of the room. "You look bored."

"These ain't my people, India."

"They're not mine, either." I sighed. "I'm sorry I dragged you here. We'll leave as soon as the lecture is over."

"Is that the toymaker magician?" he asked, nodding at Mr. Trentham.

It was the man behind Mr. Trentham who caught my attention. Oscar stood alone, his icy glare directed at Louisa and Fabian, speaking quietly to one another. She looked relieved at something Fabian said and shifted closer to him. She fingered his lapel before lightly pressing her hand to it.

Oscar stiffened and marched off. He did not head towards them but corralled Lord Coyle by the door. I could no longer see Oscar's face, but from the way Lord Coyle's nostrils flared, I suspected he was confronting his lordship over his involvement in Oscar's dismissal from the newspaper.

It was the very thing Louisa asked Oscar not to do tonight.

Lord Coyle folded both hands over the head of his walking stick and shook his head. He said something to Oscar then went to move off.

Oscar grabbed his arm. Coyle glared down at it, but Oscar did not let go. By now, several guests had stopped their conversations and watched.

"It wasn't me!" Lord Coyle bellowed.

"Wasn't it?" Oscar asked, voice also raised. "It seems like the sort of thing you'd do to force me to give up the book."

"You *have* given it up, so you tell everyone. Or is that not the case?"

All conversations stopped and an eerie hush blanketed the room. Louisa had gone very still. She appeared frozen to the spot, but I suspected I was the only one who noticed. Everyone else's attention was on her fiancé and Lord Coyle.

"You're a fool if you think it was me, Barratt." Coyle had lowered his voice but it was still audible in the quiet room. "Why would I want you dismissed from the paper when that would give you more time to work on the book?" Lord Coyle smacked the end of his walking stick into Oscar's shin. "Out of my way."

Oscar's chest heaved with his unsteady breaths. For one heart-stopping moment I thought he'd assault Lord Coyle. I'd never considered Oscar to be a violent man, but being dismissed from the *Gazette* had clearly rattled him. When added to his troubles with Louisa, it might cause him to be frustrated enough to lash out.

Louisa clapped her hands to get our attention. "Time for the lecture, everyone! Mr. Trentham, would you like to make your way to the front."

Footmen positioned chairs into rows as Louisa directed Mr. Trentham where to stand.

I sat near the back and Fabian occupied the chair beside me. "That was a curious show between Barratt and Coyle," he said. "Did Coyle lie about having Barratt dismissed, do you think?"

"It's difficult to say." I tried not to look at either Oscar or Lord Coyle and directed my gaze ahead. "He is a good liar."

"And capable of costing a man his work." Fabian clicked his tongue. "I despise him. He cares for no one but himself. But Barratt should not have confronted him here. Not in front of everyone."

"Louisa asked Oscar not to."

Fabian frowned. "Then why did he?"

"Why indeed?" The only explanation I could come up with was frustration and perhaps jealousy. When Oscar had seen Louisa touching Fabian's lapel in an intimate gesture, he'd done the very thing he knew would get her attention.

If he was jealous then that meant he loved her. Perhaps he wasn't marrying her simply for her money, after all. It explained why he continued with the engagement when he'd abandoned the book and no longer needed her money.

Poor Oscar. Louisa only had eyes for Fabian.

Fabian leaned closer to me. "There is a madness in the air tonight. Do you feel it, India?"

"A little. Why did you come? I thought you were trying to avoid Louisa."

His dark eyes sparkled. "She sent me a message this afternoon to say you would be here. Of course I want to come to see my friend. I miss you."

I chuckled. "You mean you miss making spells with me."

He pressed a hand to his heart and fought against a smile. "You wound me, India. I miss my friend."

"You can call on me whenever you like. Just because we're no longer creating spells together doesn't mean we can't see one another."

"I do not wish to make Glass jealous of me."

I laughed. "You're so French, Fabian. I assure you, Matt won't get jealous."

"Then I promise to call on you." He turned to face the front where the toymaker was inspecting the contents of the trunk while the rest of the audience took their seats. "His magic is curious but not strong. He wants to meet you, very much."

"I'll talk to him later, but I won't create a spell with him."

"I was not asking you to. *You* must come to *me* if you change your mind. I will not trouble you." He sounded genuinely disappointed in me for thinking he would.

"Sorry, Fabian." An uncomfortable silence filled the space between us which Fabian thankfully broke after a moment.

"I can bring you the carpet, if you like. I retrieved it from the field near Brighton. It was dirty but my servants cleaned it."

"It's your rug, Fabian. You keep it."

"But your magic made it fly."

"Yours too. I couldn't have managed it without your iron magic in the supports. Besides, I have nowhere to put it." I glanced at Lord Coyle, seated two rows in front. "Whatever you do, don't let his lordship know he didn't buy it."

He smiled slyly. "I would never. Tricking him makes me happy."

I smiled too. "It does give one a sense of satisfaction. Speaking of that spell, I've been meaning to ask you for it."

"You wish to keep it?"

"If you don't mind."

"Will you destroy it?"

I hesitated before saying, "I don't know."

There was nothing to stop Fabian making a copy before he gave it to me, so it didn't matter if I destroyed it. I couldn't imagine Fabian bringing himself to release the one and only written copy of our flying carpet spell, no matter how many times he said it was mine to do with as I wished. I suspected he would keep it simply for the sakes of future studies into magic. He couldn't use it himself; his magic couldn't make the rug fly, only the iron supports beneath it. Iron and wood magic needed to be used in conjunction with our new spell to make the whole structure fly.

"I will bring it to you tomorrow," he said.

Louisa called for quiet then introduced Mr. Trentham.

During the applause, Fabian bent his head to mine and whispered, "Perhaps you will use the spell to create another in secret."

I stared at his refined profile as he watched Mr. Trentham. This was one of those times when it was impossible to know if Fabian was teasing me. While he'd been upset when I first told him I no longer wanted to create new spells with him, I thought he'd come to accept it. But his response seemed to say that he held out hope I would change my mind. Fortunately he did not pressure me to change it. I liked Fabian and I didn't want to argue with him or have to stop seeing him altogether.

Mr. Trentham was an engaging speaker with interesting tales to tell about his toys and the people who came into his shop. Unfortunately his magic was somewhat less engaging. The only spell he knew made his toys move a little longer than without it. They still had to be manipulated by human hands, however.

The spinning top spun for five minutes before it lost momentum and toppled over. The wooden train traveled further than expected after he pushed it. A doll repeated the words "My name is Polly" three times with the spell and two times without it, but only after Mr. Trentham pulled on the string at her back. I was hoping it would work without the need for anyone to pull it at all.

"*You* could make it walk," Fabian whispered in my ear.

I nudged him with my elbow, but the twinkle in his eyes remained.

Polite applause followed the conclusion of Mr. Trentham's lecture and Louisa announced that refreshments would be served. As we filed into the adjoining room, the footmen removed the chairs and returned the sofa and other furniture to the drawing room while it was empty.

I accepted a cup of tea from a footman but did not want anything to eat. Cyclops and Duke made a beeline for the table along with Fabian and most of the other guests. Willie beat them all.

"Mrs. Glass?" came a soft voice from behind me.

I turned to see Mr. Trentham smiling tentatively. I put out my hand. "I'm pleased to meet you. Thank you for your lecture. It was enlightening."

His cheeks flushed and he shook his head. "I'm afraid it's the best I can do. My magic is rather weak, so I tried to make it more interesting by telling a few stories. I've never done this sort of thing before. I'm afraid I'm not a lecturer."

"You're a natural, and your magic is intriguing. I'm sure the children get great enjoyment from your toys."

"You're too kind. My magic is nothing compared to yours." He cleared his throat. "I heard about your extension spell, Mrs. Glass."

I sighed into my teacup.

Mr. Trentham heard it and put his hands up in surrender. "Please, do not think I'm trying to ingratiate myself to you. I have no intention of asking you to extend my magic."

"I'm relieved to hear it."

"Mr. Charbonneau warned me not to."

I bit the inside of my lip to stop my smile.

Fabian joined us, a questioning look on his face, but I didn't get a chance to thank him for warning Mr. Trentham as others approached. They asked Mr. Trentham about his magic and toys.

"Can you detect magic in other objects?" asked a woman.

He nodded. "All magicians can feel magical warmth."

"Are you the only toy magician in London?" Sir Charles asked.

"No."

A bespectacled fellow I'd seen at other club meetings handed Mr. Trentham a glass filled with amber liquid. "Have you ever tried frightening someone by making the doll move with a spell? You know, without touching it and while you're standing on the other side of the room."

"That would be a lark," his female companion said, laughing.

"I can't do that," Mr. Trentham said, apologetically.

The man's face fell. "Pity."

Mrs. Delancey muscled her way between two other members. One of them had to lean back to avoid being poked in the eye by the feather in her headdress. "Are any of your pieces for sale?" she asked.

Mr. Trentham nodded. "Would you like to inspect them?"

"Yes, please."

They led the way to Mr. Trentham's toy chest with a trail of onlookers in tow. He could make quite a tidy sum tonight if he played his cards right.

I found myself standing very near Hope as she watched the procession return to the drawing room. "You're not purchasing anything?" I asked her. "A gift for your husband, perhaps?"

"He adds to his collection as he sees fit." She somehow managed to seem as though she were looking down her nose at me despite being shorter. "Nor would he advise under-taking transactions at a gathering such as this. A private nego-tiation is more his style."

"I suppose he can use whatever tactics he likes in private without receiving the censure of the crowd."

She stiffened. "What is that supposed to mean?"

"It means precisely what you think it means. Your husband is ruthless. He does and says whatever is necessary to get what he wants without concern for those he walks over."

"You don't know what you're talking about."

I stepped toward her, stopping very close, and did not bend to her level. She had to crane her neck to meet my gaze. "I know your husband's tactics rather well, as it happens. I'd have a care if I were you, Hope, or he might walk over you too."

The gleam in her eyes turned hard. "Or he might teach me how to get what I want."

* * *

WE DIDN'T STAY MUCH LONGER and arrived home before Matt returned from Lord Farnsworth's club. Duke and Cyclops went to bed at midnight, but Willie and I waited up. By one-thirty, I was beginning to think Matt had found it necessary to join Farnsworth and the home secretary's friend in some nocturnal adventure or other. I only hoped it didn't involve too much imbibing, given Matt's prior battles with drink.

I was considering retiring when I heard the front door open. I'd sent Bristow to bed some time ago, so Matt let himself in.

"Thought I saw the light on in here," he said, entering. He still wore his hat and coat as he tugged on his gloves to remove them. He leaned down to kiss me. "Good evening, Wife. Did you have a good night or did someone do or say something to ruin it?"

"Was that directed at me?" Willie asked, sounding curious rather than defensive.

"Not in particular, but it could be. Why? What did you do?"

"Nothing! And that's the God's honest truth."

Matt seemed to be having trouble getting the glove off his right hand so I helped him. "Have you been drinking?"

He pulled his hand out of the glove then scrubbed it over his face. "Yes."

"Don't lecture him, India," Willie scolded. "He did what he had to do, ain't that right, Matt?"

"I was hardly scolding him," I said, standing.

Matt turned to Willie. "She wasn't scolding me."

I helped him out of his coat then directed him to sit on the sofa. He slumped into it, gathering me around my waist as he did so, and drew me onto his lap. He gave me a devilish smile as his heated gaze dipped to my mouth.

Willie made a sound of disgust in the back of her throat. "You used to be able to hold your liquor better."

Matt settled me beside him. "I'm out of practice, but I'm

not completely inebriated, either. You're correct in saying that I drank more than I usually would. Farnsworth's liver must be made of iron."

"What did you learn?" I asked.

"That he drinks a lot."

I smiled. "I meant about Sir Charles and his knighthood."

"Nothing, yet. I merely laid down the groundwork with the home secretary's friend. He promised to introduce me when the home secretary returns to the city."

"When will that be?"

Matt shrugged.

I sighed and took his hand. "Are you coming to bed or staying up awhile?"

"To bed, definitely." He rose and bade Willie goodnight.

She shot to her feet. "That's it? That's all you learned?"

Matt shrugged again. "Tonight was about getting the home secretary's friend to trust me. I couldn't come right out and ask how someone could receive a knighthood without being nominated through the usual channels. It would be too suspicious. Besides, he wouldn't know, unless the home secretary confides in him."

"But what about Farnsworth's day? Didn't you ask him how it went?"

"How what went?"

"With the girl he was meeting. His future wife."

Matt gave his cousin a lopsided grin. "Jealous?"

"No!" Willie crossed her arms over her chest. "Just curious."

Matt picked up his hat and pointed it at her. "If you are interested, you should make your feelings known to him. He might consider you a serious prospect."

"I ain't jealous. I just don't want to lose another friend to marriage. First you, next it'll be Cyclops, then Farnsworth. At least I still got Duke, but he's getting dull, too."

"Marriage is not a disease," I said.

"It's worse. At least you can recover from a disease." She stormed out of the sitting room.

Matt chuckled as he dropped the hat on the sofa and circled his arms around my waist. He nuzzled my throat beneath my ear. "She is jealous," he purred.

I pulled away. "You shouldn't encourage her to tell Farnsworth how she feels. He might not conform to some society norms, but he's still an earl. He won't wed someone like Willie."

He tightened his hold on my waist, drawing me against his body. "I don't expect them to marry, but she might form a relationship with him. Now kiss me."

I put a finger to his lips before he planted them on my mouth. "And what about Detective Inspector Brockwell?"

He sighed. "He knows he can't monopolize her. Can we stop talking about Willie and her overly complicated romantic liaisons and start talking about what I'd like to do to you when I get you into the bedroom?"

I gave him a sly smile. "Don't talk, just show me."

His lips brushed mine in a tender kiss that promised much more. "As you command, Mrs. Glass."

* * *

THE FOLLOWING morning was another gloomy day. A letter came for Aunt Letitia from her sister-in-law, Lady Rycroft, saying she and Charity were returning to London. They found the country too provincial and lacking in sophisticated society. Most of their friends wouldn't have returned to the city yet, but a few were trickling back now that Christmas festivities were behind us.

"What about my uncle?" Matt asked.

"He's not coming," Aunt Letitia said, scanning the letter again. "Beatrice says she cannot wait to see Hope. She has some suggestions for guests she ought to invite to a dinner party."

"Coyle will enjoy that," Matt muttered.

"What about Patience?" I asked. "Any word about her and Byron?"

"She doesn't mention them."

It was as if Patience no longer existed. Ever since her husband had his title stripped away and given to his older half-brother, Lady Rycroft barely acknowledged her eldest daughter's existence. She might as well be dead. Lady Rycroft probably preferred she had died to the scandal that ensued.

Matt, standing behind me, gently squeezed my shoulder. "Don't worry about them. They have one another, and I suspect Patience likes being out of her mother's sphere anyway."

Bristow entered the drawing room and announced the arrival of Fabian. He'd barely finished speaking when Fabian pushed past him. He breathed heavily, as if he'd been running, and his face was flushed.

"Bristow, fetch Mr. Charbonneau a glass of water," I said.

"Have you been exerting yourself?" Aunt Letitia asked with a slight wrinkle of her nose.

Fabian offered a shallow bow. "My apologies for my state, Miss Glass. I am in disarray." He smoothed down his hair and fidgeted with his tie. "I could not wait for the carriage to be prepared so walked here, very quickly."

"Fabian, what is the matter?" I asked.

He turned to Matt. "Glass, I have a job for you. An investigation."

"Into what?" Matt asked.

"A theft." Fabian swallowed and settled his anxious gaze on me. "Your spell has been stolen, India."

CHAPTER 3

"Stolen!" I pressed a hand to my rapidly beating heart. "When?"

"Last night," Fabian said. "The maid discovered the top drawer of my desk open and everything inside it missing."

"The spell wasn't in your safe?"

"No. It was in the drawer, but it was locked. All the papers in the drawer were stolen, and the spell was hidden among them. The thief got in through the sitting room window on the ground floor."

Matt swore under his breath, earning a glare from Aunt Letitia. "If you'd given me the spell when India first asked, it would have been safe."

"Matt," I scolded. "That's not fair. It could just as easily have been stolen from here."

He gave me a look that said he doubted it, but he kept the thought to himself, thankfully. Fabian didn't look as though he needed further censure. He dragged a trembling hand through his hair, only straightening when Bristow entered with a glass of water on a tray.

"Have you questioned the servants?" Matt asked.

Fabian accepted the glass. "Not thoroughly."

"Bristow, have the carriage brought around. India, are you coming?"

"Of course," I said, rising. "Should we send word to Brockwell?"

"Not yet."

"Nobody else should know," Fabian said. "This is magical business."

"Detective Inspector Brockwell understands magic," I told him. "You remember how discreet he was after the affair with Amelia Moreton. He hushed up the magical element to the case."

"He is still artless."

"As is Matt."

Matt settled a hand on my shoulder. "We'll notify Brockwell if we need his resources. For now, we'll keep this to ourselves. The fewer people who know, the better. I don't want someone like Coyle getting even a hint of it."

"Coyle may already know," Fabian said darkly.

My heart skipped a beat. He was right. The most likely person to steal the spell was Lord Coyle. Nobody else knew what Fabian and I had created, although many knew that we'd been working together to create spells. It was possible they suspected we'd lied, and decided to see for themselves, and had been lucky enough to stumble across the spell. But what would they do with it once they got it?

I voiced my concern once we were ensconced in the carriage and on our way to Fabian's townhouse near Berkeley Square. "Why would anyone bother to steal it? It's useless to anyone but me."

"We don't know if there are others like you in the world, India," Matt said.

"There is no other as powerful as her," Fabian told him. "I am almost sure of it."

"Almost?" Matt bit off.

"Matt does have a point," I said quickly. "There might be

another strong magician who could make it work. If Lord Coyle, or someone else, thinks there is another, he might have stolen the spell to give to them."

"Or sell it," Matt added.

Fabian, seated opposite, glanced first at Matt then me. "Or they might force *you* to use it, India."

My blood ran cold. He was right. I hadn't thought of that.

Neither had Matt, going by the way his face lost all color. He took my hand in his and caressed it with his thumb.

The first thing we did upon arriving at Fabian's townhouse was inspect the sitting room window. The lock had been snapped clean off.

"Someone used a lot of force," I said.

"Not necessarily." Matt ran his finger over the windowsill. "This wood should be splintered, but there are only scratches. Was the lock loose, Charbonneau?"

"I do not know," Fabian said.

"You didn't hear anyone moving through the house?" I asked.

"It must have happened in the dead of night. The servants' rooms are on the top level and I am a heavy sleeper."

"It wasn't like this when you returned home from the collector's club meeting?"

He shook his head then suddenly stopped. He wagged a finger at me. "The toymaker magician, Mr. Trentham, was very interested in our work. He asked me about spells we created together. I told him we are not doing that anymore, but..." He muttered something in French. "I do not think he believed me. Perhaps he suspected we created a spell before giving up, although I did not imply as much to him, I assure you."

"You think he decided to break in on the off-chance that you did have a spell?" Matt shook his head. "It seems unlikely."

"What would he do with the spell anyway?" I asked. "His magic isn't all that strong."

Fabian opened his mouth to say something but closed it again. He frowned at the window frame where the window's lock had been affixed.

Matt approached the butler, standing by the door.

I took the opportunity to have a quiet word with Fabian. He looked somewhat ill. "I know you feel violated. It's awful that someone got into your house while you were asleep under the very same roof."

"It is not that." He screwed his eyes shut. "*Mon dieu*, I cannot believe it is gone. All that hard work, for nothing."

"You made a copy, didn't you?"

He opened his eyes. They looked sadder than when I'd told him I wasn't going to work with him anymore. "No."

"Oh." I leaned against the window frame. The spell really was lost if we couldn't retrieve it. I felt somewhat bereft at the notion, as if a little piece of me had been torn off and thrown away.

Fabian suddenly grasped my hand. His eyes were bright, his cheeks flushed with color. "We must create it again, India. Do you remember the words? I think I do, but I need your help."

"No, Fabian. I told you I don't want to cast new spells."

"But it is the same spell, not a new one."

I withdrew my hand.

His face fell, but his lips pursed. "You would let the thief be the only one with the spell? That is not fair."

"We'll catch whoever it is. You'll get the spell back."

Matt strode across the room and rejoined us. "The butler will assemble the staff in here for questioning." He frowned at me. "Is everything all right?"

I folded my arms and nodded.

He studied Fabian from beneath hooded lids, only looking away when the footman entered.

Fabian joined him and the other servants filtering into the drawing room. They stood in a line, hands clasped in front of them. All bowed their heads except for a tall, pretty maid who gazed adoringly at Fabian. He didn't seem to notice as he asked each of them to tell him if they'd seen or heard anything suspicious the night before.

The housekeeper and cook lived off-premises, but the butler, maid and footman all had rooms in the attic and none heard a thing.

"Except for someone coughing," the maid said. "Real loud, he was. He coughed twice. No, three times."

"Someone outside the house?" Matt asked.

"Oh yes, not inside. I'd wager they were on the pavement near this room, in fact."

"And where is your bedchamber?"

"Pardon me?"

"Where is your bedchamber positioned in the house? Is it on this side or the other?"

"The other."

"So why do you think the coughing was outside here? I doubt you could have heard it from your room."

She bit her lip and seemed to shrink into herself. When Matt turned off his charm, he could be rather daunting when he wanted to be.

"I heard it too," Fabian said quickly. "I did not think it might be connected, but Jane is right. It did come from somewhere near here. My room is on this side." He pointed to the ceiling. "Do you think the thief coughed to cover the sound of the lock breaking?"

"It's highly likely," Matt said. "Thank you, Jane. It's fortunate both you and Mr. Charbonneau heard it. Do you recall the time?"

"No, sir. It would have been after midnight but before six, when I get up to start my chores. The coughing woke me, but I was too sleepy to check the time and it was dark anyway."

"May we have a look at the office now?" he asked Fabian.

In the office, Matt immediately crouched at the desk to inspect the top drawer. "The thief either used a key or a slender tool to open the lock. It's not a complicated mechanism." He eyed Fabian. "Please tell me you didn't leave the key lying about."

"No! It is kept on my person." He patted his waistcoat pocket.

Matt stood. "The thief knows how to pick a simple lock." He checked inside the drawer and removed some coins. The drawer was otherwise empty. "What else was in here?"

"Letters from my man of business in France, private correspondence with my brother, investment information. Nothing of value to a thief."

"Could the thief have simply taken everything in the drawer because they couldn't see the contents in the dark?" I asked. "That might mean they weren't after the spell in particular."

"It's possible," Matt conceded, looking around the office. "Are there any other locked drawers, boxes or cabinets in here, Charbonneau?"

"There is a safe behind that painting." Fabian indicated a framed landscape on the wall. "Only this drawer was broken into, and nothing but its contents were stolen. I think they wanted the spell and suspected it was in there. Perhaps *hoped* it was in there, and not the safe."

"How fortunate for them that it wasn't," Matt said pointedly.

Fabian swallowed and lowered his gaze.

Matt peered into the other drawers, checked the door, windows, and inspected the carpeted floor. Fabian watched him with an ever darkening frown.

"There is something I should tell you," he eventually said. "Something Trentham spoke of last night troubles me and might be relevant."

"Go on," I said as Matt once more inspected the top drawer.

"Trentham claims his magic is cursed. He says if the curse is lifted, it would be stronger."

"Curse?"

"It is not the curse that interests me. It is his belief that his magic could be stronger without it. If he knew of a way to lift the curse, then he might think he will be strong enough to use your spell."

"Hence he came here, hoping to find it so he could use it once his magic returns to its full strength," I finished for him. "That gives Trentham a motive. And you did say he asked you a lot of questions last night. Not only that, the timing is too coincidental for my liking. This theft happened the very night he questioned you at length about our work."

"Curses aren't real," Matt piped up.

I gave him an arched look.

"Very well, they might be real. But I still think this is the work of Coyle. He knows about your flying carpet spell. He's the only one outside our circle who does. Anyone else is simply guessing that you created a new spell. It must be him."

"Shall we pay him a call now?" I asked.

"He won't admit it, and I doubt we can trick him into saying something incriminating. He's an accomplished liar."

"It might be worth letting him think we're onto him," I pointed out.

Matt agreed, and we departed for Coyle's townhouse. Once seated in the carriage, he said, "Charbonneau is sleeping with his maid."

"I know. Isn't it positively scandalous!"

"Not to mention stupid. She could easily retrieve the key from his pocket and use it to open the desk drawer, or give it to the thief."

I gasped. "You think she lied about the coughing?"

"It's possible."

Poor Fabian, being duped like that. While I didn't believe he had feelings for her, and I didn't approve of him having a relationship with his maid, it would be a betrayal if she'd been behind the theft.

"We should have questioned her more thoroughly," I said.

"Perhaps, but she seemed a little in love with him, going by the way she looked at him. She wouldn't steal from him if that were the case. I suspect she's innocent and simply happened to be in his room when the thief broke in."

"You have a good heart, Matt." I touched his jaw so he'd look at me. "But a little too good. I think we should question her, but we can compromise and do it subtly. We'll send Duke or Willie. She's never met them."

"The footman and butler have. Besides, Willie isn't subtle. It'll have to be Duke, and somewhere away from the house so the other servants don't see him."

"Agreed. But where? And how will he encourage her to talk?"

"I'll think of something."

We traveled in silence for several minutes, the only sound coming from the rain on the roof and the rumble of wheels. I assumed Matt was pondering the problem of the maid, so his next question took me by surprise.

"Do you believe Charbonneau didn't make a copy of the spell?"

"Why would he lie?"

"I can't think of a reason, but it seems odd that something so important to him wasn't locked in the safe and he made no copies."

"Fabian wouldn't lie to us, Matt. Besides, did you see his hand shake when he told us? He's devastated by the theft. He wouldn't be if he held another copy." I turned to face him squarely. I wanted to see his reaction properly. "Have you always doubted Fabian's character?"

41

"No, and I don't doubt him now." He gathered my hands in his and gave them a gentle squeeze. "But we must consider all angles, India."

"You're worried, aren't you?"

"A little. If Fabian lied about making a copy, perhaps he's lying about other things. Like you being the only powerful magician. If there is someone else, someone who could use that spell…"

He didn't go on, but I knew what he was implying. There was nothing stopping them from using it. If the thief was unscrupulous enough to steal the spell, they probably wouldn't have the morals to refrain from using my spell to their own advantage. "It's just a flying spell, Matt. It's more harmless than Amelia Moreton's detonation spell. I'd wager Coyle had someone steal it so that he can one day make money off commercial flights." The more I thought about it, the more I warmed to the idea. It certainly made me feel a little less anxious about the theft.

Matt considered this a moment then smiled. "If anyone is mad enough to pay money to ride on a flying carpet, they should be charged a fortune for their stupidity. That thing was a death trap."

* * *

As we drove up to the house, a hackney cab drove off. The occupant's hand was raised to adjust her hat and her arm obscured her face. It was a little early to be receiving callers, but perhaps Hope was an early riser and liked to get on with the day.

Lord Coyle received us in the library, a small room of paneled wood and leather-bound books. His collection of magical objects was kept in an even smaller room hidden behind one of the shelves. Perhaps he'd just been in it, because he had no book or newspaper in hand. He sat in the only armchair, positioned by the fireplace where a small fire warmed the room, and regarded us from the shadows of his thick brow.

"I was just thinking about you two," he said with a flick of his fingers at the butler. He didn't ask the butler to bring refreshments, which meant Coyle didn't wish us to stay long. There was nowhere to sit anyway. Coyle occupied the only chair. It wasn't a room designed for receiving guests, or even for sitting quietly with his spouse.

"Why?" Matt asked.

"First things first. Why are you here?"

"To ask if you sent a thief to Charbonneau's house to burgle him."

Lord Coyle's chuckle started deep in his belly and rose to his chest. It rocked him, making his entire body shake and his jowls tremble. "Very amusing, Glass."

"Did you?" I pressed.

"To steal what, precisely? I already have enough magical iron in my collection." He indicated the shelves that were in fact a secret door that led to the hidden room. "Did Charbonneau put you up to this? The man dislikes me, you know. Can't think why."

The library door opened. "Who was that—?" Hope cut herself off when she saw us. A visible change passed over her, like a ripple. It lifted her features and put a smile on her lips. It was entirely for Matt's benefit, of course. I doubted seeing me would raise her spirits. "Dearest cousins, how lovely to see you both. Do come through to the drawing room. The library has a strange smell in it that the maids can't get rid of."

"The Glasses are about to leave," Lord Coyle told her. "They stated their business, and I suspect will have nothing further to say when I tell them they're barking up the wrong tree."

"What tree is that, Husband?"

43

"I did not send a thief to steal anything from Charbonneau."

Hope gasped. "He was robbed? How awful. What did the thieves take?"

"A magical object," Matt said.

"No wonder you think it was my husband. But I can assure you, he hasn't sent a thief to steal from Mr. Charbonneau. You ought to look elsewhere for your culprit."

"And you know everything he does?" I asked. "Every person he meets, including the woman who just left?"

Hope's spine stiffened. So I was right. She'd come in here to ask her husband who'd visited.

Lord Coyle put out his hand to her. "Come, my dear. There's no need to be jealous."

Hope's wince was almost imperceptible and I wondered if her husband noticed it. She hesitated a mere moment before going to him.

"She was a magician," he told us.

"Who?" I asked.

"No one you know. I asked her here to touch a magical object for me and confirm whether or not it does have magic in it."

"I could have done that for you," I said.

"You are the one who gave it to me, and it's fair to say I don't trust you. Indeed, I shouldn't say *gave*, I meant sold, and it was Glass, not you, who asked a considerable thing in return."

My blood chilled and my heart raced. Beside me, Matt shifted his weight to his other foot.

"I see from your faces that you realize I now know you sold me an ordinary rug, not a magical flying one." He indicated the rug beneath our feet. "I thought it was too small to be the one we saw that day."

"You didn't expect us to hand over something so valuable." Matt did not pose it as a question so Lord Coyle offered no answer.

He merely sat there, holding his wife's fingertips as if he'd just managed to catch her before she snatched her hand away. "You crossed me, Glass."

"Go on," Matt said idly. "Next you have to issue a threat. That's how these exchanges go."

I could have kicked him, but I doubted that would have shut him up. Matt was not going to bow beneath Coyle's ferocity any more than Coyle was going to let us get away with the duplicity.

"I won't threaten you," Lord Coyle said. "Not if you give me the real magical carpet."

"It's lost," I told him. "It landed in a paddock somewhere near Brighton and has since disappeared."

"Perhaps a cow ate it," Matt said without taking his cold glare off Coyle.

"I want that carpet!"

Hope and I both jumped at Coyle's bellow. Coyle's grip tightened on her fingers.

Hope swallowed. "You could speak the spell into another one." She tapped her toe on the rug beneath her feet. "Why not this one? Do it now."

"The spell was stolen from Fabian and I haven't memorized it," I said.

Her eyes widened. She turned to her husband.

He let go of her hand. "Another carpet will not suffice. I want the original. That was what I purchased."

"Why does it matter?" Hope asked. "It will still be one of two flying magical carpets in existence."

"It matters!"

I jumped again, but Hope seemed prepared this time. She regarded him with that superior air she often used on me. I wondered if it galled him as it galled me. After all, she was only on her lofty pedestal because marrying him put her there.

"No harm done," Matt said. His cheerfulness got everyone's attention in the way a sharp object down a chalkboard does. "No money exchanged hands and we hadn't yet collected our payment. As to the matter of the burglary…"

Coyle pointed at the door. "Get out."

"Can we at least look at your collection? Just to make sure, of course."

An unexpected ally came in the form of Hope. "That seems like a good idea. We can have this resolved in a moment." To her husband, she added, "We don't want them thinking you're a common thief."

Coyle's jowls took on a life of their own as he struggled to contain his rising temper. He failed, however, and his face turned a dangerous shade of puce. "I said get out!"

The door opened and the butler and a burly footman stood there.

Matt smiled at Coyle. "Why won't you listen to your wife on this? If you want us to think you innocent, you should just open the secret door."

"I don't care what you think," Coyle ground out between a locked jaw. He flicked a hand at the butler. "See Mr. and Mrs. Glass out."

The butler indicated we should exit the library ahead of him.

"Then bring me a cigar," Lord Coyle snapped.

Hope pulled a face. "You promised me you wouldn't smoke in the house. It makes the furniture smell."

"It's my bloody house, my furniture, and I like the smell."

"That's the end of that love affair," Matt said as the butler closed the front door behind us.

"I don't think love had much to do with their relationship. Certainly not on her part. Her reasons for marrying Coyle were entirely avaricious."

Matt gave Woodall the address Fabian had given for Mr. Trentham's toyshop. He'd gleaned it from the toymaker at Louisa's soiree. Once we were settled in the carriage, Matt tucked the blanket over my lap. When the horses set off, I rocked forward, bumping my forehead on his chin. He kissed the spot, his warm lips lingering invitingly.

But I wasn't in the mood for kisses. "Do you think we need to worry about Coyle's threat?" I asked.

"He didn't threaten us. Not really."

I regarded him levelly. "You know what I mean. Should we be worried that he knows we tricked him?"

"We should always worry about Coyle."

I sighed. Worrying about Coyle and what he'd do was constantly in the back of my mind of late. The problem was, we weren't entirely sure what he wanted. Money seemed the most obvious, but why? He had no heir to leave it to, unless Hope fell pregnant. Perhaps he wanted power, but I wasn't sure how collecting magical objects would get it. Collecting information certainly did, and had allowed him to manipulate people and events to his liking, but not magical things.

"I wonder why he didn't want us seeing his collection today," I said.

"Probably because your spell is in there."

"I suppose so."

The question now was, who stole it for him? And if it was the toymaker magician, would he admit it to save himself? Or did Coyle have some incriminating information against him that would see him lie, no matter what?

CHAPTER 4

*M*r. Trentham's toyshop on High Holborn was a delightful fantasy land for any child. It was crammed with everything a boy or girl could dream up, from baby rattles to sophisticated train sets. A rather intricate dolls house with miniature furniture reminded me of a carpentry magician we'd met recently. It sat at the back of the shop beside a life-sized medieval knight complete with helmet, chainmail and shield. There were also toy soldiers arranged in battle formation, board games, rocking horses, boats and a collection of puppies that looked eerily lifelike.

It was the workshop at the back that delighted me more, however. Spread over a counter, desk and on the floor itself, were half-built toys, painting tubes and brushes, and internal mechanisms that looked similar to those used in timepieces. They must be for the drum-playing monkey automaton perched on the end of the long workbench. It looked poised to make a loud bang on its drums, and going by its mischievous expression, it couldn't wait to annoy the adults of the household while delighting the children.

I picked up a toy soldier's wooden leg only to put it down again when I spotted train carriages lined up to be painted.

They were wooden too, with a pull string for a young child to tug. A metal train set on the desk looked more interesting and I bent to have a closer look.

"How does it move?" I asked. "Can I look inside to see how it works?"

Mr. Trentham chuckled softly. His wife, serving in the shop at the front, had shown us through to her husband's workshop before leaving us alone. We had not yet stated our business.

"It uses a simple winding mechanism." Mr. Trentham held up a key and inserted it into a slot at the front of the engine. "Like a clock."

"No wonder I was drawn to it."

He cleared some space on the workbench and positioned the engine at one end. He turned the key and the engine whirred then moved forward two feet before coming to a halt.

"Marvelous," I said, successfully keeping the disappointment from my voice.

"That's without magic." Mr. Trentham returned the engine to the end of the counter then spoke a spell very similar in timbre to Fabian's iron movement spell. He turned the key, released it, and the engine shot forward. It lost power about half way along the counter and stopped before it toppled off the end.

I applauded, although I was still somewhat disappointed. The counter was only about five feet long.

Mr. Trentham gave me a sheepish look. "I'm afraid that's it. The spell only works for a single use."

"It's still magical, Mr. Trentham, and all magic is marvelous."

"You're too kind. I know it's not much. My magic is…not what it ought to be."

"Mr. Charbonneau told me you think a curse was laid upon you and your magic," I said.

He picked up the engine and studied it with a sigh. "A

rival magician toymaker, Nicholas Mirnov, put the curse on me several years ago. Before the curse, that train would have traveled clean off the counter and landed gently on the floor. Now, not only can't it reach the end, but it would break if it fell."

"Your spell could control its flight?"

"I controlled its speed and direction with my mind. I had to concentrate very hard, but it almost always worked. Now, my magic is a shadow of what it once was."

It was very much how I'd made the carpet fly so I knew he must be speaking the truth. "Tell me about Nicholas Mirnov."

"Despite the foreign sounding name, he's English. He sells toys from a cart he takes around the poorer streets of Bethnal Green." He made a face. "He's friendly with the foreigners in those parts, and is part gypsy, I believe. Filthy, sticky-fingered thieves, the lot of them."

"Why did he curse you?"

"It wasn't him, it was his wife, but she did it upon his urging, I'm sure of it. She's full gypsy. Her family are travelers, living out of caravans and tents, but she and Mirnov settled down in London when they married."

"You seem to know him quite well."

"We're both members of the Toymaker's Guild. I identified him as a magician immediately I touched one of his toys and felt its heat. I thought we could become friends, but..." He shook his head. "He saw me as a rival. He wanted to be the best toymaker magician in London, without equal. Hence the curse."

"And yet he sells toys out of a cart," I pointed out. "Whereas you have this wonderful shop."

"He wants to avoid detection from the guild, but I suspect he has plans to make something marvelous, something unrivaled, and is worried I'll beat him to it. Or he was worried, before the curse." He cast a forlorn look at the engine.

Out of the corner of my eye, I saw Matt touching things on

the desk, picking them up and putting them down without properly inspecting them. He was waiting for me to finish before he asked his own questions. Considering my questions had nothing to do with the task at hand and were more to satisfy my own curiosity about curses, I decided to end my interrogation and let him take over.

"We need to ask you some questions, Mr. Trentham," I said.

"I'm honored." He fought against a smile. "My magic is humble compared to yours, Mrs. Glass. I hope I may answer to your satisfaction. What do you want to know?"

I suddenly had reservations about what we were doing. Fabian's instincts had sent us here, not solid clues. Accusing Mr. Trentham of theft seemed somewhat presumptuous given our lack of evidence.

Matt had no such qualms, however. "Where were you last night after Lady Hollingbroke's soiree?"

The question startled Mr. Trentham. "Why?"

"Mr. Charbonneau was burgled."

Mr. Trentham gasped. "That's terrible. But…do you suspect me?"

"We're asking everyone about their whereabouts last night," I said quickly.

"Everyone?"

"Everyone with an interest in magic."

"Was one of his magical artefacts stolen?"

Neither Matt nor I responded. Mr. Trentham's gaze snapped from me to Matt then back again. Needing to avert my gaze so I didn't give away too much, I picked up the automaton monkey.

"Was it something special?" Mr. Trentham pressed. "Perhaps something Mr. Charbonneau was working on with you, Mrs. Glass? Perhaps a new spell?"

"What new spell?" Matt growled.

"That's enough speculation," I said, snippily. The snippiness was for both his and Mr. Trentham's benefit. Matt needed to know that Mr. Trentham was merely guessing, and neither Fabian nor I had mentioned our flying spell to him at the soiree.

Mr. Trentham put up his hands. "It's an open secret among magicians that you were working on creating new spells. Many suspect you already created one before stopping your experiments. And since I asked a great many questions about it last night, Mr. Charbonneau suspects me of its theft. It explains why you're here today." When Matt nodded, Mr. Trentham sat heavily on the chair at the workbench. "I can assure you, it wasn't me. I'm no thief."

"Then you won't mind answering the question," Matt said. "Where were you last night?"

Mr. Trentham flipped open the lid of a paint pot. He picked up a paintbrush in one hand and a carriage in the other. "At home upstairs."

"Your wife will confirm that?"

Mr. Trentham's hand shook. "Of course."

Matt opened the door leading to the shop and waited as Mrs. Trentham finished serving a woman and her small son. Once the customer paid, Mrs. Trentham came out from behind the counter and bent to the boy's level.

"There you go, General," she said, handing the boy a box painted with a battle scene on the lid.

His face lit up as he accepted it.

"Now remember to play with the soldiers every day or they get lonely. And be firm," she said with mock sternness. "They require a strong commander, but one who is also understanding. Can you be that commander, General?"

"Yes, ma'am. I will and I promise to play with them every day."

She straightened and saluted him. He saluted back, almost dropping the box.

Matt waited for the customers to leave before asking Mrs. Trentham to join us.

She was at least ten years younger than her husband, with a milky complexion, rosy cheeks and blue eyes. Matt told Mrs. Trentham about the theft, then pointedly asked her if her husband had returned home after the soiree.

"Afterwards? Yes, of course." She sounded relieved.

"Immediately afterwards?" Matt pressed.

She hesitated and glanced at her husband. He gave an almost imperceptible nod. "Yes."

"I'm not a fool." Matt addressed them both, his tone not unkind although I'd heard him infuse more ice into it during questionings. "Mr. Trentham, leave the room."

"No! This my workshop. *You* may leave." He drew himself up, but he was rather shorter than Matt and not at all authoritative.

Matt didn't move.

Mrs. Trentham laid a hand on her husband's arm before letting it fall away. She picked up a doll from a shelf and stroked its hair. "We ought to tell them the truth. It proves you weren't out thieving, so I think we must."

Mr. Trentham glanced at me and swallowed. "Please don't think ill of me, Mrs. Glass."

Is that why he'd lied? Because he worried what I thought? How curious. "I won't judge you. Not if you tell the truth."

He blew out a breath. "I was at the Toymaker's Guild most of the night. I arrived home at dawn this morning."

"You were there all night?" Matt asked. "Doing what?"

"Playing cards, drinking, smoking." He bit the inside of his lip as he looked at me through his lashes. "I never wager more than I can afford to lose. It's just an innocent way to spend an evening with friends. My wife doesn't mind, do you, my dear?"

She smiled. "It's his evening to himself. I don't begrudge

him that. We have no children yet, so I don't mind if he makes a little wager with friends over cards. It's harmless enough."

"Then why not admit it when I first questioned you?" Matt asked.

Mr. Trentham blushed. "Your wife is something of an idol to me, sir. I didn't want her thinking me a poor husband."

"The only person whose opinion you should worry about is your wife's." Matt put out his elbow for me to take. "We'll be following this up with your guild."

"Of course. The thief must be caught." He frowned. "Why aren't the police investigating?"

"Due to the magical nature of the crime, we're not involving the police at this point. But we will, when an arrest needs to be made."

"Good, good." Mr. Trentham let his fingers run over the spine of the train carriages. He breathed deeply, no doubt taking comfort from the toy as I did when I touched a timepiece. "You ought to investigate Nicholas Mirnov. If anyone would covet one of Mrs. Glass's spells, it would be him."

"Mr. Trentham!" his wife scolded. "You can't accuse him of everything."

"Not everything, just this crime. He probably heard about the work of Mrs. Glass and Mr. Charbonneau and, like many other magicians, assumed a spell was indeed created. The man is from thieving stock; it's no stretch to assume he broke into Mr. Charbonneau's house. If I were you, I'd look at him."

Mrs. Trentham threw a censorial glare at her husband and he simply shrugged in return. It was she who showed us out through the shopfront to the door, giving us the opportunity to ask her questions without her husband being present.

"What do you think of Mr. Mirnov being the thief?" I asked her. "What's he like?"

"I wouldn't know. I've never met him."

"Oh?"

"Mr. Trentham and I have been married just shy of two

years. The curse was put on my husband's magic several years beforehand, and it's safe to say they've had little to do with one another since, except for a few guild meetings."

"The guild don't know either of them are magicians?"

"Goodness no. Neither would be allowed to sell their toys if they did. I don't know about Mr. Mirnov but my husband keeps his magic well hidden. Indeed, he rarely uses it."

We thanked her and climbed into our waiting carriage. Matt directed Woodall to take us home rather than to the Toymaker Guild's hall. He wanted to speak to Duke first.

"I'm sure Mr. Trentham's alibi is solid," I said as the carriage jerked to a start. "He didn't look particularly worried about telling us after he got over his embarrassment."

Matt gave me a wry smile. "How strange that he was worried you would think less of him for staying out all night drinking and gambling."

"He isn't to know I'm used to it."

"I think Trentham's a little in love with you."

I laughed. "Don't be ridiculous."

He grunted but he was still smiling.

"What do you think of him blaming Mirnov for the theft?" I asked.

"A man who happens to be his rival and who he claims put a curse on him? It's very suspicious."

"You still don't believe in curses, do you?"

"I'm on the fence."

I wasn't entirely sure I believed either, but Mr. Trentham certainly did. "Setting aside his quick accusation, we can easily find out if Mr. Trentham is lying about his whereabouts last night."

"Indeed. We'll call on the guild this afternoon, and then we'll go in search of Mirnov."

"You think Mr. Trentham's accusation has merit?"

"None whatsoever, but I'm wildly curious about the curse."

* * *

After giving Duke instructions to subtly question Jane, Fabian's maid, Matt and I departed again for the Toymaker's Guild. Squeezed between modern, taller buildings, the thin, half-Tudor timber structure on a lane near St Paul's looked like the creation of one of its member's young customers. Each level leaned a little more than the one below it so that the entire structure resembled a stack of blocks. The effect was rather charming.

The white-whiskered porter who answered Matt's knock invited us inside with a welcoming smile. He was dressed in the scarlet tunic of a redcoat soldier complete with tricorne hat. The livery made him look like a toy soldier, which was probably the intention.

"My name is Matthew Glass and this is my wife, India," Matt said. "Will you—"

"Glass? Mrs. India Glass?" The porter gave me a thorough inspection. "You don't look like a magician."

Matt tensed, and I thought it best to speak before he said something cutting that put the fellow in an unhelpful mood.

"Magicians come in all shapes and sizes," I said. "Very few of us carry wands or have warts."

The porter's whiskers twitched with his fleeting smile. "I was told not to let you in."

"Why? Are they worried I'll turn you into a frog?"

"The guild master says you're a danger to the integrity of the guild and its members, and if you happen to come here, you're to be turned away."

"What does he think I'm going to do?" I posed the question to Matt rather than the porter. Neither had an answer for me, however.

Matt dug some coins out of his pocket. "You seem like a reasonable fellow who wouldn't jump off a cliff just because his employer told him to. We have a few questions about one of your members. Answering them won't get you into trouble. No one else in the guild will even know we were here asking them."

"And we don't need to step a foot inside," I added.

The porter hesitated before taking the coins. "Answering a few questions never hurt anybody."

"Is Mr. Trentham a member here?"

"He is."

"Was he here last night?"

"He was." He pointed to the top of the staircase behind him. "He was in the hall with the others from about eleven to six this morning."

"Are you sure?"

"I was stationed on the door last night, like I always am when they have their social evenings once a month. No one gets in or out without me seeing them." He rocked back on his heels, pleased with himself. "Mr. Trentham arrived late and was one of the last to leave this morning." He indicated the open ledger on the small desk near the door. "I can check if you like, but my memory's excellent."

Matt asked him to check anyway. He did so and showed us the entry for Mr. Trentham. It stated he arrived at 10:54 PM and left at 6:07 AM.

"You keep precise times," I told him. "Thank you for your assistance."

He closed the ledger. "Is that it?"

"Yes."

"That was easier than I expected."

"I reserve my frog spells for the weekends."

The porter chuckled. He touched the brim of his hat and gave me a nod. "You're not as troublesome as Mr. Abercrombie made out."

"Abercrombie!" both Matt and I cried.

"Was it he who warned your guild master not to talk to my wife?" Matt asked.

The porter looked as though he regretted mentioning the name of the former Watchmaker's Guild master. "I, er, I'd rather not say."

Mr. Abercrombie had been the bane of my existence before the guild had removed him as master. He'd tried to block my entry into the guild when I worked for my father, and that was before he or anyone knew I was a magician. He had suspected, however, long before I became aware of my family's history.

Since he'd been forced to resign as master, he'd almost disappeared from my life, only reappearing recently when we learned he told Mrs. Mason about Cyclops and Catherine's relationship.

It seemed he was still warning people against me, too; specifically other craft guild masters. The only reason I could fathom was that he was trying to hinder our investigations. Fortunately it wasn't working.

We thanked the porter and departed. Woodall already had his instructions and we set off immediately when the carriage door closed. We'd decided earlier not to ask about Nicholas Mirnov at the Toymaker's Guild, and I was doubly glad now that we hadn't. By asking after Mr. Trentham, we'd associated his name with mine. If word got back to the members that I'd asked after him, they might suspect him of being a magician and cause him all sorts of problems. I felt awful that I'd implicated one man; I would feel even worse if I implicated two.

"Damned Abercrombie," Matt growled.

I placed my hand over the top of his balled fist, resting on his thigh. "Don't worry about him. His attempts to blacken my name have come to naught. That porter didn't care, and I suspect others wouldn't either."

He uncurled his fist and turned his hand over to clasp mine. "You're right."

"I wonder if his reaction is indicative of how the wider public will react to magicians."

"He's one man, India. I wouldn't wager your life on his reaction."

Nor would I. But it was gratifying nevertheless.

* * *

WOODALL DROVE through the streets of Bethnal Green to Brick Lane but could not drive along it. The narrow thoroughfare was made even narrower by the many food stalls and carts positioned at the front of the shops. A throng of pedestrians moved between them, adding items to their baskets or stopping to talk to neighbors. Hawkers bellowed, each trying to be heard over the others. They watched Matt and me with open curiosity as we alighted from the carriage, making me feel conspicuous in my burgundy velvet trimmed coat and matching hat. We were an oddity, in our sleek conveyance and fine clothes, in an area where the residents were one ladder rung away from the pit of poverty.

We were prepared to ask as many stall holders as necessary if they knew where to find Mr. Mirnov, but the first costermonger we asked directed us to the end of Brick Lane. There, we spotted the toymaker with the side of his cart open and his toys laid out for the dozen or so small children to play with while they waited for their mothers to finish shopping.

"That cart is a lot bigger than I expected," Matt said.

It was as large as the cabin of our carriage, and painted in bright colors of red, yellow, blue, and green with bold lettering. The sides flipped down to form benches, however only one side was set out that way. The toys were similar to those in Mr. Trentham's shop, and the children delighted in playing with them.

A man crouched down to show a little boy how to wind up the toy court jester. The boy's fingers had trouble with the mechanism, but he eventually managed it with the man's encouragement. When he set it down on the pavement and the jester clapped its hands, the boy squealed with delight and clapped along.

"Mr. Mirnov?" Matt asked.

The man stood. He was as tall as Matt but very thin, with a thick black moustache and narrow, sharp face. He wore a long coat that skimmed his shins and a faded cap pulled low over his forehead. He'd been smiling at the boy, but it vanished upon seeing us.

"Who're you and what do you want?" he asked.

Matt introduced us, mentioning that Mr. Trentham had given us his name. He showed no recognition at hearing mine, but his eyebrows crashed together upon hearing Trentham's. "What is he accusing me of now?"

"Theft."

Mr. Mirnov waved a hand in the air as if batting off the suggestion. "Why would *I* steal from *him*? His toys are ordinary. Mine are better."

Matt took a step closer and glanced around to make sure no one was close enough to overhear. "A spell was taken from the house of Mr. Charbonneau. Do you know him?"

"No." He frowned. "This is about magic?"

I was pleased to see he whispered the word, and Matt looked relieved too.

Mr. Mirnov wagged a finger at Matt. "Now I understand. Trentham stole the spell to make his magic stronger and when suspicion falls on him, he blames me. He's jealous of me. He'd like me to go to prison so he can become the best toymaker in London. He hates that I'm the best. *Hates* it!"

"He says you placed a curse on him," Matt went on.

Mr. Mirnov huffed out a humorless laugh. "Do you believe that?"

"So your wife didn't curse him?"

Mr. Mirnov shrugged. "Maybe she did. She was Romany gypsy, and the Romany like to believe they can curse people, but I'm not sure. I'm only half-Romany on my mother's side, so I was never immersed in their culture."

"You said your wife *was* Romany," I pointed out.

"She died three months ago."

"I'm sorry."

He studied the toys in the cart for a moment before turning back to me. "Trentham should look to his own lack of skill and not blame a curse for his poor work."

"Actually his work is very good," I said. "His toys are marvelous."

He indicated his cart full of toys and games. "Mine are better. My automatons work for longer, the spinning tops spin longer. Children love them. Look at their happy faces."

The child sitting on the ground was struggling with the toy jester again, so I bent and wound it for him. He giggled as it clapped and waddled along the pavement.

The toy's magical warmth had been so strong I felt it through my gloves.

I stood and inspected the other toys in the cart. Even with a light touch, I felt their warmth. It was in all of them. Not a single spinning top, wooden soldier, skipping rope or jack-in-the-box lacked magic.

"Was your wife a magician?" Matt asked.

"No."

"Why would she curse Mr. Trentham?"

"I didn't say she did. You said it." Mr. Mirnov grinned, revealing crooked brown teeth.

"Did you ask your wife to place a curse on him?"

"No."

"I'd like to learn more about curses," Matt said, his tone turning conversational. He sounded genuinely interested. "Do you know someone who can teach me?"

"Any Romany can tell you what you need to know, but that doesn't mean they will. Expect to pay for the information."

"Where will I find a Romany at this time of year?"

Mr. Mirnov picked up a small mechanical drummer from his cart and wound it up. "Here and there." He crouched and set the drummer next to the child and smiled as the boy squealed with delight as the drumsticks hit the drum.

"Do they camp in London over winter?" Matt pressed.

"Not usually."

I was about to thank him and leave, but Matt hesitated. A small frown connected his eyebrows. He had detected something in Mr. Mirnov's answers that didn't sit well with him.

"Come now," Matt urged. "There is a group camping here, isn't there? One that would usually be elsewhere at this time of year?"

Mr. Mirnov stood and continued to watch the child and the toy drummer.

"It must be your wife's family. Am I correct in thinking you have no contact with other Romany?"

"I don't have contact with her family, either. Not anymore. They're mad. Don't believe everything they tell you."

Matt thanked him and we departed. His determined step cut a path through the crowded market to our carriage. I picked up my skirts and raced after him.

"Why didn't you press him for a location?" I asked as he held the door open for me. "Or are you not interested in learning about curses anymore?"

"Not right now. We must find the spell thief first." His eyes twinkled as he assisted me into the carriage. "But I don't need to ask him where to find them. I can just ask Brockwell. He'll know where to find the only Romany group to camp in London this winter."

"Very clever. But you're right. Curses must wait. Magic first." I moved my skirt out of the way so he could sit next to me. "Why are you so interested? Is there someone you wish to curse?"

"You never know when it might come in handy. Besides, I

62

need a special power to keep up with you." He kissed my cheek.

"You already have a special power, and it's better than magic. You know how to get the best out of people, how to talk to them and gain their trust so they'll do what you want."

He grunted. "Not always."

"You also know how to handle Willie. Now *that* is a monumental feat in itself."

He chuckled. "Very well. You win. But I still want to learn more about curses."

CHAPTER 5

*W*illie was restless at breakfast. She kept glancing at the clock or the door and took little notice of her food. It was just the three of us seated at the table—her, Matt and me. It was too early for Aunt Letitia, Cyclops had already left for his police training, and Duke hadn't come home all night. I suspected the latter bothered Willie.

"Did you go out with Lord Farnsworth last night?" I asked her.

"No. I went to see Jasper."

"Brockwell? How lovely. How is he?"

"Fine."

Bristow entered, carrying a pot of coffee. Willie clicked her tongue when she realized it was him and got up to pour herself a cup from the sideboard where the butler set it down.

Matt held out his cup. "Thanks Willie," he said from behind his newspaper. I wondered if he'd noticed her distracted state this morning and was ignoring her, or whether the newspaper had taken up his entire attention.

"Is something the matter?" I asked Willie as she sat again, coffee cup clutched between both hands. "Did it not go well with Brockwell last night?"

"Well enough."

"Then it's Duke, isn't it?"

"He ain't been home all night, and I know he was out seeing Charbonneau's maid, not his merry widow."

"So?"

"He's a one-woman man. He doesn't flit from flower to flower like me."

I nodded. "His heart is constant."

She slumped down in the chair and muttered, "I didn't think his heart had anything to do with it."

I sat forward. This conversation had suddenly become more interesting. Even Matt had lowered his newspaper and peered over the top of it at Willie. "But now you're not so certain?" I prompted. "Do you think Duke has taken a deeper interest in Jane the maid than you expected, hence him not returning yet?"

She lifted a shoulder in a morose shrug.

Matt folded up the newspaper and set it on the table beside his plate. "Willie, you can't have your cake and eat it too."

"What's that supposed to mean?"

"It means you claim to have no interest in Duke and yet you get jealous when you think he developed true feelings for someone. You can't have it both ways."

"I ain't jealous. I just...don't like it."

Matt's gaze connected with mine then he rolled his eyes.

"*Do* you have feelings for Duke?" I pressed.

She sighed. "It ain't that. It's like I said the other day. Cyclops is settling down and Farnsworth probably will too. I gave up on Matt long ago, but I always thought I'd have Duke to keep me company. The widow is just an occasional distraction, but maybe Charbonneau's maid could be more."

Matt picked up his coffee cup. "You're being selfish. You have to let Duke be with whomever he wants."

"It's too soon to tell if the maid will prove to be more than an occasional distraction," I said. "Besides, you've still got Brockwell for company."

"And I like my time with him, but he doesn't go out gambling and drinking with me. I need a *friend*. I thought that would always be Duke."

"Everyone grows up at some point," Matt said.

"Not me."

"Amen to that," he muttered into his cup.

Duke strolled in at that moment, looking tired but pleased with himself. He bade us good morning and headed directly to the sideboard and the dishes laid out there. He filled a plate, poured himself a coffee, and joined us at the table. He ate two rashers of bacon before he finally looked up, fork paused halfway to his mouth.

"Why are you all staring at me?"

"We're keen to hear how it went with Jane," I said.

He shoveled the third rasher of bacon into his mouth and chewed. Willie huffed her frustration at the delay. She drained her coffee cup then got up to pour another from the pot.

"Jane was careful," Duke finally told us. "She didn't give much away. I had to resort to questioning the maid who works at the neighboring house. They've become friends."

"I hope you were discreet," Matt said.

"Her mistress was out so she had the evening off. I bought her a drink at the Hound and Thistle. She told me Jane's infatuated with Charbonneau."

"Oh dear," I said on a sigh. "The poor girl. Fabian isn't likely to be serious about her."

"That's what Betty reckons."

"Betty, eh?" Willie snorted. "You're on first name basis already?"

Duke gave her a smug smile. "Wouldn't be right to call her Miss after spending the night with her."

Willie screwed up her nose.

"Did you sneak into her employer's house?" I asked, shocked.

"She doesn't live at her mistress's house. She lives in Soho with her sister and her sister's baby." He sliced the top off his boiled egg. "Betty left early to return to work and I stayed a little longer to help with the baby while the sister did some chores."

Willie watched as he spooned egg into his mouth. "This is your second breakfast, ain't it?"

He smiled around his mouthful of egg.

"You're going to get fat."

He rubbed his stomach. "Fat but happy."

She made a sound of disgust in the back of her throat.

"Can we talk about the investigation for a moment?" Matt said with a pointed glare for Willie. He turned back to Duke. "So Betty thinks Jane was in Charbonneau's bedchamber on the night of the theft."

Duke nodded. "According to Betty, Jane spends most nights with him. I reckon she told you the truth about the coughs when you questioned her."

Matt drummed his fingers on the table in thought. "It seems so." He stopped drumming. "Good work, Duke. Well done."

"You're praising him for that?" Willie cried. "He hardly did a thing! I could have got that much out of the maid."

Duke set his cup down with a *thunk* on the table. "Don't you go near her."

Willie sat back in the chair, arms crossed over her chest. "Why not?"

"Because I found her first and you're supposed to be my friend."

She lowered her arms with a sigh. "Fine. But only because you're so worried she'd like me more, which we all know she would."

He rolled his eyes. "You need a hobby."

"I got hobbies. It's just that no one will join me in them."

"Come to my office after breakfast," Matt said to her. "I've got something for you to do."

While they discussed his plans for her, I sat silently sipping my tea, thinking about Fabian and Jane. While I didn't expect him to live like a monk, I was still a little surprised that he'd take his maid to bed.

I could hear Willie's voice in my head, telling me I was being a prude, that Jane knew what she was doing just much as Fabian did. It wasn't my business anyway and I had no right to even dwell on it. Fabian would probably be embarrassed if he knew that I knew.

I spent the morning with Aunt Letitia while Matt and Willie questioned Fabian's neighbors. They returned after luncheon to report that nobody had heard anything on the night of the robbery, including coughs, nor had they seen anyone behaving suspiciously in the area.

We were at a loss as to how to proceed. We had no witnesses, no evidence left behind by the thief, and the only suspect had an alibi.

No, not the *only* suspect. Mr. Trentham had been Fabian's suspect, but ours was Lord Coyle. If anyone coveted that spell, it was him. If anyone had the means to hire a skillful thief, it was Coyle. He must be top of our list.

But how to prove that he was behind the theft?

It was looking rather hopeless. Matt considered questioning Coyle's coachman for locations where he'd taken his master lately, but I dismissed the idea. Coyle probably paid his servants handsomely for their loyalty. It wouldn't surprise me if he'd also threatened them if they ever spoke against him. Short of breaking into Coyle's house and searching it, I had no other ideas.

Matt, however, had one more. "We'll ask Brockwell for the names of the city's most skillful thieves. If Coyle hired one to break into Charbonneau's house, he would hire the best."

It seemed like a good idea, and we resolved to visit the detective inspector at Scotland Yard. Unfortunately our plan was thwarted by unexpected visitors.

"Are you home for Lord and Lady Coyle?" Bristow asked after answering the front door.

Matt and I exchanged glances. "Speak of the devil," Matt said, giving Bristow a nod to see our guests through to the drawing room.

"Two devils," I added.

"Indeed," Aunt Letitia said, rising from the sofa. "Please give them my apologies. I have a headache and need to lie down."

Willie rose too. "I ain't got a headache, but I'm leaving. No need to give anyone my apologies on account of I ain't sorry to miss them. Want me to go speak to Jasper, Matt?"

"Invite him to dine with us tonight."

Duke followed Willie while Matt and I headed to the drawing room. I steeled myself for what I expected to be another trying meeting with the Coyles.

"I wonder what they want?" I asked Matt before we reached the drawing room.

"I don't know but I doubt it's merely a social call."

We greeted them curtly and received the same stiff manner in response. There was no point pretending civility anymore. We'd gone beyond polite niceties.

"To what do we owe this unexpected visit?" Matt asked as he sat.

Hope smiled at him as I sat beside her on the sofa. "I wanted to pay a call on my dearest cousin." By the way she gazed upon Matt, clearly she wasn't including me.

Lord Coyle's heavy lids lowered to half-mast as he regarded his wife. He'd detected the slight too. What he thought of it, however, was not obvious.

"I doubt this is purely a social call," Matt said to her.

"It is for me. *I* like seeing you, very much."

Was she flirting with him? In front of both her husband and me? Hope had never been shy about her attraction to Matt, and while I doubted those feelings had been eliminated, I thought marriage would have made her set them aside. It would seem not.

Matt was rarely unchivalrous where women were concerned, but he completely ignored Hope and focused his full attention on Lord Coyle. Hope's chin slowly sank and she stared down at her clasped hands in her lap. An outside observer would think Matt's slight had wounded her, but I suspected it was all part of her act.

Lord Coyle shifted his weight in the chair. "How is your investigation into the spell theft proceeding?"

Matt arched a brow. "You can't possibly expect us to answer that considering you're a suspect."

"Come now, Glass. I'm not a common thief. You know that."

"This is not a common theft."

Lord Coyle stroked his long white moustache. "Mind if I smoke?"

"Yes."

"I thought you'd given up," I said.

Lord Coyle grunted. "I came to realize what a foolish mistake I'd made. Let it be a lesson to you younger ones. Don't give up a habit you enjoy, particularly one you've had for many years. The change is…unpleasant."

I tried to watch for Hope's reaction out of the corner of my eye, but her head was still bowed. The knuckles of her clasped hands turned white, however. She knew every word in her husband's warning was directed at her and was about his bachelorhood, not his smoking.

The exchange left me feeling uncomfortable. I shouldn't feel sorry for Hope. I didn't *want* to feel sorry for her. She'd married the earl for his money and power, and her greed had given her what she deserved. Yet a small part of me felt sympathy. I knew all too well from my past with Eddie Hardacre how a woman's position in this man's world was a precarious one. We were at the mercy of our fathers, brothers, employers and husbands, and if none championed you, life could be difficult. Indeed, if the man who was supposed to champion you worked against you instead, life could be a living nightmare. If Matt had not crossed my path when he did, everything would have turned out so differently for me.

"What clues do you have?" Lord Coyle asked.

"We're not discussing the theft," Matt said, voice raised. "If that's all you came for, you may leave."

Lord Coyle stroked his moustache again. "We came for something else, as it happens."

Hope raised her head to look at her husband. Whatever he was about to say, she'd not been informed of it.

Coyle turned to me. "You might be interested to know Chronos is selling his services to other magicians."

I frowned. "What services?"

"He'll use the time spell to extend the magic of others for a considerable sum."

Damnation. My grandfather was doing precisely what I refused to do. I'd been afraid every magician would come pounding on my door, demanding I extend their magic so that it didn't fade too quickly. I'd refused for fear it would give magicians an even bigger advantage over the artless, therefore deepen divisions further.

Chronos seemed to have no such dilemma. He could perform the spell as well as I could, being a horology magician, and yet I hadn't expected him to do it. I thought he possessed enough common sense to see the dangers. He was a bigger fool than I thought, and more selfish.

"How do you know?" Matt asked Coyle.

Coyle smiled. "Come now, Glass, you can't expect me to reveal my sources when you won't give me information about your investigation. Tell Chronos to desist, Mrs. Glass.

He might listen to you." His eyes turned hard. "If not, I'm sure he'll listen to me."

I bristled. "Why? What will you threaten him with?"

Lord Coyle merely pushed himself to his feet with a grunt of exertion.

"Why do you want him to stop?" I asked.

"Isn't it obvious? He's ruining the balance of magic. There's an order in the magical collector's world, a hierarchy. Rare magical objects have a higher value, naturally, and strong magic holds its value longer than weaker. But what happens when the extension spell is added to another's magic? Chaos. Weak magic becomes strong. Objects with Chronos's spell become rare when previously they might have had low value. I can't allow it."

Matt scoffed. "You're worried about your collection losing its value."

Lord Coyle picked up his walking stick from where it was leaning against the mantelpiece. "Balance is important. We can't have chaos. Isn't that right, my dear?"

Hope gave him a tight smile. "You are correct, of course. But who is to say what the balance is and what is chaos? Does not chaos become the new balance, in time?"

Lord Coyle passed her on his way to the door. "You are in a defiant frame of mind today, my dear. I do hope it changes by dinnertime."

The muscles in Hope's face twitched, as if she were trying to suppress a physical reaction. Once Lord Coyle was gone from sight, she seemed to relax a little. She even managed a smile for Matt as they both stood. "I do hope your dislike of my husband doesn't extend to me, Cousin."

"I'm afraid we won't be seeing much of one another," he said.

She suddenly grasped his hand "Please, Matt. You're my cousin, my father's heir. Can we not be friends too?"

"I doubt it."

She blinked rapidly at him and stepped away. "Oh. I see. I'm sorry to hear that. Very sorry indeed." She gave him a rallying smile. "At least we will always be cousins, and one day you will be the head of the Glass family, which includes me."

"You're a Coyle now."

She glanced at the door. "In name only." She picked up her skirts and raced after her husband.

Matt joined me on the sofa, shaking his head. "I always feel like a strong drink after an encounter with one of them. An encounter with both makes me want the entire bottle."

"Did you find Hope's speech odd?" I asked, frowning at the door through which she'd left.

"Very. Do you think she's going mad?"

"It's possible. Marriage to Coyle would cause even a strong-willed woman to lose her mind."

"But she wanted to marry him, even knowing what he's like." He threw his hands in the air and let them fall to his sides. "I thought I understood women well, but she's a mystery to me. I can't decide if I ought to protect her from Coyle or wish her luck."

I tugged on the bell pull and when Bristow arrived, I asked him to bring tea as well as pen, ink and a sheet of stationery.

"Who are you writing to?" Matt asked.

"Chronos. I'm inviting him to dine with us tonight. When he's comfortably full of Mrs. Potter's delicious food, I'll demand he cease using the extension spell."

"And if he won't?"

"I'll tell him Coyle has him in his sights. That ought to be enough to frighten him into submission."

* * *

73

DINNER ENDED up being a grander affair than we'd antici-
pated. In addition to Chronos and Brockwell, Catherine and
Lord Farnsworth joined us too. Farnsworth had come to visit
in the late afternoon and simply never left, while Cyclops had
invited Catherine when he'd called in to see her at the shop
after his classes finished for the day.

"I told my mother that you'd invited me, India," she said
before we entered the dining room. "She wouldn't have let
me come if I'd told the truth."

"Perhaps you should be honest with her," I said.

"Then Nate and I will never get to see one another." She
lifted her gaze to Cyclops's and smiled. He smiled back.
"Don't worry about us, India. My mother will come around.
You'll see."

Her confidence gave me hope. If she could be positive, so
could I. "Are you going to invite Cyclops to tea until she
comes to realize he has a good heart?"

"That'll take too long, considering he can only come to tea
on Sundays now that he's joined the police. Besides, she can
easily make her excuses then we'd have to cancel altogether."

"So what do you have in mind?"

"You'll see."

The dinner gong sounded and we filed into the dining
room, taking our seats as directed by Aunt Letitia. I'd prefer it
if we sat next to whomever we wished, but she was a stickler
for the correct order, although it was difficult with so many
men compared to women, and with Willie being, well, Willie.

We hadn't all been together since Christmas, and as I
gazed down the length of the table, I realized how much I
enjoyed having everyone's company. We were a family. A
mismatched, strange kind of family, but one bound together
as much as the regular kind. The only one missing was Fabian
and I wished I'd thought to invite him.

The food arrived and the many voices in conversation
began to rise in volume as each tried to be heard over the

other. At one point my gaze connected with Matt's over the platters and tureens. He lifted his glass in salute and I smiled back.

"You know, you ought to consider it, Brockwell," Lord Farnsworth said in his clear, refined tones that somehow cut through the noise.

The detective inspector, seated two places down from his lordship, hadn't been listening. "Sorry, my lord, I missed what you were saying. What should I consider?"

"Marriage."

All the other conversations stopped.

Brockwell's face turned scarlet. "I, er…" He studied his plate. Opposite him, Willie studied hers.

"I'm considering it, you know," Lord Farnsworth went on, oblivious to the awkward silence. "I've found myself a nice filly from good stock. She appears to be in excellent health and has a good temperament. I think she'll do well."

"You realize she's a woman, not a horse," Matt said.

"Even so, I'm prepared to take her on." Lord Farnsworth chuckled. "What say you, Steele? You've got more experience than anyone here. Got any advice for a fellow considering the institution?"

Chronos dabbed at the corner of his mouth with a napkin. "Institution is an appropriate word in the instance of marriage." He hiccoughed at that very moment, giving me the opportunity to take over.

"My grandfather's advice on marriage shouldn't be heeded. He wasn't the best husband."

Chronos surprised me by nodding along. To be fair, he'd never claimed to be a good husband. He'd simply accused my grandmother of being an equally poor spouse.

"Marriage isn't something to be entered into lightly," Aunt Letitia said with all the authority of an expert. "Particularly for a woman. It's better to remain a spinster than marry the wrong man. Isn't that right, Willemina?"

Willie choked on her sip of wine. "Are you calling me a spinster?"

"One should marry a friend rather than blindly follow the heart. Passion fades while friendship lasts."

Lord Farnsworth nodded thoughtfully. "Thank you, Miss Glass. Very wise words. So what you're saying is, I ought to look closer to home, so to speak."

Aunt Letitia smiled. "Precisely. Look to your current circle and consider a woman of marriageable age whose company you enjoy. It doesn't matter if she's the wrong sort."

"Quite right. Marrying me will raise her up."

"And soon no one will remember what her station was before the marriage. Society's memory is short."

"Depends on the woman," Duke muttered with a glance at Willie.

Brockwell went quite still.

What a disaster! Aunt Letitia wanted Farnsworth to consider marrying Willie while her lover was seated at the same table! I didn't know whether to laugh or gasp in shock. All I could do was cringe. As hostess, it was my duty to avoid such awkward conversations, but I had no idea how to proceed.

In the end, it was Matt who expertly steered the conversation away. "You never used to think that way, Aunt, but I'm glad you've changed your tune. Speaking of institutions, how is the training coming along, Cyclops?"

Brockwell listened in to the conversation with Cyclops, thankfully. I worried he might continue to frown so hard at Lord Farnsworth that his lordship would notice. I wanted to scold Aunt Letitia for causing such awkwardness at the dinner table but she was too far away from me. I suspected she was avoiding looking at me on purpose.

We adjourned to the drawing room after dinner. Usually the men would remain behind or retreat to the smoking room, but we didn't like such formality and segregation in our household. It was easier to move around in the drawing room, which meant we could have quiet conversations on topics that others shouldn't hear, particularly Aunt Letitia with her delicate mind.

"You should confront Chronos now," Matt whispered in my ear as everyone took their seats or decided to remain standing.

I quickly scanned the room, but couldn't see my grandfather. "Where did he go?"

He returned ten minutes later, a hand to his stomach. "Indigestion," he said with an apologetic look.

"I need to speak to you." I grasped his elbow. "Come and sit with me in the corner."

"The corner, eh? So I can expect a scolding then?" He chuckled, but stopped when I glared at him. He sighed. "So what is it now?"

"I've been informed you're using the extension spell with the magic of others."

"Who told you that?"

"Is it true?"

He tugged on his cuffs. "So what if it is? I've a right to earn a little extra ready in my old age to fund my retirement."

"You already get the rent from the shop. Why do you need more?"

"My rooms are expensive. They're in a nice part of the city. I've also had some big expenses lately." He indicated his suit. "The best tailors aren't cheap."

"Why do you need to go to the best?"

"Because my granddaughter is the future baroness of Rycroft. I can't be seen in poorly tailored suits."

I pressed my fingers to my temple where a headache was beginning to tap away.

"And dining out is costly these days," he added.

"Doesn't your landlady cook for you?"

He screwed up his nose. "She's a terrible cook. Her stew tastes like old boots."

"You need to learn to live within your means."

"That's easy for you to say." He waved a hand to indicate the room. "We can't all marry money."

I sighed. I couldn't win this conversation. "I'll have Mrs. Potter send you leftovers every day. Sometimes I'll put a little extra money in the package for you. Will that be enough to stop you selling your extension magic?"

"Dearest India." He patted my cheek. "You are generous to your poor old grandfather. I knew there was a good reason for you to marry an artless."

I rolled my eyes. Sometimes I wondered if he liked vexing me as punishment for marrying Matt. While Chronos liked the status and wealth that my marriage gave me, and him by extension, he would have preferred I'd married a magician to keep the Steele lineage strong.

Chronos hiccoughed. He pressed a hand to his stomach and winced. "I think I'll say goodnight now."

I asked Bristow to have our carriage prepared to take Chronos home. Once my grandfather was gone, I joined Matt and Brockwell by the fireplace. Brockwell was in the middle of giving Matt the directions to Mitcham Common.

"What's at Mitcham Common?" I asked.

"A Romany camp," Brockwell said. "Usually they only camp there in the summertime, but one family group returned."

That must be Mr. Mirnov's late wife's family.

"Why do you want to know about gypsies?" he asked.

"We're investigating a theft," Matt said.

"Why wasn't it reported to the police?"

"The victim has his reasons."

"And who is the victim?"

"That information is confidential."

Brockwell scrubbed his sideburns. "I assume the theft is

related to magic and the victim wishes to avoid exposing magic to the authorities. Very well, I'll allow your private investigation to go ahead."

Matt laughed softly. "You don't have a choice in the matter."

"However, if there are more thefts, I must be informed."

"Of course," I said before Matt could say otherwise. "In the spirit of working collaboratively, can you tell us of any expert thieves operating in London who are known to the police?"

Brockwell smirked. "No clues, eh?"

I arched a brow, waiting.

"I can think of only two who are not currently serving time at one of Her Majesty's establishments. One happens to be a member of the Romany clan camped in Mitcham Common. I'd begin my inquiries there."

"India!" Aunt Letitia called from where she sat alone on the sofa. "Come and keep me company."

Lord Farnsworth looked up from where he stood with Catherine, Cyclops and Willie. He joined me and sat on Aunt Letitia's left while I sat on her right. The serious look on his face had me intrigued. One never quite knew what would come out of his mouth.

"I've been considering what you said over dinner about marrying a friend, Miss Glass. While I think it's a good idea and very modern, I'm afraid I don't have any eligible female friends."

I pressed my lips together to suppress my smile.

"Don't you?" Aunt Letitia asked, her gaze on Willie. When she saw that he didn't follow her gaze, she thrust her chin in Willie's direction.

He still didn't notice. "Alas, India is already married."

Well, that was unexpected. "I'm honored you consider me a friend, my lord."

"Do call me Davide."

"I thought your name was David."

"It is, but I like the way my former French mistress used to say it. It has an exotic ring to it."

"Very well. I'll call you Davide from now on. Do you mean to say, you don't have any other female friends? Are you *quite* sure?"

He frowned hard. "Oh! You're referring to Willie." He chuckled. "Marrying her would be a lark, I suppose, and we do get along. But I doubt she'd agree to an arrangement that leaves her shackled to a man."

"Very true. She's a unique individual."

Aunt Letitia sighed. "I suppose you're right. And marrying someone so far beneath you would have been rather shocking."

He laughed. "I'll say!"

Peter the footman entered with a message that he handed to Matt. Matt approached and handed the paper to Lord Farnsworth.

Farnsworth read it. "It's from the club. I asked the manager to send me a message when the home secretary shows up, and my butler has sent the message on to me here." He folded up the note. "Want to go tonight, Glass? Might be a good opportunity to chat to him."

Matt and Farnsworth left together at eleven and I went to bed. Matt didn't return until after four. He briefly reported that he'd become friends with the home secretary over their shared interest in poker. I didn't ask how much money he'd lost to earn that friendship because I didn't want to know. It was a necessary expense to learn more about Sir Charles Whittaker.

I left Matt asleep in bed in the morning and ate breakfast with Aunt Letitia, Duke and Willie. Cyclops had already departed for the day. We were just about to finish when Bristow announced that Detective Inspector Brockwell had arrived.

"It's breakfast," Willie said, knowingly. The inspector did have a habit of turning up at meal times and accepting my invitation to stay.

"Tell him to join us," I said to Bristow.

Brockwell had no intention of sitting down, however. "I'm here on official business," he said. "There's been a murder, and according to the wife, you and Mr. Glass were among the last people to see the victim."

"Murder! Good lord, who is it?"

"Mr. Trentham, a toymaker with premises on High Holborn."

I sat back, the wind knocked out of me. Poor Mr. Trentham.

"I have to question you and Mr. Glass about your reason for visiting him."

I nodded numbly and indicated a chair. "You might as well question us over breakfast."

Brockwell inspected the array of dishes on the sideboard. "Thank you, Mrs. Glass. I don't mind if I do."

CHAPTER 6

"He was strangled," Detective Inspector Brockwell said in response to Matt's question. He'd already finished a plate of eggs and sausages by the time Matt joined us and was nursing a cup of coffee. He'd told us he'd been called out to the scene of the murder at six, just after Mrs. Trentham found her husband dead in his workshop.

"Strangled with what?" Duke asked.

Brockwell took another sip of his coffee, set the cup down then wiped his top lip with a napkin. He folded it up before placing it on the table again and finally meeting Duke's gaze. "The bruises match the shape of fingers."

"Bare hands!" Willie looked impressed. "The killer must have been strong."

"He wasn't incapacitated first?" Matt asked.

Brockwell shook his head. "There are signs he tried to fight off his killer. I won't go into details for Mrs. Glass's sake."

Usually I would protest at being treated like a weakling, but this time I was rather grateful. The thought of poor Mr. Trentham struggling with his killer had left me feeling somewhat ill.

"The murderer must have been a man," Duke said, with one eye on Willie.

To everyone's surprise, she didn't disagree. "He'll have the marks of the struggle on his hands and face."

Brockwell picked up his cup again. "If you don't mind answering some questions for me, I'd be most grateful. What was the nature of your discussion with the victim?"

"He's a suspect in our investigation," Matt said.

"Ah, yes, the theft. The one you were reluctant to discuss with me."

Matt shrugged off the pointed remark. "The victim didn't want the police involved, but his wishes will now have to be ignored in light of the murder. The victim of the theft is Fabian Charbonneau. A spell was stolen from his house. Charbonneau had been engaged in a long conversation earlier in the evening with Trentham whereby the toymaker asked many questions about the potential of the spell's existence, so we began our investigations there."

"What's so special about the spell that someone would want to steal it?"

"Fabian and I made the spell," I said. "It's the one we used to reach Brighton."

"Ah. *That* spell."

"It's not only rare, it could be collectible, and therefore valuable."

"But not useful?"

"Fabian's quite sure there are no other magicians capable of making it work."

Brockwell rubbed his sideburns. "So why would Trentham want it? Is he a collector?"

"We don't think he stole it for himself," Matt said. "He probably didn't steal it at all. We suspect Lord Coyle is involved somehow. Outside of our own intimate circle of friends, he's the only one who knew for certain the spell not only existed, but worked. He tried to buy the magic carpet from us and would covet the spell that made it fly."

Brockwell took this information in with a slow nod then a sip of coffee. I was used to his pedantic ways now, but they still grated on my nerves at times, particularly when we wanted information.

"How has your investigation proceeded so far?" I asked.

"You'd like to be involved?"

"Yes," we all said.

He twisted his mouth one way then the other as he regarded each of us in turn.

Willie clicked her tongue and leaned forward. "You know you need our help considering there's a magical connection."

"I will admit that your involvement will make it easier and my superiors won't blink an eye."

"Good," I said. "They've become used to us helping you from time to time, have they?"

"No. I simply won't inform them." He flashed me a rare smile before removing the notepad from his jacket pocket. He licked the pad of his thumb and flipped the pages until he found the one he wanted. "The victim was discovered by his wife early this morning. She says she awoke at about five and wondered why her husband hadn't come to bed. Apparently he sometimes works late, but never that late, and he hadn't gone out to his guild. She went in search of him and discovered him in the workshop. She was very distressed during her interview at the scene, so I discontinued it." He removed his watch from his waistcoat pocket, checked the time then returned it. "She might be ready now. Shall we resume the interview together?"

Matt informed Bristow to prepare the carriage while I went to see if Aunt Letitia had everything she needed for the day and to inform her of our new investigation. By the time I returned, the carriage was waiting and so were the others.

"I'm glad you're coming, Mrs. Glass," Brockwell said as

we set off. "A woman's touch might be useful in getting information from Mrs. Trentham."

Willie frowned. "What about me?"

"Will you offer words of comfort to the distraught widow?"

"Only if I must."

He gave her a flat smile. "You may investigate the scene with Duke while we talk to Mrs. Trentham."

Her gaze narrowed. "Haven't your men already looked over the scene?"

"Perhaps they missed something."

She crossed her arms. "You don't really think that. Come on, Jasper, give me something useful to do. I can ask Mrs. Trentham questions too. I can be sympathetic if I have to."

"You can talk to the neighbors with me," Matt told her.

She gave him a sloppy salute.

When she turned to look out the window, Brockwell mouthed "Thank you" to Matt.

The constable stationed outside the toyshop nodded at Brockwell as we alighted from the carriage. Matt and Willie peeled away to speak to the neighboring shopkeepers, while the inspector, Duke, and I entered.

It was dark inside. No lamps were lit and little of the dull morning light filtered through the windows. It was difficult to imagine children leaving here with smiles, clutching a new treasure. The small toys now looked like forgotten trinkets, waiting futilely for a child to notice them, while the larger ones loomed in the shadows with a sinister air about them.

We wove our way past tables and shelves, careful not to knock anything. Some of the toys had been rearranged since our last visit. The doll's house had been moved to the front and others sat on different tables.

Brockwell pushed open the door to the workshop at the back, only to stop suddenly in the doorway. "My apologies, Mrs. Trentham. I thought you'd be resting upstairs."

I peered past him to see Mrs. Trentham sitting on the same stool her husband had occupied when we'd last seen him. The lamp on the counter cast a pale light across her tear-stained cheeks. She dabbed at her nose with her handkerchief.

"Do come in, Inspector. I was just..." She indicated the room with her handkerchief but didn't finish her sentence.

"I have more questions for you, if you don't mind. Are you feeling up to answering them?"

She nodded. "I know this is necessary, so please go ahead. Ask me anything." She blinked watery eyes at me. "Mrs. Glass? What are you doing here?"

Brockwell explained how Matt and I got involved whenever Scotland Yard needed to investigate a crime related to magic.

She looked taken aback. "If my husband knew that, he might not have been so dismissive when you asked him questions yesterday." She gasped. "Do you think the theft is related to his murder?"

"We're not yet sure," I said.

Brockwell introduced Duke and informed Mrs. Trentham he was going to look over the workshop again then he asked her to repeat what she'd already told him about finding her husband's body. She did, and it was the same story the inspector had passed on to us. He indicated that I should continue with the questions.

"Yesterday, your husband directed us to a rival toymaker," I began. "Do you think Mr. Mirnov capable of murder?"

"I don't know. I've never met him."

"Your husband claimed Mr. Mirnov put a curse on him." At Brockwell's raised eyebrows, I added, "The curse supposedly weakened Mr. Trentham's magic."

She sighed. "I don't believe in curses, Mrs. Glass."

"Even though magic is real?"

She lifted a shoulder in a shrug.

"Did your husband have any other business rivals?" Brockwell asked.

"No. At least, he never mentioned any in a bad light. Only Mirnov."

"What about members of the Toymaker's Guild?" I asked. "Perhaps one of them learned he was a magician and became worried for their own business. If they suspected he used magic, they might kill him out of jealousy or fear."

She picked up a small wooden horse in need of painting. "Do my husband's toys seem special to you, Mrs. Glass?" She set the horse down. "His magic wasn't strong enough to make the sort of pieces that would make another toymaker jealous. Besides, he didn't use magic in many of his toys."

"That's not true. All of the toys I touched yesterday had magic in them."

"Oh." She looked down at her handkerchief, scrunched in her fist. "He told me he rarely used it."

"Has anyone called on your husband lately?" Brockwell asked. "Anyone who wasn't a regular customer or supplier?"

"You mean besides Mr. and Mrs. Glass?" She began to shake her head but stopped. "There was a gentleman last week who comes to mind. He was well dressed and arrived by a private conveyance which is why I remember his visit. He came into the shop and asked to see my husband. I directed him in here."

"Do you know his name?"

She looked down at her handkerchief again. "My husband wouldn't tell me when I inquired."

Brockwell and I exchanged frowns. "Is it odd for him not to confide in you?" I asked gently.

"Somewhat." She sniffed and dabbed at her nose.

The inspector removed his notepad and short pencil from his jacket pocket. "What did the gentleman look like?"

"Older, very large in girth but not height, with a long white moustache."

Everything inside me tightened. It was Lord Coyle. That put a connection between him and Trentham *before* the collector's club soiree.

Brockwell's pencil paused before he continued taking notes. "Do you know what he spoke to your husband about?"

"No." She blinked up at him. "Do you think it was him, Inspector? Do you think that man murdered my husband?"

"I don't think anything yet, Mrs. Trentham." He snapped the notebook closed. "Did your husband keep any private correspondence upstairs?"

"All of his work papers, including correspondence, are kept down here." She indicated the desk in the corner where Duke had just finished going through the drawers. "He keeps nothing in our rooms, not even private letters. He has no family, you see, and no friends outside the guild. Inspector, that gentleman…"

"Yes?"

"There was something about him I didn't like. I can't quite put my finger on it, but I got a feeling of dread when I looked into his eyes."

Brockwell gave a curt, "Thank you," then led the way outside. "Feelings are all well and good, but they're not evidence," he said to us.

There was no sign of Matt or Willie so we waited by the carriage for them. It was one of London's typical wintry days with a sky of solid gray and a chill that made one want to hunker down by the fireplace with a good book. At least it wasn't raining. Yet.

"Find anything?" Brockwell asked Duke.

Duke shook his head. "I went through the papers in the desk, but found nothing from Coyle. There were just unpaid bills, orders, and receipts."

Brockwell turned to me. "Tell me more about Mirnov and the curse he is supposed to have put on Trentham."

"Mirnov is another magician toymaker who sells his

wares from a cart," I said. "He seems to work in the poorer areas of the city. We visited him after Trentham blamed him for the theft. Mirnov's late wife was Romany and it was she who cursed Trentham's magic."

"That's why you were interested in the gypsy camp."

"We think the Romany family in Mitcham Common is Mirnov's wife's family. He suggested as much and didn't deny it when pressed."

"Why have they stayed here through winter?" Duke asked.

Brockwell flipped up the collar of his coat as a freezing wind whipped along the street. "We should visit them and ask."

Duke shivered. "I don't like gypsies."

"They're ordinary people," I told him. "They just live differently to us. There's no need to fear them."

"They curse their enemies!"

"We don't know that. We don't even know if curses are real." Two figures emerged from a tobacconist two doors down. "Here come Matt and Willie. Let's hope they discovered something."

Going by Willie's smug look, I suspected they had learned something of use. We all piled into the carriage with Duke and Brockwell sharing one seat while Matt, Willie and I squeezed together on the opposite side.

We had hardly settled when Willie, unable to remain silent any longer, blurted out, "A figure was seen leaving the premises last night."

"Now that is intriguing." Brockwell took out his notepad and pencil again. "Go on."

Willie leaned forward to watch as he wrote. "The pharmacist's son saw him when he came home." She indicated the shop directly opposite. "According to the father, the son is a bit of a scoundrel, stays out late drinking and gambling. Anyway, when he came home last night at about one, he saw a man leaving the toy shop. He couldn't see his face, but he reckons it was definitely a man."

"Although we all know how deceptive clothing can be," Matt pointed out.

"Aye, but we reckon the murderer was a man on account of the strength needed to strangle someone," Duke said.

"Did he describe the man's physique? His gait?" Brockwell asked.

"He was slim, so it ain't Coyle," Willie said. "Coyle wouldn't do his own dirty work anyway."

"Did he walk or get into a conveyance?" Brockwell asked.

"He was on foot."

Brockwell wrote that down then glanced up, pencil hovering over the page. "Anything else?"

"One more thing," Matt said, more to me than the inspector. "The figure leaving the toyshop last night wore a long coat."

I drew in a breath. "Mirnov. He's slim and wears a long coat."

Brockwell resumed writing. "Then we'll question him next. Glass, be so good as to inform your driver."

Duke opened the door. "I'll do it, and I'll sit with Woodall. There ain't no room in here. I've got to say, I'm glad we're not going to the gypsy camp."

Willie snorted. "You scared of gypsies, Duke?"

"I'm scared of their curses."

She rolled her eyes.

Duke climbed out, but didn't shut the door. He leaned against the doorframe, frowning. "Why did the killer strangle Trentham with his bare hands?"

"What do you mean?" Matt asked.

"The workshop didn't look like much had been moved since the murder. There were toy parts all over the place, and tools too. Both a hammer and screwdriver were near where Trentham's body was found. Why not just use either of them and bash him in the head? It would be easier than strangulation and over in an instant."

It was a good point and one that I pondered on the drive to Brick Lane in Bethnal Green. I couldn't come up with a conclusion, however.

We found Mr. Mirnov standing with his cart at the end of the street market, crouched in front of a group of wide-eyed children watching him perform a sleight-of-hand trick with a deck of cards. Three of them had cards stuck to their foreheads, as did Mr. Mirnov. When he accurately guessed the card on his forehead, the children squealed and applauded with delight.

Upon seeing us, Mr. Mirnov unfolded his long limbs and straightened. He directed the children to run off and find their parents. "What's this? You have more questions?"

"We do," Matt said. He introduced Brockwell, Duke and Willie.

"Detective?" He looked Brockwell up and down. "I'm not a thief! I told them that, but they don't believe me because I'm half-Romany and have a foreign name."

"This isn't about the theft," Brockwell said.

"And it has nothing to do with your ancestry or culture and everything to do with your connection to Trentham," Matt added.

"What has he said now?"

"Nothing. He's dead."

Mr. Mirnov went very still. "How did he die?"

"He was strangled by hand."

He blinked. "Strangled!" He muttered something under his breath in what sounded like a foreign language. "That's terrible. Are you here because you think I killed him?"

"We're interviewing people who knew him and may have held a grudge against him," Brockwell said. "My colleagues informed me that Mr. Trentham accused you of theft, and now he is dead."

"I didn't kill him! I don't hold grudges." He stabbed his chest with his finger. "*He* held a grudge against *me*."

"Because he believed your wife cursed his magic. Is that correct?"

"Yes."

"And did she curse him?"

"She did, but if you're asking me if curses are real and if it worked, I don't know. The Romany believe they do, my wife believed she cursed him, but I can't say for sure."

"Where were you last night?"

"Home." He gave an address in Shoreditch which Brockwell noted in his little book.

"Can anyone confirm you were there all night?"

"No."

"Have you been to Mr. Trentham's toy shop lately?"

"No. I have no reason to go there, just as I have no reason to kill him. Now, are you finished? I have to work."

"In a moment," Brockwell said in his most plodding voice. "Do you know why your wife's family returned to Mitcham Common?"

Again, he went quite still before answering. "No. You'll have to ask them. Do you think one of them is Trentham's murderer?"

"Should we have reason to think that?"

He shook his head slowly. "No, but nothing about the Shaw family would surprise me. Be careful not to believe everything they tell you, Inspector. They're liars, the lot of them."

"Are they also thieves?" Matt asked.

Mr. Mirnov gave a harsh chuckle. "Yes, Mr. Glass, they're thieves and very good ones. Perhaps one of them stole that spell."

"What would they want with it?"

He threw his hands in the air. "I don't know. Ask them."

92

Beside me, Duke heaved a sigh. He knew where we were heading next and he didn't like it.

Brockwell thanked Mr. Mirnov and closed his notebook. He walked off through the market with Duke and Willie flanking him. Matt remained behind and I waited too.

"Just one more question," Matt said. "Do you know a gentleman by the name of Coyle?"

Mr. Mirnov shook his head. "No."

We followed the others back to the carriage. Matt gave Woodall instructions to drive to Mitcham Common on the other side of the river. Thankfully the rain held off, but the grassland was too soggy for the carriage to traverse so we walked from the road across the common. It was quite a vast area with some sheep grazing in the distance, several ponds, and some small copses of trees. A plume of smoke signaled the location of the Shaw family.

A dog tied to a tree stump announced our arrival at the camp with a vicious bark and was immediately joined by two more. Three young boys kicking a small sack stopped and stared. The tallest settled his feet apart, crossed his arms and lifted his chin. His trouser legs were two inches too short and his jacket bore more patches than original fabric, but at least he wore shoes, unlike one of the smaller boys.

An elderly woman with steel-gray hair poking out from beneath a faded red scarf and a young girl seated by the campfire looked up from the cooking pots. The woman rose, adjusting her shawl, but her gaze was more curious than confrontational. Once it fell on me, it didn't leave.

A man aged about thirty emerged from the tent, pitched beside the caravan. He wiped his hands on a rag and stopped by one of the dogs. He spoke quietly to it and the dog fell silent. The others soon followed suit.

"I don't like this," Duke murmured.

Willie hissed at him to be quiet.

We'd already decided in the carriage that Matt should do

the talking, and we wouldn't tell them Brockwell was with Scotland Yard unless it became necessary. The inspector had protested but been outvoted.

"Is this the Shaw family encampment?" Matt asked.

The man approached. Now that he was closer, I could make out the terrible scarring on his ear. Half of the lobe was missing, as if it had been bitten off. He continued to wipe his hands on the rag. Both rag and hands were filthy with grease and dirt.

"Who're you?"

Matt introduced us all. "We have some questions about Nicholas Mirnov we hope the Shaw family can answer for us. Are you the Shaws?"

The man spat into the ground.

"We are the Shaws," the woman said. "What do you want to know about that snake?"

"He was married to a member of your family, wasn't he?"

"My daughter, Albina."

Matt indicated the children. "Is this your entire family?"

The woman laughed a brittle, thin laugh that ended with a dry cough. "All of this just for us?" She indicated the caravan and tent. "Course not. The others are out working."

"What sort of work do they do?"

"Stealing and fighting," the man said with a crooked grin.

"Lancelot!" the woman snapped.

Lancelot's grin turned bitter.

"He's my son," Mrs. Shaw said. "My other son is a tinker. My two daughters-in-law are out selling pegs, baskets, and odds and ends. My husband's dead."

"Does that meet with your approval?" Lancelot asked Matt in a mocking upper class accent.

"I don't care what you do," Matt told him.

"Unless it's illegal," Brockwell added. "*You're* not a tinker, are you, Lancelot?"

Lancelot Shaw must be the name of the master thief Brockwell had identified. I wanted to kick him for inferring that he knew it with his tone. Willie shot him a glare, but Brockwell was too intent on the Romany man to notice. Lancelot's grin widened.

"I want to know about a curse your daughter, Albina, might have placed on a toymaker by the name of Trentham," Matt said.

The woman thrust a hand on her hip. A loose strand of hair fluttered across her face in the breeze and she swiped at it with her shoulder. "A curse, eh? What do you want to know about it?"

"You can start by telling us if they're real or not."

Lancelot tossed the rag over his shoulder and held out his palm. His mother merely smiled as she waited for us to pay him.

"Duke," Matt said.

Duke didn't move. He swallowed hard as he stared at the dog, sitting by its master.

Willie swore under her breath and dug into her pocket. She handed Lancelot a coin, patted the dog and stepped back next to me.

"Curses are real," Mrs. Shaw said. "They work if done properly."

"Did your daughter tell you about the curse she placed on Mr. Trentham?"

Lancelot put out his palm again.

Willie hesitated but when Mrs. Shaw didn't respond, she handed over another coin.

"No, she didn't tell me she cursed a man by that name. She tell you, Lancelot?"

"No, Ma."

"Then why'd you take my money?" Willie asked.

"You want answers, you got to pay for them," Lancelot said. "Even if the answer's not what you want to hear."

Her jaw firmed. "I don't like it when someone takes advantage."

"Then what're you doing in a Romany camp?" Lancelot spread out his arms, indicating the site. "Don't you know we take advantage of *gorja*?"

Willie pushed back her jacket to reveal the gun tucked into her waistband. The moment she did so, Mrs. Shaw whipped out a pistol from the folds of her skirt. All of the children, including the girl, suddenly held knives.

Duke swore. Matt moved to stand in front of me, and Brockwell put his hands up for calm.

Willie chuckled and let her jacket fall back into place. "You're my kind of people. Ever played poker, Lancelot?"

"What's that?"

"A card game from America. Maybe one day I'll teach you."

Duke groaned.

"Willie," I hissed. "I know you want a new friend, but I suspect he'll be a bad influence on you."

"Maybe I'll be a bad influence on him."

"Lancelot is married," Mrs. Shaw said with a scowl for Willie. "Both my sons are. If you want to learn about your future husband, come here and I'll read your palm."

Duke laughed. "She won't get married. There you go, Willie, I just saved you a penny."

"It costs more than that." Mrs. Shaw's thin-lipped smile stretched wide and her dark eyes sparkled. "Do you dare, Miss? Or are you afraid of what you'll learn?"

Duke's laughter died. He knew accusing Willie of being afraid was the best way to get her to do something. Mrs. Shaw had read Willie well.

"Why not?" Willie said. "Just don't tell me when I die. I don't want to know that." She handed over another coin, this time to Mrs. Shaw, and put out her palm.

Mrs. Shaw squinted and bent to give Willie's palm a close inspection. "You will not have children."

"Thank God for that."

"Amen," Matt muttered.

I nudged him with my elbow.

"You will not return to your homeland," Mrs. Shaw went on.

Willie pulled her hand free. "I damn well will."

Mrs. Shaw grabbed Willie's hand and held it tightly. "You paid for a full reading, so I must give you one or it will be bad luck for both of us."

Willie sighed. "So what other nonsense you going to tell me?"

Mrs. Shaw smiled and released her hand. "You'll marry twice. One of your husbands is standing here today."

Willie stared at her. Then she burst out laughing. She laughed so hard she frightened the horse tied to the nearest tree and set one of the dogs barking. "You should have said one husband and I might have believed you." She wiped the tears from her eyes, still chuckling. "Nope, not even then. Jasper knows it too, don't you, Jasper?"

"I do," Brockwell said without looking at her. "Now can we set aside the parlor tricks and focus on the questions we have for the Shaws?"

Willie stepped back, hands up. "Carry on."

"You say you don't know if your daughter cursed Trentham specifically," he said to Mrs. Shaw. "But do you know if she cursed someone for her husband's sake? A rival, perhaps, or an acquaintance?"

"This is the second part of the earlier question," Willie clarified for Lancelot's sake. "We ain't paying more."

"She did curse someone once," Mrs. Shaw said. "Years ago. And I think it was a business rival of her husband's." Her nose wrinkled and the corners of her mouth turned down, as if talking about him left a bad taste in her mouth.

"Nicholas didn't believe in curses, in our culture. He pretended to, at first, but later..."

Lancelot spat into the ground.

"Later?" Matt prompted.

"Nicholas tried to change Albina. He tried to keep her away from us, keep her from her family, her people. He became ashamed of who she was. But Albina always found a way to see us when we came to London. She was a clever girl. A good girl." She looked away, but not before I saw the shine of tears in her eyes.

"Why all these questions about our Albina now?" Lancelot asked.

Willie put up her finger. "Wait. That's a question. You want answers, give me back a coin." She put out her palm.

Duke slapped it away. "Don't antagonize them."

"Mr. Trentham, the man Albina cursed, is dead," Brockwell said in his uniquely blunt way. "He was murdered last night."

"And you think my sister's curse had something to do with it?" Lancelot snarled.

"No." Mrs. Shaw pressed a hand to her stomach. Her sharp eyes drilled into Brockwell. "They think Nicholas Mirnov did it. That's why you're here, isn't it? To find out if he had reason? If he's capable of murder?"

Lancelot released a breath. "He's capable all right. He's more than capable. That bastard's murdered once, he'd do it again."

"Who has he murdered?" Matt asked.

Mrs. Shaw's eyes flashed. "He killed my daughter. He killed my Albina."

CHAPTER 7

*M*rs. Shaw clutched her shawl tightly at her throat. "We didn't want Albina to marry Nicholas Mirnov because he was never taught the Romany ways by his mother. But she insisted."

"Albina was pigheaded," Lancelot said.

"She was strong," his mother countered. "When Albina wanted something, she always got it in the end."

"What makes you think Nicholas Mirnov killed her?" Matt asked.

Mrs. Shaw tapped her chest. "A feeling in here. They grew distant this last year. They argued all the time and he called her names. Terrible names." She shook her head. "He made her feel worthless, like she was dirt under his shoe."

Lancelot spat into the ground. "Because she was Romany. He despised us."

"Did he abuse her physically?" Brockwell asked.

Mrs. Shaw indicated her cheek. "One day in the summer, she visited us. She had bruises on the left side of her face and body. She said she fell down the stairs, but…" She shook her head. "A mother knows when her daughter is lying. It was him. Nicholas gave her those bruises, I'm sure of it."

"Did you confront him at the time?" Matt asked Lancelot.

"Don't answer that," Mrs. Shaw said before Lancelot could speak.

Lancelot shrugged. "I don't remember."

"How did your daughter die?" Brockwell asked.

"The doctor claimed her heart stopped," Mrs. Shaw said. "But how can that be? She was young and healthy. He *must* have done something to her."

"Did you ever take your suspicions to the police?"

Lancelot snorted.

"We had no proof," Mrs. Shaw said with a lift of her chin. "And the police don't liked the Romany. They wouldn't listen to us."

Brockwell shifted his weight and stared down at his shuffling feet. He knew she was right and couldn't defend the organization he respected. While Brockwell was a good man who wanted justice for victims, not all of his colleagues were as fair-minded.

"That's why you came back to London, isn't it?" I asked. "To find proof that Mr. Mirnov killed Albina."

"We wanted to remind him that we know what he did." She indicated her eyes with two fingers. "We want him to know that we see him and see into his empty heart."

Brockwell looked up. "Do not try to get retribution. Vigilante justice is not justice. It's just breaking the law."

Lancelot cracked his knuckles. "Don't worry, Mr. Policeman. We don't break the law in this family."

Brockwell squared his shoulders. "It's Detective Inspector Brockwell. And I know for a fact that you've broken the law on several occasions, Mr. Lancelot Shaw. You've served time for theft, twice, the first time when you were just sixteen. And that's only here in London."

Lancelot merely smiled a rather irritating conceited smile.

"Mr. Shaw," Matt said, "do you know a man named Fabian Charbonneau?"

"No."

"What about Lord Coyle?"

Lancelot shook his head.

"Where were you two nights ago?"

Lancelot jerked his thumb at the tent. "Here. Why?"

"Mind if we look through your abodes?" Brockwell asked.

"Course I bloody well mind!"

Mr. Shaw blocked access to the short ladder leading up to the caravan's door. He cracked his knuckles again.

His mother advanced toward us, shooing us with robust sweeps of her arms. "You can't just come in here and search an innocent man's home. Now get out! Go on! Clear off!"

Duke grabbed Willie's arm and pulled her away. He must have been worried she'd draw her gun, and from the fierce look in her eyes, he was right to be worried.

Brockwell followed them and Matt placed a hand to my lower back to steer me off too. But I wasn't ready to go yet.

I stepped closer and lowered my voice. "Can you tell me which man she's going to marry?"

Mrs. Shaw thrust out her palm for a coin.

"India," Matt warned.

I sighed. "Never mind. I'll enjoy guessing." I picked up my skirts and raced after the others.

"If you become friends with that gypsy then our friend-ship ends," Brockwell was saying to Willie when we caught up to them.

"Don't worry, Jasper. Even I know he'd be nothing but trouble."

We all looked at her in surprise, although Brockwell's gaze held a measure of relief. Ordinarily a directive such as the one he'd given her would fall on deaf ears, at best, or end in a petulant argument, at worse. This change was curious, and very pleasing.

"You settling down, Willie?" Duke asked.

"Ha! I don't believe in fortune telling. I ain't getting married."

"That ain't what I meant, but it's interesting that you *think* that's what I meant."

She shot him a withering glare and lengthened her strides. "You're a turd, Duke."

Duke sidled closer to Brockwell. "She's calling me names. That means I hit close to the bone."

Brockwell watched Willie's back as she forged on, not stopping until she reached our waiting carriage. She scraped the mud off her boots on the back wheel before climbing in. She was sulking in the corner when we joined her. I thought it best to ignore her altogether and focus on the investigation.

Matt gave Woodall instructions to return to the Brick Lane market and as we traveled there, we debated whether we believed Mirnov or his late wife's family. They clearly hated one another.

"I doubt the hatred is recent," Brockwell said. "Seems to me the Shaws never liked that their daughter married a half-Romany non-believer."

"To think he murdered her," I muttered. "He seemed so nice, particularly to the children."

"We only have the Shaws' word for it," Brockwell said. "Don't condemn him based on their opinion."

Matt agreed but had another point to make. "Whether he did or did not kill her, the fact is, the Shaws believe he did. That belief could mean they want to cause him trouble by accusing him of Trentham's death."

"You think they killed him just to implicate Mirnov?" Duke asked. "Seems extreme to me."

Brockwell remained silent as he slowly scratched his sideburns. I thought he was thinking about our encounter with the Shaws until I followed his gaze to Willie. She was staring out the window, her arms crossed over her chest. It would seem that Mrs. Shaw's declaration after reading Willie's palm had got them both thinking.

I smiled to myself.

"I still want to know if curses are real," Matt said. "We need to talk to an independent source who has studied them."

"Who?" I asked. "We don't know any experts."

"We know an expert in magic and its history. It's possible Professor Nash's expertise extends to curses too."

He seemed like a good place to start, but questioning the professor would have to wait. We had more pressing leads to investigate, starting with yet another interview with Mr. Mirnov.

He was not at the market, however. The place where his cart had been was now occupied by a costermonger's barrow. We drove slowly through the nearby streets, and even went to his place of residence, but couldn't find him.

We returned home to Park Street in the afternoon for refreshments and to see that Aunt Letitia had everything she required. She happened to be passing the front door as Bristow greeted us, and smiled at each of us in turn. Until she saw me.

"India! Look at you! You're covered in mud."

I glanced down at my skirt. The bottom three inches were indeed filthy. "So is everyone else."

"Yes, but you're a lady. What if one of our friends saw you?"

"Then I would explain to them that I was meeting a Romany family on Mitcham Common."

She gasped. "Gypsies! Matthew, why did you take your wife to see gypsies?"

He took her elbow and steered her toward the stairs. "Willie wanted her fortune told."

"That's all nonsense. No one can tell the future." She

glanced over her shoulder at Willie. "What did the fortune teller say?"

"Nothing," Willie grumbled. When Duke opened his mouth to speak, she stabbed him with a sharp glare and he closed it again.

I changed my outfit then rejoined the others in the drawing room. Cyclops had arrived home from police training in my absence, and Duke was telling him how our investigation was coming along. Cyclops sighed when Duke got to the part where we had to return here after searching in vain for Mirnov.

"I miss it," he said on another sigh. "I miss talking to suspects, finding clues, and putting together the pieces of the puzzle."

"You don't like training?" Matt asked.

"I do, but I like investigating more."

"It won't be long before you join the ranks of detective," Brockwell told him. "You're a natural."

"And you've got Jasper in your corner," Willie added with a wink for Cyclops and a smile for Brockwell.

The inspector smiled back.

Duke, watching the exchange, leaned toward Cyclops. "You won't believe what the gypsy fortune teller said to Willie when she read her palm."

* * *

MATT, Brockwell and I departed a short while later as the bleak day became an even bleaker dusk. A damp fog was already settling into the narrow lanes and dead-end courts of the slums where the streetlamps provided little comfort and no security. The Shoreditch tenement where Mirnov rented a room on the second floor was one of many built of uniform brown brick. There were no streetlamps here and no lanterns to welcome residents home, only the squalid gutters and the smell of urine. The only light came from our carriage lamps.

The lane appeared deserted. If it wasn't for a child crying, I'd have thought the tenements empty. Brockwell knocked on Mirnov's door, but there was no answer. He tried the neighbor's and a heavily pregnant woman answered. She seemed neither concerned nor curious to greet three strangers on her doorstep. She was utterly indifferent to our presence, even when Brockwell introduced himself as a detective inspector from Scotland Yard.

"We're after Nicholas Mirnov," he said. "Have you seen or heard him return home?"

"No." The woman began to close the door, but Matt put his hand up to stop it.

He offered her a coin. "When does he usually get in?"

"Why should I know? I'm his neighbor, not his wife."

"What can you tell us about his habits?"

She put out her hand. He hesitated before placing another coin on her palm. It disappeared into the pocket of her apron in the blink of an eye. "He lives alone now after his wife passed, God rest her soul."

"Is he a good neighbor?" Brockwell asked.

"He's quiet these days."

"These days?"

"When his wife was alive, they used to have terrible fights. They'd shout at each other then be loud when they made up, if you know what I mean, sir." She rubbed her round belly and chuckled.

"What did they argue about?" I asked.

"This and that. Money, mostly, or her family. He called them thieving, lying gypsies. Sometimes he didn't like the way she looked at a man."

"He was jealous?"

"Aye, but so was she. She'd tell him he flirted with too

many women. He is a terrible flirt, it's true." She winked at me. "Does he flirt with you, ma'am?"

"He wouldn't dare," Matt said before I could answer.

The woman leaned her shoulder against the door frame and gazed up at him. I knew that look. She thought him dashing. He could probably ask whatever he wanted and she'd answer.

Brockwell took over the questioning, however. "Did Mirnov ever hit his wife?"

She shrugged. "I don't think so. It was just a lot of shouting. Was she really a gypsy?"

"Yes."

The woman winced and rubbed her pregnant belly. "If I'd known, I wouldn't have loaned her my cooking pot that time."

"That's probably why they didn't tell you," Matt said.

She bristled. "Her family have given Nicholas nothing but grief since his wife died."

I would have expected his wife's death would have given him grief too, but I kept my mouth shut.

"They used to steal the toys from his cart overnight when he left it outside here. Once, they stole a wheel off it. He found somewhere safe to store it after that."

"How do you know it wasn't a random theft?" Brockwell asked. "Perhaps it was youths having a lark."

"Because after he stored it away, they got frustrated and left him little gifts." She folded her arms over her belly. "Once, they threw dung at his window. Another time, they broke in when he was out and ruined his carpet. It was personal, not random, and youths don't just break into a house in the middle of the day. Now I know her family are gypsies, I reckon it must have been them."

"When do you think Mirnov will return home?" Matt asked.

"Not for an hour or more. Ever since his wife died, he goes

for a drink at The Rose and Crown on Bunhill Row after he locks up his cart."

Matt thanked her and she went to close the door, but I had one more question to ask. "Does Mr. Mirnov receive many visitors here?"

"Not often."

"What about a man named Trentham?"

"I don't know." She ran her tongue over her top teeth beneath her lip. "There was a fellow who came here some time ago, but I remember him on account of his fancy carriage." She nodded at our conveyance then thrust out her hand again. "I could be persuaded to remember more."

Brockwell sighed, but Matt handed over another coin without comment.

The woman rubbed her stomach again. "He was a real fat gen'leman with a long white moustache."

So Mirnov had lied about never meeting Lord Coyle. His lordship had even visited the toymaker here. The question was, why? What did they discuss?

Unfortunately the neighbor had no more answers for us. We returned to our carriage and Matt gave Woodall instructions to find the Rose and Crown on Bunhill Row.

Brockwell wasn't keen for me to enter the pub, but Matt knew better than to forbid me. While Shoreditch wasn't the worst area of London, it was close, and we were very conspicuous. With Matt and Brockwell flanking me, I felt safe, only enduring some curious stares from the patrons we passed. Aside from the serving women, I was the only female and my attire was vastly different to theirs. My shoulders were covered, for one thing, and my décolletage hidden beneath a fur-lined coat.

There was no point trying to blend in since we stuck out like elephants, so Matt asked one of the serving women if she knew Nicholas Mirnov. She nodded toward a fellow with his back to us at the end of the counter. Even seated on the stool, his height was distinctive.

Matt removed his hat and ducked his head to avoid hitting a beam and Brockwell and I followed behind. The deeper we moved into the pub, the more crowded it became. It was warmer too, and the pungent mix of odors grew thicker.

"Mirnov," Matt said. "We have more questions."

Mr. Mirnov groaned as he turned to face us. "Can't a man drink in peace after a long day?"

Brockwell indicated the people surrounding us, talking loudly so they could be heard over the other patrons, and the violinist standing on a chair in the corner, torturing his instrument. "You call this peaceful?"

"No one bothers me here. Until now. What do you want? I've answered everything you've asked of me."

"We have more questions which we'd also be much obliged if you answer." Brockwell angled himself so that he could rest an elbow on the counter. The barman, wiping a tankard with a dirty gray cloth, waited for an order, but Brockwell didn't notice him.

Matt signaled for the barman to pour Mr. Mirnov another drink.

"We've just been speaking to your late wife's mother and brother," Brockwell began.

Mr. Mirnov's lips pinched. "Liars, all of them. Which brother? Lancelot? He's a no-good character. Been in and out of prison his whole life." He accepted the tankard of ale from the barman and saluted Matt with it before taking a sip.

"We know you said they can't be trusted, but we needed to speak to them anyway," Matt said.

Mr. Mirnov swung around to face us fully. "Let me guess what Mrs. Shaw said. Did she say I killed my wife? That I used to beat her and abuse her?"

"Your neighbors confirmed that you and your wife argued."

Mr. Mirnov blinked rapidly. "Did my neighbors also tell you I received abuse from my wife in return?"

Matt didn't answer.

Mr. Mirnov grunted. "Well I did. She shouted at me, I shouted at her...it was just part of being married to a woman with a fiery nature. But I can assure you, I never harmed her. I never beat her or pushed her, and I certainly didn't kill her." He pointed his tankard at me. "You believe me, don't you, Mrs. Glass?"

"I don't know you," I said. "What happened, Mr. Mirnov? Your relationship with your wife wasn't always such a fractured one, was it? The problems came later?"

He took a long sip of his drink before setting it down and wiping his mouth with the back of his hand. "I discovered my wife wasn't faithful." It was spoken so quietly that I wasn't sure I'd heard correctly at first.

Not until Brockwell asked what evidence Mr. Mirnov had to substantiate the claim.

Mr. Mirnov gave me an apologetic glance. "It was her smell. She'd come home reeking like a man. Then one evening I followed her and saw her meet a fellow at the Blue Anchor. They left together and I followed them to a place not far from there. When I asked her later where she'd been, she said she'd visited a friend." He shook his head. "I called her a liar, we argued, and things never improved after that. On the day she died, we'd been having another one of our arguments." He cradled the tankard between both hands and stared at the contents. "She shouted herself to death."

"We're sorry for your loss," I said gently.

He gave me a grim smile. "I did love her once, Mrs. Glass, and I believe she used to love me too. I don't know why her feelings towards me changed. Maybe it was because her family never liked me. They'd say things to her about me, make things up, poisoning her against me. Maybe she eventually believed them."

"Did your wife have heart problems before her death?" Matt asked.

He shook his head. "I know it seems suspicious. She was young and healthy. If I hadn't seen her die myself, I wouldn't believe it either. But she died of natural causes. I only wished her family would believe it and stop accusing me. The problem is, they don't like to admit she was an unfaithful wife. They'd rather think me a murderer than she was a *whore*."

The vehemence with which he spoke the word startled me after hearing the sorrow in his voice. Just when I thought I'd made my mind up about Mr. Mirnov, he gave me reason to change it again.

He turned to Brockwell. "I didn't kill her, Inspector. I'm a toymaker. I like to make people smile. I couldn't hurt her, or anyone."

Brockwell's face gave nothing away. He was unperturbed by Mr. Mirnov's pleas, or his changing tone. He was used to speaking to suspects who were excellent liars.

So was Matt, and it was he who took over the questioning. "Was Trentham one of your wife's lovers?"

Mr. Mirnov's eyes widened. "No! Well, not that I know of. I certainly doubt it. Trentham doesn't strike me as the type to interest Albina. He was too quiet, too much of a mouse for her. She preferred lions and bears."

He would say that if he wanted to avoid suspicion in the murder of Mr. Trentham. If his wife was having a liaison with the rival toymaker, it would give Mr. Mirnov a solid motive to kill him.

"You also told us you didn't know a man named Lord Coyle," I said.

"I don't."

"He was seen at your place of residence."

Mr. Mirnov scoffed into his ale. "That doesn't mean he was there to see me."

"Who else would he call upon?"

He drained the cup and stood. He peered down at me, his teeth bared in a snarl. "Who do you think?"

I refused to be intimidated by this man. Indeed, I suspected he didn't want to be intimidating, he was merely upset at having his wife's infidelity openly discussed. It must be doubly humiliating to talk about it in front of a woman.

"My wife asked you a question," Matt said, his tone as harsh as Mirnov's.

Mr. Mirnov looked away. "He must have been visiting Albina."

Ever the policeman, Brockwell wasn't satisfied with that answer. "Are you certain they knew one another?"

"No, Inspector, I'm not. It's speculation. However, my wife was an adulteress. It's a reasonable assumption that a male visitor to my residence when I'm not home would be there to be intimate with her."

"No, Mr. Mirnov," I bit off. "It's not a reasonable assumption at all." I turned and walked off, pushing my way through the crowd, not caring if Matt and Brockwell followed. It bothered me that men assumed a woman who'd been unfaithful once would be unfaithful again and again, even with a man as revolting as Lord Coyle.

Matt had followed me and he assisted me into the carriage. "Are you all right?" he asked as we waited for the inspector.

"I'm just a little riled by Mirnov's opinion of his wife." I picked up the fur muff I'd left on the seat and dug my hands inside. "What do you think of his suggestion that Albina was having an affair with Coyle?"

Brockwell entered the carriage and sat opposite. He'd heard my question and seemed quite interested in Matt's response too.

C.J. ARCHER

"I think it's nonsense," Matt said. "Coyle has never shown much interest in women until Hope came along. I suspect his interest in her went beyond the physical."

I pulled a face. The notion of Coyle and Hope being intimate was very unappealing.

"He also wouldn't call on Albina at her home," Matt went on. "If Coyle had a mistress, he'd meet her in nice rooms in a good area that was easy for him to get to. Visiting her in her Shoreditch tenement is not Coyle's style."

Brockwell nodded. "You know him best, Glass, so I will bow to your judgement in this. So if Coyle wasn't there to visit Albina, Mirnov must have lied. Coyle *was* there to see him."

"The question is, why?" Matt's gaze connected with mine. "Because of your flying spell? Perhaps he asked him to steal it."

"But the neighbor said Coyle visited months ago," I pointed out. "Fabian and I only created the spell a few weeks ago. We weren't even creating spells until a few weeks before that." Something else was going on here, I was sure of it. Something that had nothing to do with my flying carpet spell.

But I couldn't fathom how Mirnov, Trentham and Coyle were all connected.

* * *

FABIAN CALLED on me the following morning, but I could tell him very little about our progress. Indeed, we hadn't progressed far at all. Trentham's murder had become more important than the theft of the spell, but when I admitted as much to Fabian, he gave me a dubious look.

"The theft is very important," he said. "We do not know what the thief intends to do with it."

"I'm sure the theft and murder are linked. If we find the

112

murderer, we'll also find the thief. Have faith in us, Fabian. Please."

He clasped my hand and gave me a grim smile. "I do, India. I do."

We sat in the drawing room while Matt was in his study, writing letters to his man of business. Brockwell was due to arrive soon and together we would continue with the investigation. Willie had spent the night with him and I suspected would insist on coming, as would Duke. With Cyclops out every day, he was growing increasingly restless. Indeed, before this investigation, he'd mentioned returning home to America. Having received an unenthusiastic response from the others, even Willie, he'd not brought the subject up again.

"Tell me, have you found evidence that Coyle is involved?" Fabian asked.

"He was seen at Trentham's shop as well as at the home of our main suspect, Mr. Mirnov, the other toymaker magician. We're going to question his lordship again this morning."

Fabian's lips pinched. "It must be him."

Brockwell and Willie arrived, and Fabian took his leave. Duke and Willie did indeed want to join us, and we five set off for Lord Coyle's Belgravia townhouse. I spent the short journey trying to determine if Willie and Brockwell had discussed Mrs. Shaw's predictions for Willie's matrimonial prospects, but neither appeared any different this morning. Brockwell was as expressionless as ever, and Willie filled the silence by disagreeing with Duke about a point of American Civil War history. I was rather glad when we arrived at our destination and they called a ceasefire.

We waited in the drawing room for Lord Coyle. It would seem Hope was out or possibly in another part of the house where she preferred to remain to avoid seeing us. The drawing room was showing signs that a lady now resided there. A sofa and chairs upholstered in buttercup yellow had replaced the dark furniture with the thick legs, and a painting of a hunting scene was missing. A gilt-edged mirror now occupied the spot above the fireplace. A vase on the sofa table was filled with pink and peach hothouse roses.

Thankfully Coyle didn't keep us waiting long. He walked with a slight limp to the chair by the fireplace, passing by the sofa where I sat with Duke on one side of me and Brockwell on the other. The smell of cigar smoke trailed him.

"You've brought along the cavalry today, Glass." He groaned as he eased himself into an armchair. "Or should I say the fairground freaks?"

Willie, who'd been inspecting a painting of a sour-faced woman, bristled. "Are you calling me a freak?"

Duke snickered.

Lord Coyle's gaze didn't waver from Matt, standing on the other side of the mantelpiece. "So what do you want to accuse me of now?"

"You previously denied any knowledge of Mr. Nicholas Mirnov," Matt said.

"And I continue to deny it."

"You were seen at his place of residence by a witness."

Lord Coyle's heavy brow plunged. "Where does he live?"

Matt gave him the Shoreditch address.

Lord Coyle's jowls settled into bulldoggish folds and his gaze shifted to the burning coals in the grate. "Well, well," he muttered.

"So you were there," Brockwell said.

Lord Coyle looked up. "It seems someone wants you to think I'm guilty."

Matt folded his arms over his chest and leaned against the mantel. One corner of his mouth lifted with his sneer. "Is that so?"

"Go on, my lord," Brockwell said.

"Some months ago, I did indeed travel to that address. I was sent a message to meet an acquaintance there. My acquaintance didn't show so I left. When I inquired into why, I was informed the invitation didn't originate from them."

"So who did send you the message?" I asked.

"I don't know."

Matt's eyes narrowed. "Can we have the name of your acquaintance?"

"No. Now, if you don't mind, I'm busy." He pushed himself up from the chair and bellowed for his butler.

Brockwell rose, clearing his throat. "Just one more question. You were also seen at the victim's toyshop. Were you—"

"I was purchasing a toy for the grandchild of a friend. It was several weeks ago."

"What about last week?"

"No. I believe it's still legal to go shopping, Inspector?"

Brockwell swallowed. The poor man had shown backbone until now, but Lord Coyle's intimidating glare appeared to be working. Brockwell knew that Coyle could destroy his career if he chose to.

Willie, however, didn't have a career to worry about. She pointed her finger at Lord Coyle's chest. "It ain't illegal, but your story is just that, ain't it? A story."

Lord Coyle gave a harsh chuckle. "And why is that?"

"You ain't got no friends."

Lord Coyle's nostrils flared and his jowls shook. "You need to keep your cousin on a tighter leash, Glass. You don't want her biting innocent people."

Willie charged toward him, only to be caught by Duke and Matt. Duke bundled her out of the drawing room under the disdainful eye of the butler. She swore at the top of her lungs all the way to the carriage.

It was not a peaceful journey to Trentham's shop with Willie spitting angry words about Lord Coyle most of the way. Duke, Brockwell and I tried to calm her down but she ignored us. The only person she would potentially listen to—

Matt—was too distracted to notice. He continually turned to look behind him out of the rear window.

"What is it?" I asked, following his gaze. All I could see was a black growler pulled by two horses.

"That same carriage has been following us since we left Coyle's," he said.

Brockwell, Duke and Willie all tried to look until Matt ordered them to sit down and act normally.

"Do you think it's one of Coyle's spies?" Duke asked.

"It's possible."

Willie reached for the window. "I'll tell Woodall to speed up and lose it."

"No," Matt said. "Let them follow. They're not going to learn anything important by doing so. Besides, it gives us a better chance of seeing who's in that vehicle. If Woodall succeeds in losing them, we might never discover their identity."

"Darn it." Willie slumped in the seat, pouting. "I'm in the mood for a chase at high speed."

When Woodall pulled to the curb outside the toyshop, the other vehicle passed by without slowing. The curtain was pulled across the window and the driver had a scarf covering his lower face. It continued on and turned the corner.

I released a breath and stepped across the threshold into the shop. Mrs. Trentham stood behind the counter, but her smile slipped upon seeing us.

"I thought you were customers," she said, picking up a cloth and wiping over the counter.

"Business is slow?" Matt asked.

She nodded. "No one wants to bring their child to a toyshop where a murder took place."

I approached the counter along with the others, but stopped. I turned around slowly, taking in my surroundings. Something was amiss. Not *missing*, just different.

"Of course!" I strode up to the knight automaton standing

at the back of the shop. "This wasn't here last time we visited, although it was the time before that."

The knight dressed in a full suit of armor was just a little shorter than me but taller than Willie. It stood sentinel by the doll's house as if protecting the damsel inside. It was covered in metal from head to toe; even the hands were made of metal. The face, however, couldn't be seen behind the helmet's visor.

I traced a small indentation with my finger. "The visor is damaged."

Mrs. Trentham joined me and lifted the visor. There was nothing inside, just a dark cavity where the face should have been. It was an empty suit of armor, albeit one that could move when wound up.

"Someone found it in an alley yesterday and returned it," she said. "They'd seen it in here before and knew it was one of my husband's creations." She closed the visor on the void. "I hadn't noticed until then that it was missing. My husband moved a few things around on the day of his death, and then in the chaos I failed to notice it wasn't here. It must have been stolen that night but the thieves couldn't carry it far and decided to leave it behind."

Matt moved up behind us. "You think the murderer stole it?"

"Who else could it be?"

"Are any other toys missing?" Brockwell asked.

"Not that I know of, but I haven't done a full count of the stock. I'm still…out of sorts."

"May I ask you to check when you're feeling up to it?"

"Of course, Inspector. That seems like a wise thing to do. It might help your investigation."

Duke peered behind the automaton. "Does it work?"

"Yes. The key is in a drawer behind the counter, away from inquisitive little fingers. I'm afraid it will knock things off tables if it was wound up in here."

Duke backed away. "Did your husband install his magic into it?"

Mrs. Trentham shrugged. "I don't know."

I touched the knight's arm. The metal was warm. "Yes, he did."

"What would the magic do to it?" Matt asked.

"Make it move a little longer," Mrs. Trentham said. "His magic was too weak to make it work for any length of time."

Matt's gaze connected with mine and he gave a small nod. I took that as my signal to ask the question that needed to be asked. We had decided in the carriage that I must be the one to do it. Matt moved out of earshot, and the others followed. Even Willie, who'd argued that she was a woman too and therefore it was entirely appropriate for her to ask Mrs. Trentham about her husband's infidelity.

I studied the automaton before turning to her. "I have to ask you something delicate, Mrs. Trentham. Please forgive me."

Her gaze narrowed. "Go on."

"Was your husband having a liaison with another woman?"

She blinked hard. "No."

"Not even a few months ago?"

"No! Why?"

"It's a routine question in these sorts of unsolved murders. It means nothing. The inspector wanted me to ask you as he finds it awkward to talk to women."

A fleeting smile touched her lips. "While I cannot be perfectly sure, of course, I doubt it. My husband was either here, in the workshop or at his guild's hall. He didn't have time for other women."

I thanked her and signaled to others that we could go. We were about to exit when Mrs. Trentham called out.

"I almost forgot. I wanted to tell you that I was wrong about something the other day."

"And what is that?" Brockwell asked.

"I didn't see that large gentleman with the long white moustache in the days before my husband's death. It was some time ago. Weeks, I think. He bought a toy."

Brockwell frowned. "You said he only spoke to your husband. You never mention him buying something."

"I was a little muddled last time we spoke. I hope my confusion hasn't caused any problems."

"Not at all." He thanked her for the information and opened the front door.

Matt wasn't quite ready to leave, however. "Are you sure he wasn't here last week?"

She shook her head. "I'm sure."

"Just think for a moment."

Her face crumpled. "Yes. I think so."

I placed a hand on Matt's arm then followed the others out. He exited behind me. I crossed the pavement and had one foot on the carriage step when a gunshot rang out.

A woman screamed. Willie leaped out of the carriage, knocking me aside. Her face was ashen, her eyes full of raw fear. I would have fallen if Duke hadn't caught me by the shoulders. His alarmed gaze didn't seem to see me, however. It focused on the entrance to the toyshop.

Then he let me go and crouched beside Matt, lying in the doorway. A patch of blood bloomed on Matt's clothes. The patch grew and grew as his eyelids fluttered closed.

CHAPTER 8

"*M*att!" Willie's scream drowned out the voices of those who'd stopped to look. "MATT!"

I fell to my knees at his side. He breathed, thank God, and his eyes re-opened. His gaze connected with mine. It was full of pain that I knew he was trying to suppress for my sake. For his sake, I tried not to cry, but my cheeks were damp and I found it hard to breathe. Matt's own breathing suddenly turned ragged and shallow.

He didn't have much time.

My blood thundered between my ears, but it didn't block out Willie's and Duke's shouts.

"The watch! Where's the goddamned watch?" Willie tore open Matt's jacket, then fumbled with his waistcoat. She swore when her trembling fingers couldn't manage the buttons.

I took over, my hands surprisingly steady. My tears stopped and my heart ceased its manic rhythm. Calm settled over me. I couldn't crumble and fall in a heap. Not yet. Not when Matt needed me to be sensible, to be the strength he didn't have.

My fingers found the hidden pocket on the inside of his

waistcoat and I pulled out the watch. Someone had removed his gloves so I placed the watch in his bare hand. The magic bloomed. It was the most beautiful sight in the world and I would never tire of seeing it move through him, mixing with the blood in his veins, giving them an unnatural color that was like nothing else in nature. I watched as it disappeared beneath his sleeve and reappeared at his collar, spreading along the veins, both large and small, of his neck and face.

When it reached his heart, he drew in a deep breath and suddenly sat up. I threw my arms around him, trapping the watch between us. Its intense magical heat warmed me through to my bones.

Before he closed the watch case, I whispered the extension spell for good measure. Then I fell into a sobbing mess.

A set of arms came around us and Willie's voice muttered a string of expletives in my ear. But I could tell she was both smiling and crying as she said them.

After a few moments, she stood and stepped back, her hand out to help Matt to his feet. He took it, gave it a squeeze, smiled at her, and returned his watch to his pocket. He then drew me against his body and kissed my forehead.

"I'm all right." He caressed my cheek with his thumb and smiled down at me. "You saved my life, India. Again."

I tried to smile up at him but it was wobbly and unconvincing.

Matt broke the tender moment upon Mrs. Trentham's gasp.

"I can't believe you're alive," she whispered from the doorway.

I looked around and saw that Brockwell kept onlookers at bay. Duke had disappeared and Matt asked after him.

Brockwell peered along the street. "He went after the carriage, but it was going fast."

I followed his gaze. "The shooter was inside?"

"Was it the same carriage that followed us?" Matt asked.

Brockwell shook his head. "I don't know. It looked the same, but unmarked black growlers are as common as mud around London. I couldn't see the shooter, I'm afraid."

Two constables ran up to us, breathing heavily. Brockwell identified himself then directed the policemen to speak to witnesses.

Willie pushed Matt in the back, urging him toward our conveyance. "Get in. It ain't safe for you out here."

Matt hesitated until he caught sight of my glare. With a grim smile, he obliged, and we waited in the carriage for Duke's return. I clung to Matt's hand lest he decide to get out again, and also because I simply needed to hold him.

"We'll have Gabe Seaford check you over," I said. As a magician doctor, he was the only one I trusted to tell me that Matt had fully recovered. Anyone else would wonder why he wasn't dead.

"That won't be necessary," Matt said. "I feel fine."

With his jacket and waistcoat still open, the bullet hole in the shirt was clearly visible. I tore it to widen it and gingerly touched his stomach. His skin was still slick with blood, but there was no wound. Not even a scratch.

"The magic is strong in that watch," he murmured. "I feel normal. Better than normal. I feel—"

"Don't you dare say invincible," Willie snapped.

"I was going to say I feel like a youth again."

She grunted. "Sometimes you acted like you were invincible back then."

"That was the bourbon."

Duke returned and squeezed next to Willie. He was puffing hard. "You all right?" he asked Matt in between deep breaths.

"Fine. Did you see who fired the shot?"

Duke shook his head. "He wore a low hat and a scarf covered most of his face."

"Could have been a she, not a he," Willie reminded us.

She fixed Matt with a stern glare. "So who's trying to kill you?"

"I might not have been the target."

I rounded on him. "No, Matt. You're not denying it this time. That bullet was meant for you."

"This time?" Brockwell echoed from where he stood on the pavement.

"Someone tried to shoot him outside the *The Weekly Gazette's* office before Christmas."

Brockwell leaned into the cabin. "I remember, but I thought Barratt was the target."

"We assumed he was because Sir Charles Whittaker sent a thug to beat him up, but there was always doubt. After today, I'm convinced Matt was the intended victim then. It's too coincidental for it to be otherwise."

Matt opened his mouth to speak, but Willie stabbed her finger into the air near his nose. "Don't you dare try to deny it. You hear me? India's right and you know it."

Matt clamped his mouth shut and eyed me sideways.

"So who wants to kill you?" Brockwell pressed.

Matt shrugged. "Coyle, perhaps."

"Why?"

"Because I'm a thorn in his side. Or Whittaker, for the same reason."

My fingers tightened around Matt's. Both men would deny it if we confronted them about the shootings. So what should we do?

"You have to stay inside the house until the gunman is caught," Willie said, her mind following the same path as mine.

"I can't. We're in the middle of an investigation."

She wagged her finger at him. "You listen to me, Matt. This ain't a negotiation. You're staying home until we find out who's trying to kill you."

Before Matt could respond, I leaned across him to speak to

Brockwell. "Inspector, please ask Woodall to drive to the Belgrave Hospital for Children in Pimlico."

Brockwell waved us off and the carriage jerked forward. Willie and Duke glared at Matt, while Matt pretended not to notice. We sat in taut silence until we arrived at the hospital where Gabe Seaford worked.

* * *

GABE DECLARED Matt to be in perfect health and sent him home. I insisted on checking him over myself, however, and ordered him to the bedroom. I threw his ruined shirt into the corner, but saved the jacket and waistcoat for cleaning. Mrs. Bristow was going to get a shock when she saw the bloodstains.

Gabe had cleaned the immediate area on Matt's stomach where the bullet had entered so I cleaned the rest. The damp cloth revealed the muscular ridges of his body, but no sign of the wound. It had completely healed. It was miraculous, but I felt more relieved than awed. Tears filled my eyes as I washed him, blurring my vision until I could no longer see what I was doing.

"India," he purred. He took the cloth from me and returned it to the basin of water. "Come here." He drew me against him and I buried my face in his shoulder. He held me as I sobbed, stroking my back and neck, up into my hair.

When my crying eased, he clasped my face between his hands, wiping my damp cheeks with his thumbs. I blinked up at him.

"I'm fine," he said with a smile. "So no more tears. Be happy that your magic is strong. I feel fitter than I ever have."

I removed his hands and clasped them against my chest. "Today was...awful. I don't ever want to feel such panic and dread again. It's happened too many times already, and I thought after Sheriff Payne was caught that it was over. But it's not."

"We'll find who did it."

"How? Where do we even begin?"

"Someone might have seen something. We'll wait for Brockwell's report." He kissed my forehead. "We can't do much more than that."

"We *can*, Matt!"

"I can confront Whittaker, I suppose. Along with Coyle, he's the most likely—"

"*You* will do no such thing." I clasped his hands tighter. "You're not leaving this house until the shooter is caught."

He gave me an arched look. "Be serious, India. I can't hide away."

"It's not hiding, it's staying safe. If you don't want to stay here, we can go to the country or the seaside."

He shook his head. "I'll continue on as normal. We have an investigation—"

"Forget the investigation! Brockwell and I can continue without you."

"Oh, so *you* can investigate, but *I* must remain holed up in here?"

I ground my back teeth together. He was being purposely stubborn. I should have expected his masculine pride to be dented, but I didn't think he'd be stupid. "Matt, this is important. You have to stay safe until the gunman is caught."

He let me go and sat on the bed with a heavy sigh. He leaned his elbows on his knees and dragged a hand through his hair. When his hand came away, he peered up at me through the dark strands. "My life has been on borrowed time for years."

"I wouldn't put it like that."

"Call it what you want, India, but it's true. I shouldn't even be here. I should have died years ago."

"Stop it, Matt!"

He took my hand. "Every day of living since I almost died in Broken Creek is a gift. Every moment after your grandfather and the doctor magician placed the magic into my watch is one I should never have lived. I won't waste this second chance by doing nothing. I'm going to live well and by my own rules. That doesn't involve staying indoors like an invalid. I am healthy and strong and *alive*. I owe it to the magic to live the best life I can." His thumb caressed my knuckles. "Do you understand?"

I jerked my hand free. "Can you not do this for me? For the others who love you?"

"I would do anything for you, India. Anything. Even this, if you insist." The pain in his voice grated on my already frayed nerves. "But you'll be caging me for an indefinite period of time. You know that. So please don't ask." He reached for me, but I stepped away.

I turned my back to him and fussed with the objects on my dressing table without really seeing them. Matt wrapped his fingers around my upper arms, but I shrugged him off. My throat tightened and my eyes stung with more tears, but after a few deep breaths I calmed down. I couldn't look at him, however. Not yet. My heart felt so exposed that I knew I'd burst into tears if I saw the anguish in his eyes.

"India, please, accept my decision."

I swallowed the lump in my throat and lifted my chin. "Get dressed and come downstairs to inform the others. I'll see you in the drawing room."

"India!"

I marched out and closed the door on him. He could have opened it but he chose not to. I leaned back against the wall and expelled a ragged breath. *Damn it, Matt.*

I made my way to the drawing room where Duke, Willie and Aunt Letitia sat. From Aunt Letitia's cheerful conversation, I knew the others hadn't told her what happened. I arched a brow at Duke and he gave a slight shake of his head in confirmation.

We spent the afternoon in a strange kind of fog. If Aunt Letitia thought it odd that we were all home, yet hardly spoke a word to one another, she didn't say. Perhaps she assumed it was because the weather had turned nasty. Sleet battered the windows and a cold wind blew down the chimney, fanning the flames. She insisted we pass the time by playing cards.

It was a relief when Cyclops arrived home. He immediately knew something was amiss but thankfully refrained from asking. It wasn't until Aunt Letitia left the room to dress for dinner that we were able to inform him.

There followed the same discussion that Matt and I'd had upstairs. I didn't participate, but the other three made the same case in increasingly loud voices. Matt continued to refuse to stay safely off the street. When they argued back, his temper rose. It rarely made an appearance, but when it did, it was rather ferocious.

"You're being stubborn, Matt." Willie was on her feet, wagging her finger at him.

He batted it away. "That's enough. All of you. I've made my decision, and it's final."

"Be reasonable," Cyclops begged. "You *have* to stay home."

"Would you?" Matt shot back. Upon Cyclops's sigh, Matt marched across the floor only to return. "This is my decision to make. Nobody else's. Is that clear?"

Willie crossed her arms with a *humph.* "Goddamned stubborn *idiot.*"

Duke snapped his fingers. "I got an idea. India, you can have him committed."

"To an asylum?" Matt barked a humorless laugh. "You're the mad one if you think India would do that."

Duke ignored him and continued to address me. "You

need a doctor's approval. Dr. Seaford would write a letter, I reckon."

Willie nodded enthusiastically. "We'll visit Gabe tomorrow. Well, India? What do you say?"

I turned to Cyclops. "What do you think? About staying home, I mean, not about the asylum."

"Thank you," Matt muttered wryly.

"Don't ask me that, India," Cyclops said.

"I am asking."

Cyclops rubbed the back of his neck and winced. "The thing is...he's right. If it were me, I wouldn't stay home either." He put his hands up to ward off Duke and Willie's protests. "He's still a target if he remains here. That won't change. But if he maintains an unpredictable schedule of coming and going, it makes it harder for the shooter to try again."

Willie threw her hands in the air. "That's the stupidest thing to ever come out of your mouth, Cyclops. If Matt stays in here, he won't answer the door, he won't go near the windows, he'll just stay inside and be safe."

"What kind of life is that for a man like him?" Cyclops turned to me. "I can't ask him to do something I wouldn't do myself."

Matt sat beside me and took my hand in both of his. The intensity in his eyes alarmed me. "India."

Bristow entered and announced Brockwell's arrival. The inspector shuffled in, scratching his scruffy sideburns. His cheeks were flushed from the cold and his hair flat from his hat. He didn't look like he belonged in a Mayfair drawing room, but this was no typical Mayfair house.

He greeted Willie with a small smile, the sort that he reserved just for her, and she attempted a smile in return. I wanted to smile too, but my heart wasn't in it. Not tonight. I was too upset and too aware of the man sitting beside me.

Even though I didn't look at him, I sensed Matt hadn't taken that intense gaze off me.

"India," he pressed. "Say something."

I pulled my hand free. "Bristow, is dinner almost ready?"

"I believe it's five minutes away, madam."

"Then please sound the gong to alert Miss Glass. We'll make our way to the dining room now."

With Aunt Letitia present, we kept our conversations to innocuous topics. I asked after Catherine, which made Cyclops smile.

"She's well," he said. "She likes working in the shop. She's getting real good at knowing all the different names for clock and watch parts too."

"And her parents?"

His smile faded. "Her mother is still trying to convince her to look for a...suitable husband. Not that Catherine told me that. Ronnie did after I asked him to keep me informed. He also told me Abercrombie dined at their house last week."

I pulled a face. "No doubt he complained about me the entire time."

"I believe your name came up."

"And yours?"

"Ronnie said I wasn't mentioned. I don't think the Masons want to acknowledge my existence by speaking my name to their friends."

"They will have to acknowledge you soon, or they'll lose Catherine. And I wouldn't call Abercrombie their friend. Mr. Mason detests him."

"Then why was he dining there?"

That was a good question. I suspected it was because he'd somehow wormed his way into their good graces.

"Catherine was angry with them for inviting him, so Ronnie told me. She stood up to her parents over it." He sounded proud of her.

As was I. Catherine had matured so much since she'd fallen in love with Cyclops. Although she was only a few years younger than me, sometimes the age gap had felt larger. She could be silly at times, and an incorrigible flirt, but that had all changed in recent months. "What do you think Catherine has planned to convince her mother that you're worthy of her?"

He shrugged. "I don't know."

Wondering about it gave me something other than the attempt on Matt's life to think about. I avoided his gaze throughout dinner but could not continue to do so afterwards. He sat next to me on the sofa in the drawing room, holding my hand, his thumb rubbing my knuckles. It felt nice, but I wanted to send him a message that I was still angry at him for refusing to protect himself. Torn between withdrawing my hand and enjoying the sensation of close proximity, I ended up doing nothing.

We all breathed a sigh of relief when Aunt Letitia retired early. As soon as the drawing room door closed, we turned to Brockwell.

He dug into his inside jacket pocket and pulled out the notebook. He licked a fingertip and flipped the pages, one at a time, until he found the one he wanted. "According to witnesses, the carriage was pulled by two brown horses."

"Any distinguishing marks?" Matt asked.

"One witness says no, another says one of the horses had white fetlocks, and a third witness says they think one of the horses had a white patch on its forehead."

"One of the horses pulling the carriage that followed us from Coyle's had a white star on its forehead."

Willie swore under her breath. "What about the driver or passenger?"

"The coachman wore a greatcoat and broad hat for the rain. No one saw the gunman inside, but witnesses believe he used a pistol." He glanced at Matt. "The bullet wasn't found at the scene."

"Nor will it be," Matt said.

Brockwell swallowed and his gaze lowered to Matt's stomach. "Unfortunately, we learned nothing else. In my estimation, we're looking for a shooter with a steady hand and good aim."

"Excellent aim," Willie countered. "You'd need the skill of me or Annie Oakley to hit a man from a fast moving vehicle with a pistol."

"Or luck," Duke muttered.

"Or, he wasn't trying to shoot me at all." Matt turned to me. "I might not have been the intended target."

"So who was?" Willie burst out. "Me or Duke? India?"

Matt's lips flattened. "Or someone else entirely."

"You were shot at outside the *Gazette's* office," I said. "On that occasion, the bullet missed, but we both saw where it hit the wall. You were closest, Matt. Not Oscar and not me. I think Duke's right. The shooter had luck on his side this time."

"Or *her* side," Willie chimed in.

Brockwell closed his notebook. "Until we apprehend the gunman, you should remain in the house."

Matt, who'd been dragging his hand through his hair, lowered it to glare at the inspector. "Not you too."

"I really don't think you should tempt the gunman again."

Matt stood and paced the room, already acting like a caged tiger. "Everyone needs to stop telling me to stay home. I'm not going to. I have my watch—"

"And what if the next bullet hits your heart?" I cried. "You'll die before anyone can put that watch in your hand."

He crouched in front of me and rested his hands on my knees. "The chances of him getting lucky twice are very slim. I may not gamble much of late, but I will gamble on that."

I pushed his hands off and stood. "Then you're gambling with your life."

I stormed up to our bedroom and closed the door, wanting

to slam it but not wanting to wake Aunt Letitia. Matt joined me a few minutes later and we undressed for bed in silence. I felt his gaze on me, however. It didn't have the usual tenderness in it, or desire. He was just as angry with me as I was with him.

His anger faded faster than mine. An hour later, with us both still awake, he snuggled me from behind. "Will you turn around to look at me?"

"It's dark. There's no point."

"Then I'll just have to do this." He climbed over me, and went to settle on my other side, but didn't realize I was close to the edge of the bed. He fell off.

I laughed.

"That's better." He climbed back into bed and I made way for him. "I prefer you to laugh at me than be silent."

"I said everything I wanted to say, and we have nothing more to talk about."

He tried to kiss me, but I put a hand to his chest to ward him off. "You're going to remain angry with me, aren't you?" he asked.

"You can be very wise for a stubborn idiot."

He flopped onto his back with a sigh. "For how long?"

"Until you come to your senses."

"That could be a while."

"That's entirely up to you."

He sighed again.

* * *

I AWOKE EARLY. A sliver of wan light edged the curtains, giving the room enough light for me to see Matt by. He was asleep, one muscular arm on top of the covers. I took a moment to admire his form, the rise and fall of his chest with his even breaths, and the way his eyelids twitched as he dreamed.

Then I climbed out of bed and tiptoed to the wardrobe. He awoke while I dressed.

"It's early," he said, voice rough from sleep. "Come back to bed."

"I'm hungry."

"I thought we could have breakfast in here today."

"*You* have breakfast in bed. I'm going downstairs."

He propped himself up on his elbow. "You're still angry."

I finished dressing and left without looking at him. If I looked at him, I might be tempted to give in and rejoin him. It was freezing this morning, and he was warm and very inviting.

But I had something to do, and it did not involve snuggling in bed or eating breakfast. I tiptoed along the hallway, glancing over my shoulder every few steps. He didn't follow. I lightly knocked on Willie's door before opening it. Until that moment, I hadn't considered that Brockwell might have spent the night. He never had, out of deference to Aunt Letitia, but there was a first time for everything. Thankfully there was only one body in the bed.

"Willie, wake up." I shook her shoulder.

She rolled over and squinted at me. "India?"

"Get dressed and meet me downstairs. Be quick and be quiet."

She joined me in the entrance hall a few minutes later. Bristow had sent word to the mews for Woodall and the carriage waited for us outside. Wrapped to my chin in warm clothes, I accepted my muff and coat from Bristow and exited with Willie.

The horses' breaths billowed from their nostrils in the cold morning air. Woodall greeted us, his voice muffled beneath his thick scarf. He already had his instructions, relayed by Bristow, so I didn't need to give him directions. I removed one gloved hand from the muff to hold onto Willie's arm to steady myself. The pavement was slippery with ice and Willie's sturdy boots were made for this sort of weather.

"Where are we going?" she asked as she placed the blanket over our laps in the cabin.

"Sir Charles Whittaker's house."

She gave an emphatic nod. "Good." After a long moment, she added, "Thanks for asking me and not Cyclops or Duke."

"No need to thank me. For this mission, you were my only choice. Neither Cyclops nor Duke would accompany me. They're more likely to alert Matt and stop me going altogether. Besides, they don't regularly carry weapons."

She pulled back her coat to reveal the gun strapped to her hip. "So what's the plan?"

* * *

I wanted to catch Sir Charles before he left for his place of business, hence the early morning visit. That and it was the best time to leave without Matt noticing. Sir Charles looked up from his breakfast when the landlady showed us into his parlor.

"Mrs. Glass! This is unexpected. Do come in." He removed a newspaper from a chair and invited me to sit.

I refused. "This is not a social call."

He glanced at Willie, standing with her feet apart, her hand hovering at her hip to quickly flip her coat aside and draw her gun if necessary. "What is this about?"

"Did you shoot at my husband yesterday?"

He blinked. "No! Good lord, Mrs. Glass. Why would I do that?"

"Because he's getting too close to the truth."

"The truth of what?" He frowned. "Is this to do with your investigation into the murder of the toymaker magician? I read his name in the papers and assumed you would be assisting the police. Tragic business. He seemed like a decent fellow."

"Don't play the fool, Sir Charles."

He laughed nervously, but it withered on his lips. "I did not try to kill your husband, Mrs. Glass. I swear to you."

Willie drew her gun and aimed it at him.

He put his hands up, his eyes huge as he stared at her. "Don't shoot! Please. I'm innocent. I don't even know what you're talking about. Is your husband all right, Mrs. Glass?"

Willie took a step forward and aimed the gun at Sir Charles's head. "If he dies, I'm coming for you. You got that? I'm going to blow your brains out. So you better hope nothing happens to him."

Sir Charles swallowed loudly.

Willie lowered her weapon and we left without another word. I didn't draw a proper breath until the carriage jerked forward and we were on our way.

"He looked real scared," Willie said with satisfaction.

"I think your threat got through to him."

"I reckon it did." After a while, she added, "Do you reckon it was him?"

"If it was, he now knows that we're onto him and he'll not try again."

Willie nudged me with her elbow. "We make a good team."

"We do. I'm the calm one and you're the mad one. Together, we put him off his guard."

"I mean me and my Colt make a good team."

"Oh."

She snickered. "Just joking."

I smiled, despite myself. It did feel rather good to confront him. Whether Sir Charles was the gunman or not, I felt sure he would think twice about crossing us now.

Matt, Duke and Cyclops were at breakfast when we

arrived home. All three stopped eating and glared at us upon our entry into the dining room.

"You can wipe that smile off your face, Willie," Duke snapped.

"What smile?" She headed for the sideboard and poured herself a cup of coffee.

I remained near the door and arched a brow at Matt, inviting him to get it off his chest.

He leaned back in the chair and crossed his arms. "I assume he denied it."

"Who?" I asked innocently.

"Whittaker. Bristow informed me where you went."

"He did deny it, but I never expected him to admit it."

He nodded at Willie, taking a seat at the table. "Did she shoot anything?"

"She was very restrained and merely threatened him. If Sir Charles was the gunman, he won't try again."

His jaw hardened. It would seem he hadn't got it off his chest yet.

Willie frowned at Matt over the rim of her cup. "You knew we went to Whittaker's and didn't try to stop us?"

"It wouldn't have made a difference."

"Even though India could have been walking into danger?"

"I doubt Whittaker was the gunman." Matt uncrossed his arms and picked up his knife and fork. "We were followed from Coyle's, but how could Whittaker have known we'd be there?"

"Perhaps he simply happened to be there at the same time," I said. "He could have decided to follow us on the spur of the moment. Or perhaps he followed us from here, but we didn't notice until after we left Coyle's."

Matt paused before slicing a rasher of bacon. "Do you feel better after speaking to Whittaker?"

"Yes."

"So you're no longer angry with me for refusing to stay home?"

"I've conceded that I can't change your mind."

He gave me an uncertain smile. "Thank you."

I added bacon and toast to a plate from the sideboard and poured myself a cup of coffee. I took a seat beside Cyclops. "Shouldn't you be at the training facility by now?"

"I'm taking the day off," he said.

"Are you unwell?"

"I'm feeling a little sick." He picked up his cup and nodded at Matt opposite. "Sick with worry. I'm joining you on your investigation."

I clasped his forearm. "Thank you, Cyclops."

While my mind couldn't focus on anything except the shooting, Matt was already thinking about the investigation. As we finished breakfast, he informed us that he wanted to speak with Mrs. Trentham again.

"She changed her mind about the timing of Coyle's visit to the shop," he said. "It seems too coincidental that her new story fits neatly with the one Coyle gave us about shopping there several weeks ago."

"You think they're working together?" Duke asked.

"I don't know. But it's worth questioning her again."

"She just lost her husband, Matt," I said. "Shouldn't we leave her to mourn him in peace?"

"I can't. Not until we know for certain she and Coyle are not connected." He rose and came around the table to me. He stood beside my chair as the others exited the dining room, then reached out a hand and caressed my jaw. "I know you don't want to return there so soon after what happened, but we must strike while the iron is hot."

"I know."

"So…" He tilted his head to the side and gave me one of his crooked grins. It was a look designed to disarm my heart. It worked. "Am I in your good books again?"

I stood and kissed him lightly on the lips. "Are you staying home while we go to the toyshop?"

"No."

I walked out of the dining room.

* * *

Mrs. Trentham was with a customer when we arrived, so we wandered around the shop inspecting the toys while we waited. I touched as many as I could, just to confirm that they did indeed contain magic. It was weak and present in most of them but not all.

The woman completed her purchase and beckoned to her daughter who was playing with a wooden horse pull-toy. The girl cast a last longing look at the toy before taking her mother's hand.

I joined Willie at the medieval suit of armor automaton.

She regarded it with one hand on her hip, the other rubbing her chin. "I reckon I could fit inside it."

"You are not going to try it on," I snapped.

"I wonder what it costs."

She stepped closer and searched the suit of armor for a card with the price. She'd just lifted one of its arms when the automaton's hand whipped out and grabbed her wrist.

CHAPTER 9

I screamed.

Willie yelped and smashed her fist into the automaton's arm, but it didn't release her. "Get it off me! Get it off!"

Duke and Cyclops tried to pry open the metal fingers, but only succeeded in snapping one off.

"Careful!" Mrs. Trentham hurried over, key in hand.

"Don't wind it up!" Willie cried.

"Calm down," Duke chided. "She knows what she's doing."

"You calm down. I've got a goddamned metal monster trying to break my wrist."

Mrs. Trentham inserted the key into a panel in the automaton's back and turned it twice. The mechanisms inside the automaton whirred and clanked, and the suit of armor took a step forward, closer to Willie.

She yelped again and jumped backwards, her fingers scrabbling at the automaton's hand. It took another step. Willie stumbled into a table stacked with toys arranged in a three-tiered display. The toys crashed to the floor. The automaton stopped and released her. Its arms fell to its sides, lifeless.

Mrs. Trentham breathed a sigh of relief.

Willie rubbed her wrist, keeping a wary eye on the automaton. "That thing's dangerous."

"I'm sorry, it does that sometimes," Mrs. Trentham said. "Are you hurt?"

"No."

Matt and Cyclops returned the automaton to its original position. Once back in place, Matt inspected it from head to toe. "Why did it move?"

"I don't know." Mrs. Trentham picked up the automaton's severed finger from the floor where Duke had dropped it. "Perhaps my husband's magic is faulty."

Matt looked to me, but I merely shrugged. My magic had always worked when I intended, even if it behaved in ways that I hadn't expected, like the first time I'd tried the flying carpet spell. It never worked when I *didn't* intend it to.

"How often does it do that?" Matt asked Mrs. Trentham.

"Not often. Once, after it frightened a little boy, my husband put it in the storeroom. It was there for months before he brought it out again." She returned to the counter and placed the automaton's finger and key in the drawer.

I took Willie's hand and pushed up her sleeve. The skin was starting to bruise, but it didn't seem too bad.

Duke and Cyclops picked up the fallen toys and returned them to the display table. "You squealed like a pig," Duke said, chuckling.

Willie bristled. "I did not."

Cyclops grinned. "You did."

"Well you would too if that thing grabbed you."

"I'd have smashed it to pieces before it got the chance."

"And then you would have run out of here, screaming in terror."

Duke laughed until tears filled his eyes, only to stop

suddenly when Cyclops punched him in the arm. Willie punched Duke's other arm for good measure.

Matt and I joined Mrs. Trentham at the counter. She looked somewhat ruffled by the automaton's attack on Willie, but that was quickly overwhelmed by her reaction to seeing Matt. She stared wide-eyed at his middle.

"The bullet merely grazed me," he said, anticipating her question.

"There was so much blood."

My stomach suddenly lurched. I pressed a hand to it and closed my eyes against the image of Matt lying on the pavement, so close to death.

He took my elbow. His steady, solid presence was a comfort. "I'm fine." Whether he said it for her benefit or mine, I couldn't tell.

"So I see," she said softly. "Tell me, Mr. Glass, do you think the shooting yesterday was related to my husband's murder?"

"What else could it be?"

Her face paled and she clutched the edge of the counter.

"But I'm quite sure I was the intended target," Matt quickly reassured her. "Someone wanted to warn us to stop investigating."

She blew out a breath. "Oh. Yes, of course."

"You're not in danger," I told her.

She gave me a relieved smile, but I could not return it. "Do you have more questions about what I saw yesterday or about my husband's murder?"

"The latter," Matt said. "Can you tell us more about the time Lord Coyle came here?"

"Who?"

"The gentleman with the long white moustache."

"He bought a toy, but I can't recall what it was. My husband served him. I was rearranging shelves."

"When was this?"

She lifted a shoulder. "Some weeks ago. Perhaps even months. I can't be more certain than that, I'm afraid. Why is it important? Do you think he killed my husband?"

"Why did you initially say he was here in the days before your husband's death? Why single him out?"

"I—I don't know. I was confused." She touched her temple. "My mind has been somewhat muddled since that night." A customer entered and Mrs. Trentham straightened. "Is there anything else?"

"Thank you. That's all for now. Have a good day."

Matt led the way to the door then waited as the others filed out. I didn't follow. I removed my glove and passed the automaton knight, letting my fingers brush against the metal. It was warm. Warmer than the other toys in the shop.

"Mrs. Trentham, has anyone taken particular notice of this automaton lately?" I asked.

"I don't know. It usually captures the attention of most who come in, particularly children. It's a very striking toy."

"Yes. Yes, it is."

I rushed past Matt to be first outside the doorway and checked the vicinity before ushering him to our waiting carriage. I didn't breathe again until he was safely ensconced in the cabin with the door closed.

"That automaton shouldn't be allowed on the shop floor," Willie said, rubbing her wrist.

Duke took her hand and studied the bruise. His face turned grave. "Aye. What if it attacked a child?"

Matt went to open the window, but I slapped his hand away. "What are you doing?" I asked.

"Telling Woodall to take us home. Do you have a better idea?"

"I do, as it happens. We should visit Mirnov again. The automaton felt warmer than the other toys in the shop that have magic in them. The magic in it is stronger."

"You think Mirnov spoke a spell into it, not Trentham?"

"It's a possibility."

"It's certainly worth exploring since we appear to be at a dead end. I'll tell Woodall to go to Brick Lane."

I slapped his hand again as he reached past me for the latch. "Stay away from the window. I'll give Woodall his instructions."

We arrived at Brick Lane twenty minutes later. The toymaker groaned when he saw us approaching through the market stalls. "Are you expecting trouble?" He eyed Cyclops up and down. While they were of a height, Mr. Mirnov was a twig where Cyclops was the trunk of a mature oak.

"We've just come from Trentham's toyshop," I said as my gaze swept past him. We had not been followed, but we needed to stay alert. "There's a life-sized suit of armor near the back. Have you seen it?"

"No. Why?"

"It contains magic."

"So Trentham put his magic into it." He shrugged and gave me an expectant look.

"It was stronger magic than that in the other toys."

"As strong as this?" He picked up a spinning top from his cart and handed it to me.

I removed my glove and closed my fingers around it. It was warm. Warmer than Trentham's toys, except for the automaton. "Yes." I held out the spinning top, but he didn't accept it. He simply stared at me.

"Are you sure, Mrs. Glass?"

I nodded. "There are—were—only two toy magicians in London. You and Mr. Trentham. If the magic in that automaton wasn't his, it must be yours."

He took back the top. "It's not," he growled. "You must believe me, Mrs. Glass. I have not put magic into an automaton suit of armor. What sort of toy magician would make such an object anyway? It sounds frightening."

A group of small children shyly approached the cart, and

Mr. Mirnov bent to their level to speak to them. We hurried back to the carriage. With no further ideas about our next movements, we drove home.

Fabian was there, talking with Aunt Letitia in the drawing room. He looked relieved to see us and greeted us enthusiastically. "How is your investigation coming along?" he asked as he sat again.

"Which one?" I asked. "The theft or the murder?"

Aunt Letitia made a sound of protest and rose. "I have some correspondence to attend to. Excuse me, Mr. Charbonneau."

The men stood and returned to their seats once she was gone.

"The theft, of course," Fabian said to me.

"It's not going very well."

"And the murder?"

"Also not well." I sighed. "We suspect Coyle is involved somehow, but proving it won't be easy."

Fabian turned to Matt. "You are very quiet, Glass. Do you have an idea of how to get the truth from that cur?"

"No."

Fabian frowned. "But something is on your mind, yes?"

"He was shot at yesterday," Willie said.

"*Mon dieu*! Thank God you are not hurt."

"His magic watch saved his life."

"Ah, yes, of course. Then thank God for magic. You must be very shaken."

"We are," I said, also frowning at Matt. He drummed his fingers on the chair arm and stared into the middle distance. "*Is* something the matter?"

His gaze focused again. "I was just thinking about the automaton. What do you think it was made of?"

"Metal," Duke said.

"Tin," Cyclops countered.

Matt turned to Fabian. "Do you know any tin magicians?"

"No. Why?"

I told him about the automaton at Trentham's toyshop, and how the magic in it was stronger than the rest of the toys, meaning it probably wasn't Trentham's magic. "The only other toy magician in London denies it was his magic in that automaton."

Fabian's breath caught. He passed a hand over his jaw and down to the column of his throat. "You think *it* killed Trentham?"

My blood chilled. I hadn't thought of that, but clearly Matt had, if the absence of surprise on his face was a sign.

"I reckon it could have." Willie rubbed her wrist. "That thing was strong."

"It was mindless," I told her. "It needs magic to make it work and the right kind of magician to infuse magic through it. That's the flaw in your idea, Matt. A tin magician can't make an automaton work, just like a brass magician can't make a clock run on time even though it contains brass components."

"Brass is an alloy of copper and zinc," Cyclops said.

Willie hissed at him to be quiet. "That ain't the point."

"The automaton is more than its tin shell," I went on. "Its mechanism is made up of different components. Only a toy magician can make it move without turning a key, just as only a watch magician can make a timepiece work perfectly."

Fabian suddenly sat forward, his eyes bright. "Both of you are right. A tin magician cannot make an automaton move. But a tin magician with our new spell can."

"The flying spell?" Duke asked.

"Moving spell. We chose to use it to make a carpet fly, but it can be used to move anything containing the magic of *another* magician. In this instance, an automaton made mostly of tin. The metal of its components will be insignificant in quantity for any other type of magician to make it move."

Fabian's gaze settled on me. "You must find a tin magician, India."

I rose and all the men followed suit. Willie remained seated, shaking her head. "Can't any magician make it move with your new spell? Why does it need to be a tin magician?"

Fabian tapped the rug with the toe of his shoe. "Just as I could not make the carpet fly on its own, just my iron rods, a magician who is not a tin magician or toymaker magician cannot make the automaton move."

"Unless their magic is as strong as India's," Matt pointed out. "Then it wouldn't matter what type of magician they are or what type of object they are trying to move."

Fabian smiled at me.

"But there ain't none like her," Willie said, finally standing. "Come on. We've got to find us a tin magician. Any ideas how we do that?"

"Oscar," I said at the same time Matt said, "Barratt."

Willie fastened her jacket buttons. "Then let's visit him now before lunch."

* * *

FABIAN BADE us farewell on the front steps of our townhouse just as Detective Inspector Brockwell alighted from a hansom. We invited him to join us, and filled him in on what we'd learned so far as we drove to Oscar's place of residence. He sighed heavily when we mentioned the likelihood of a tin magician moving the automaton with the stolen spell.

"Is that a problem?" Matt asked.

Brockwell sighed again. "Just once I'd like an investigation that didn't involve magic."

"We were always sure this one involved magic."

"I know. Sometimes I just miss the old days where the criminals were merely brutes fueled by liquor, carnal desire or petty disputes."

Willie barked a laugh. "You love this, Jasper. Admit it. You were bored before we came along."

Brockwell's lips twitched, the closest he ever came to actually smiling. "I suppose you're right." The smile quickly vanished, replaced by a frown directed at Matt. "Should you be venturing out of doors, Glass, considering someone shot you?"

Matt turned a frosty glare onto him. "Say that again and you can walk."

Brockwell's Adam's apple bobbed with his hard swallow and he made a point of looking out the window. "I wonder if we'll get snow tonight."

We arrived at Oscar's accommodation only to be told by his landlady that he wasn't at home and hadn't been home all night. We tried Louisa's townhouse next where she invited us inside, confirming that Oscar was there. I was wildly curious as to whether he'd spent the night but could never ask. Besides, she'd never admit it. The damage to her reputation if it got out would be catastrophic. Not that Louisa would greatly care. She wasn't looking to make a match with a suitable nobleman, nor did she want to mix in society. Still, the gossip might upset the elderly aunt she lived with.

The aunt was nowhere in sight, which meant we could speak freely. Louisa sent the ancient butler away after he'd fetched Oscar, and we sat in the drawing room with the door closed.

"You look well, India," Oscar said as we sat.

"Thank you."

Ordinarily I would make a comment that he looked well too, but I couldn't bring myself to lie. He seemed harried, and the shadows under his eyes dark against the stark white of the rest of his face. His hair was unkempt and his tie crooked, but it was the ink stained fingers of his right hand that drew my attention.

When she saw me looking, Louisa placed a hand over his,

clasping it as a loving fiancée would. "Considering the Inspector's presence, I assume this is not a social call."

"We need to ask Barratt about tin magicians," Matt said. "Do you know any, Barratt?"

"Tin?" Oscar shook his head. "I'm afraid not. Why do you need a tin magician?"

Matt didn't respond so Oscar turned to me.

"We're investigating the murder of Mr. Trentham," I said.

Oscar placed his other hand over Louisa's. "We read about it in the newspaper and wondered if you were looking into it. So he was murdered because of his magic?"

"We don't know."

"We must look at all possibilities," Brockwell added. "It would seem a tin magician may have wielded the murder weapon."

Oscar's brows shot up. "What was the murder weapon?"

No one answered him.

"I see," he murmured. "I'm sorry I can't help you, but I don't know any tin magicians."

Louisa slipped her hand out from between his and leaned forward. "How is your spell making with Fabian coming along, India?"

"I told you, we have given up."

"You *claimed* to do so for Coyle's benefit, and anyone else in that group whose interest in new spells borders on maniacal."

"Whereas your interest is purely for the benefit of mankind," Matt said with chilling idleness.

Her lips thinned with her strained smile. "I am on the side of good, Mr. Glass. I want magicians to thrive and magic to be explored. Have you considered that *you* are the villain here? You want magic suppressed. I want it to bloom."

Matt's hand curled into a fist where it rested on his thigh.

"We *have* given up," I said quickly, before the situation escalated. "That was not a lie."

Louisa leveled her gaze with mine and seemed to be trying to decide if I were telling the truth or not. "Then I am sorry for it. I know that for magicians like you and Fabian, giving up making spells is like me giving up breathing."

"That's being a little dramatic," I said icily. "And why do you presume to know what Fabian or I think?"

"He told me. In fact, that comparison was one he made."

My gaze flicked to Oscar. His cheek indented, as if he were biting the inside of it, and he stared down at his lap. "Fabian doesn't speak for me," I said. "I'm content with my magic as it is."

"Mr. Barratt," Brockwell said, "what do you know about curses?"

Oscar blinked at the sudden change in topic. "Curses?"

"Romany curses."

"Trentham's murder is linked to a gypsy curse?"

"Just answer the question, please."

Oscar shifted his weight and stroked his goatee beard. "Some believe curses are a branch of magic, but I'm not so sure. They seem entirely unconnected to me."

"Both use words," I pointed out. "Curses are a kind of spell."

"True, but magic is grounded in an object or natural resource, like a watch, iron or ink. Curses aren't."

"Are there any books on the subject?"

"I can do better than a book. I can give you the name of an expert. Indeed, you already know him. Professor Nash can help you."

Matt rose, apparently not wanting to stay in their presence a moment longer than necessary. "Thank you for your time, Barratt. Louisa."

"I'll see you out," she said, taking my arm. She slowed her pace and we fell behind the others. "How is Fabian?" she whispered.

Oscar, walking a little in front, turned his head to hear.

"He's well," I said.

"I'm worried about him. If he has given up creating new spells, he'll be out of sorts. Are you sure he doesn't seem unhappy?"

"Louisa, if you're worried about him, why not visit him yourself?"

She blinked rapidly. "Please tell him I think of him every day."

Oscar's shoulders slumped as he looked forward again.

I extricated myself from Louisa and joined him. "How are you?" I asked. "Be honest."

He gave me a tired smile. "Don't worry about me, India. I have much to keep me occupied and a marriage to look forward to."

"The evidence of your occupation is all over your fingers."

He closed his hand into a fist, hiding the ink stains.

"You're writing the book, aren't you?" I leaned closer and checked to see that Louisa was far enough away that she couldn't hear. She watched us, but Willie had engaged her in conversation several steps behind. "She's making you work all hours to finish it, isn't she?"

"I want to write it."

"But at such a cracking pace? Oscar, you're working yourself to exhaustion."

"Louisa makes sure I have enough breaks throughout the day. She's taking good care of me, don't worry."

"Is she? Because from what I see, she doesn't care *for* you. She only cares about your book." I strode off to where Matt waited at the front door, feeling a little sick about how bold I'd been.

But my words wouldn't have come as a surprise to Oscar. He knew Louisa didn't love him. He knew she was marrying him so her children could have a chance of being magicians. That didn't mean I liked letting him know that I knew. It would hurt his masculine pride.

"I thought we were following the tin magician lead," Duke said when we reached our waiting carriage.

"We still are," Brockwell said. "But in the absence of a name, we need to follow all leads. Mirnov is still our main suspect, and Mr. Mirnov's wife put a curse on Trentham."

Duke glanced at Matt. Matt nodded. "We'll call on the professor. Hopefully he can enlighten us about tin magic as well as curses."

Students had not yet returned to University College from the winter break, but staff were on campus to prepare for the resumption of lectures. We found Professor Nash in what must have been the college's smallest office in the history department. We couldn't all fit, so Duke and Cyclops volunteered to stay outside and dragged Willie with them.

Professor Nash beamed as he shook Brockwell's hand after we introduced them, making him seem even younger. With a youthful face, he couldn't be too old, but his thinning hair made it impossible to tell for sure.

"What a pleasure it is to see you again, Mrs. Glass. And Mr. Glass too, of course." He indicated we should sit. "I apologize for having only two chairs. It's a little too tight to fit more."

Even if he tidied up the stacks of books piled on the floor, there wouldn't be enough space for another chair. Nor would there be anywhere to put the books anyway. The shelves were crammed with leather-bound volumes, as was the top of the filing cabinet, and the surface of the desk was covered with papers. I sat while Matt and Brockwell remained standing behind me.

Nash squeezed between the wall and end of the desk and resumed his seat. He rested his clasped hands on the papers and smiled at me. "How can I help you?"

"Do you know any tin magicians?" I asked.

His smile slipped. "I'm afraid not."

"Oh."

"I know iron, copper and lead magicians. Will one of them do?"

"No. We're investigating a murder and believe a tin magician may be able to answer some of our questions."

"Murder!"

"A toymaker magician by the name of Trentham was killed in his workshop."

"I read about it but had no idea he was a magician. How dreadful."

"Mr. Trentham's death may be related to magic, but we don't know for sure."

"Well, I'm very sorry I can't be of more help."

"What do you know about curses?" Matt asked. "Romany curses, to be specific."

"Those are the only kind, as far as I am aware." Professor Nash pointed to the floor-to-ceiling bookshelf. "There's a volume about the Romany on the top shelf. The small one with the red cover."

Matt, the closest to the shelves, plucked off the book and opened it to the contents page. His finger scanned the lines until he found the chapter he needed. "It's a short book."

"So little is known about curses, and those who do know, the Romany families, don't like writing down their knowledge." He indicated the book. "You may borrow it if you like, but perhaps I can answer your questions now. Is there something specific you need to know?"

"Are curses real?" I asked.

He chuckled. "As real as magic."

"Oscar Barratt says some believe curses are a branch of magic, but he personally doubted it."

"Then he's wrong. Historical research points to the likelihood the two were once one and separated at some point in the distant past." He settled into the chair, and I suspected we were in for a history lesson. "Curses and most magic operate on the natural plane, not the manufactured one."

"Time pieces and toys are manufactured."

"Those are two exceptions. As a rule of thumb, if it's created by a craftsman, or is a raw material that can be manipulated by a craftsman, magic can be used on it. Do you recall when I told you that horology magic is a relatively modern magic? Its rise coincided with the new science of horology which is merely hundreds of years old instead of the thousands of the other magics, like gold, for example. If you disregard those modern, manufactured magics, the other, older ones work on natural materials. Wood, clay, cloth fibers, minerals, that sort of thing. Do you follow?"

"So far," I said. "So if curses and most magic work on natural materials, can curses only work on natural objects?"

Professor Nash looked pleased. "Precisely. In fact, they work on only *one* natural object. The body."

"I don't understand."

Matt closed the book, giving Nash his full attention too. "Like medical magic?"

Professor Nash pointed a finger at Matt. "Correct. The theory is that curses and medical magic are linked. Perhaps one grew out of the other. Both curses and medical magic manipulate the body in some way, you see."

Brockwell shook his head. "I'm confused. What if a Romany put a curse on someone to lose their key, for example, or to lose a wager? That's nothing to do with bodies."

Professor Nash chuckled. "That kind of curse is *not* real, Inspector. They're the stuff of fairy tales and sensation novels. The only true curses, ones that actually work, operate on the human body. That's why so many curses are about making the victim fall ill, or for their hair to fall out, their nose to grow warts, that sort of thing. All natural phenomena to do with the body, but helped along by a curse, so to speak."

He tilted his head to the side, smiling, as he waited for one of us to speak. I remained silent as I tried to digest what it meant for our case.

"Does that help you?" the professor prompted.

Matt was the first to form his thoughts into words. "It has been suggested that a curse was placed on the victim by a Romany to diminish the effectiveness of his magic. By your reckoning, that should be possible because magic is also natural."

"I suppose so, yes." Professor Nash pushed his spectacles up his nose. "Magic is an extension of the magician's natural makeup, as it were." He indicated me. "Magic cannot be extracted from Mrs. Glass. It is a part of her as much as any organ within her body. It makes sense that a curse could manipulate her magic, just as it could give her an earache or warts." He suddenly rifled through the papers on his desk until he found a blank one. He dipped a pen in the inkwell and began furiously writing. "This is an interesting development, and one that hasn't been explored. Nobody has conducted research on curses affecting a magician's magic."

"Thank you, Professor," I said, rising. "You've been very helpful."

He continued writing, his spectacles slipping slowly down his nose as he bent over the paper. With a final flourish of the pen, he finally looked up and saw that we were leaving. He returned the pen to the inkstand and rose.

"I'm so pleased I could be of help." He edged around the desk to see us out. "Keep the book as long as you need."

"One more thing," I said before we joined the others in the corridor. "Have you ever heard of magic being faulty?"

He frowned. "I don't understand."

I couldn't think of any way to explain it except by using the real example of the automaton. "There is a toy in Mr. Trentham's shop that has magic in it. It's a wind-up toy and the magic was supposed to make the movements last longer after it's wound. This particular toy still operates on occasion without anyone winding it up, however. Considering Mr. Trentham's magic wasn't very strong, and didn't last long by all accounts, it shouldn't do that, so we wondered if perhaps his magic is faulty."

"Is it made of tin? Is this why you wanted to find a tin magician? You think it's actually tin magic in the toy, not Trentham's toymaker magic? You do know that a wind-up toy is made from several different metals, not just its outer shell, so only a toymaker magician's magic can make it work."

"Just answer the question, Professor," Matt said.

Professor Nash pushed his spectacles up his nose. "I've never heard of faulty magic before. It either works or doesn't."

I put out my hand and he shook it. "Thank you. You've been very helpful."

We walked off, but he followed us into the corridor. "Perhaps it was Mr. Trentham's intention for this particular toy to operate that way, without being wound up. Perhaps the magic is working precisely as it should."

Given that Mr. Trentham's magic wasn't particularly strong, I doubted it, and voiced my opinion once we were ensconced in the carriage and heading home.

"Mr. Mirnov's magic is stronger, however," I pointed out.

Brockwell agreed. "The magic in that automaton must be Mirnov's. The question is, did he direct it to kill Trentham?"

Matt had been reading the book and he handed it to me with a gleam in his eyes. "According to this, Romany families have been intermarrying over the centuries, so any single magic lineage is almost impossible to trace."

"And?" I prompted.

"And Mirnov told us he's half-Romany on his mother's side. If he inherited his magic from his mother, then toymaker magic probably exists within the wider Romany community, not just his mother's family."

"His *wife's* family could be toymaker magicians too," I said, nodding along. It was a good theory.

"One of the Shaws could have used their magic on the automaton to make it move," Brockwell said. "But why? There is no good reason why they would kill Trentham. They don't benefit from his death, except that it throws suspicion onto Mirnov."

He was right. The theory was built on flimsy foundations. Matt knew it too. He sighed and accepted the book when I returned it to him.

"Maybe we'll have some ideas over lunch." Brockwell rubbed his hands together. "Is Mrs. Potter cooking something special?"

* * *

THE ONLY IDEA we had over lunch was to visit Mr. Mirnov once again. He would not be happy to see us, and I suggested waiting for the market to close and speaking to him at the Rose and Crown instead. Cyclops, Duke and Willie insisted on coming with us and acting as bodyguards to Matt. I felt a little better knowing they were looking out for suspicions persons, but the dread never quite left me. The shooter had fired from a passing carriage, and if he did so again, their presence would not save Matt. He was as exposed now as he was when he was shot outside the toyshop. I just had to hope the gunman had been lucky last time and that his luck had run out.

We spotted Mirnov sitting in the same spot at the end of the counter as last time. But he was not alone.

"Well, well," Matt said as he forged a path through the crowd.

Mr. Mirnov saw us first. He looked up and wrinkled his nose. Mrs. Trentham followed his gaze and gasped.

"What a surprise to see you here," Matt said cheerfully. "I didn't think you two knew each other."

"We don't," she said. "But I had a business proposition for

Mr. Mirnov. I found his home address in my husband's papers, and Mr. Mirnov's neighbor said I would find him here."

Mr. Mirnov narrowed his gaze at her.

"I want to sell some of my stock, and I thought Mr. Mirnov might purchase it for a fair price. I don't want to keep the shop, you see. The task is too much for me without my husband. I simply don't have the skills to keep it going."

Mr. Mirnov gave Matt a smug look. "You thought we were colluding about Trentham's murder, didn't you?"

Mrs. Trentham clasped her throat. "Good lord." She eyed Mirnov warily, as if just realizing she could be speaking to her husband's murderer. "Good day to you. I'll leave you to think about my offer."

She picked up her skirts and hurried off.

Mr. Mirnov chuckled into his tankard. "What do you want now, Inspector?"

"We have some questions about your family history," Brockwell said.

"Go on."

"Did you inherit your magic from your mother or father?"

"Father."

Damnation. That dashed our theory to pieces.

"Do you know if your mother's and father's families were in any way related?"

Mr. Mirnov barked a laugh and pointed the cup at Brockwell. "That's a disturbing thought, coming from a policeman."

"It's not unusual for Romany families to intermarry."

"True, but my father's family are not Romany. I told you that. Nor was he even born in this country. He and my mother were not distant cousins, as far as I'm aware." He frowned at me. "Is this something to do with magic lineages? Are you trying to find out if there could be toymaker magic in the Shaws?" He nodded, answering his own question. "Interesting."

"Do you think the Shaws have any magic?" Matt asked.

Mr. Mirnov shrugged. "If they do, they kept it from me." He finished his ale and waved the empty tankard in Matt's face.

Matt paid for another and we left.

"Now where?" I asked.

"Now we go home," Matt said. "I'm at a loss as to what to do next."

I was quite happy with that suggestion since it kept him off the street and out of danger.

* * *

WE WERE SITTING down for dinner when a constable arrived with an urgent message for Brockwell. Bristow brought him into the dining room. The constable must have run to the house because he puffed heavily and needed a moment before he could speak.

"The widow said you might be with the Glasses, sir," he finally managed to say between breaths. "You must come quickly."

"Where?" Brockwell asked, rising. "What widow?"

"Mrs. Trentham. We were called to her shop after a disturbance was reported. We have the culprit under arrest, sir, and await your instructions."

Brockwell sighed with longing as Peter the footman brought in a platter of roast pork. "Very well. I'm coming. Who is the culprit? Do you have a name?"

"Well, sir, that's the thing." The constable shifted from foot to foot and chewed on his lip. "It's real strange."

"Just tell me!"

"The perpetrator is dressed in a medieval suit of armor."

CHAPTER 10

The sight of police handcuffs around the wrists of the automaton made me giggle during what should have been a worrying time. Matt also looked as though he was attempting to suppress his smile as we picked our way across the floor littered with toys.

Brockwell, however, was taking the situation seriously. He lifted the knight's visor, even though one of the constables said there was no one inside, and removed his notebook from his coat pocket.

"Can I take off the cuffs now, sir?" asked the constable. "The perpetrator fled before we arrived, but the widow insisted we leave them on the armor."

Mrs. Trentham was sitting on a stool behind the counter, her hair down and a black woolen shawl wrapped tightly around her shoulders. She must have been settling in for the night in her rooms upstairs.

"Keep them on for now," Brockwell said.

"Yes, sir." The constable gave his superior a dubious look. "I don't know how he got out of that thing so quickly. It doesn't look like it'd be easy to take on and off."

"There must be a way." Brockwell indicated the toys

159

strewn around the shop. "Start setting the shop to rights as best you can."

Duke helped the constables return fallen toys to tables while Willie and Cyclops remained near the door in their self-appointed role as Matt's guardians.

The shop was a mess, and many of the toys were broken. Two display tables had been overturned and a shelf hung from the wall by a hinge. Mrs. Trentham was close to tears as the inspector forged a path through the mess toward her. Matt and I joined him.

"Can I get you anything?" I asked gently.

She shook her head. "No, thank you, Mrs. Glass."

"Are you hurt?" Matt asked.

"No."

Brockwell opened his notebook to a blank page. "Tell me what happened."

She adjusted her shawl. "I was upstairs when I heard loud noises down here. Crashing, banging...it was terrible."

"That must have been frightening," I said.

"It was. I knew it couldn't be a burglary. No burglar would make that much noise." She indicated the door leading to the workshop and the stairs beyond that led up to her private rooms. "I opened the door a little to peek through. I was too scared to confront the intruder. But then I saw it was the automaton. I knew instantly that it was acting of its own accord."

"What movements was it making?" Brockwell asked.

"Stepping this way and that without any clear sense of direction. If it bumped into a table, it would turn and head in a different direction. Sometimes it would spin around or flail its arms."

"Do you think it was trying to get out?"

She shrugged.

"It's mindless, Inspector," Matt said.

He was right, but if a magician was operating it, then it

likely had a purpose for moving. I didn't want to point that out in front of Mrs. Trentham, however. It was probably best if she thought it was simply the automaton acting without aim and without a person controlling it.

"My husband's magic is proving to be faulty," she said.

We didn't tell her that we'd learned there was no such thing as faulty magic. Once again, it was probably better for her to assume that was the case. If she suspected another magician was manipulating the automaton, she would be even more frightened than she already was.

"Did you see anyone else here?" I asked.

She shook her head. "Just the automaton, but it was quite dark."

"What happened after you saw it acting wildly?" Brockwell asked.

"I ran out the back way, along the lane to the street. I shouted for help and two constables came running. They tried the front door, but it was locked, so we returned via the back way. By the time we arrived, it had calmed down considerably and was just sort of shuffling from foot to foot without going anywhere. One of them handcuffed it. When he opened the visor and saw no one was inside, I suggested they find you." She blinked large watery eyes at the inspector. "I didn't know who else they should speak to. I didn't want to mention magic, you see, and since you seemed aware of magic…"

"You did very well, Mrs. Trentham," Brockwell assured her.

"You will take it away, won't you? I don't want it here anymore."

"Of course." Brockwell flipped his notebook closed. "Thank you for your assistance."

I touched her shoulder. "Will you be all right?"

She gave me a small smile. "Yes, thank you, Mrs. Glass. You're very kind."

C.J. ARCHER

"Glass," Brockwell whispered to Matt as we moved away from the counter, "can you keep the automaton at your house?"

"No! I don't want it anywhere near my family. What if it moves again?"

"Can't you put it in an empty cell at the Yard?" I asked.

"This city is full of criminals," Brockwell said. "We don't have empty cells. Besides, even if we did put it an empty one, it would attract attention from the officers on duty. My superiors won't want that."

He was right. We didn't want the police gossiping about the empty suit of armor occupying one of the cells. What if it moved again? "I have an idea," I said. "We can keep it in the stables, handcuffed to something so it can't create a scene like it did here."

Brockwell grunted a humorless laugh. "Your coachman will like that."

"Woodall wouldn't be perturbed," Matt said. "He lives above the coach house and is as tough as iron. It's the horses that'll hate it. It goes with you, Brockwell. Store it deep in the evidence room."

* * *

WITH THE AUTOMATON safely handcuffed to a large shelving unit in Scotland Yard's basement storeroom, we finally got to enjoy our dinner. Aunt Letitia had dined in our absence but she'd not been alone. Lord Farnsworth was with her.

"What a pleasant surprise," I said and meant it. I rather enjoyed his eccentric company. "Have you had dessert?"

"Not yet," Aunt Letitia said.

I signaled for Bristow to bring them something while the rest of us ate our main course. While I wanted to discuss the latest development in our case, I didn't want to do so in front of Aunt Letitia or Farnsworth. I sensed the others were frustrated by the delay too.

We started our meal in silence since it was late and we were quite hungry. The only thing that filled it was Lord Farnsworth's deep sighs.

"Is something the matter?" I asked when it became too obvious.

"Not at all, India. Everything's wonderful. I enjoyed an excellent meal with your dear aunt and drank some first class wine. Your butler knows his stuff, Glass."

Aunt Letitia dabbed at her mouth with the napkin. "Tell them, Davide. They'll want to know." Even she was calling him by his first name now? What was the world coming to?

"The woman I'd chosen to be my wife refused me."

I lowered my knife and fork. "What a shame. Did you have your heart set on her?"

"She would have made a fine wife. Our children would have been perfect with her common sense and my wit, charm and good looks."

Willie snickered.

Duke regarded Farnsworth with a frown that was more serious than the situation warranted. "Why'd she refuse you when you're so witty, charming and good looking?"

I kicked him under the table and his grin broke free.

Lord Farnsworth didn't notice. He sighed again. "She wouldn't say. I suspect she has another suitor, someone with a higher rank than mine. Perhaps a duke."

"There can be no other reason why she'd refuse him," Aunt Letitia said, bestowing a sympathetic smile on him.

He smiled back. "Thank you, Letitia. You're too kind."

Matt muttered something under his breath.

"What will you do now?" I asked.

"Find another, I suppose. Someone less…" He fluttered his fingers in the air, searching for the right word.

"Sensible?" Matt offered.

"Someone less appealing to dukes."

I wasn't sure what sort of woman wouldn't appeal to a duke, but I didn't want to hear the answer in case he meant someone like Willie, so I didn't ask.

Aunt Letitia rose, excusing herself, and headed for the door. As she passed Willie, she tapped her shoulder and nodded at Lord Farnsworth. Willie arched an eyebrow. Aunt Letitia jerked her head at Farnsworth. The movement was so aggressive, we all noticed it. Farnsworth pretended not to, as did Brockwell, but the rest of us watched with interest.

Aunt Letitia whispered something in Willie's ear. Willie's eyes widened and her jaw hardened.

"Goodnight, Letty," she said before giving her meal her full attention once again.

I had to wait until we were in the drawing room to ask her what Aunt Letitia had said.

"She told me she'd told Farnsworth about the gypsy reading my fortune."

"She told him you were going to marry?"

"Twice."

I smothered my laugh with my hand.

She crossed her arms. "It ain't funny, India. I don't want things to change between me and Farnsworth. I like our friendship the way it is, with no complications. You've seen the ups and downs me and Jasper have, and that nurse. But with Farnsworth, everything's simple. We have fun."

"You're right. I'm sorry."

"Now that Farnsworth's betrothal fell through, Letty's going to keep trying to match us."

"I'll tell her to stop."

"Good." She watched Lord Farnsworth talk to Cyclops. "Can't say I'm disappointed his betrothal didn't pan out. Now he can go out with me again without worrying about it getting back to a fiancée. In fact, I reckon we should go out tonight. I'm in the mood for gambling."

I eyed Brockwell where he sat on the sofa with Duke. "Is that wise, considering Brockwell is here too?"

She rested a hand on my shoulder. "India, you should understand me and my ways by now. Jasper does. He won't mind. Besides, he's more interested in the investigation than me right now."

She was right. As soon as she and Lord Farnsworth left, Brockwell wanted to discuss the situation with the automaton. We all did. Dozens of thoughts had been racing through my head during dinner, and now I could finally voice them.

"I have a theory," I blurted out. "I think Trentham stole the spell from Fabian's house and used it on the automaton. But something went wrong and the automaton turned on him and killed him." I regarded each of them in turn. "What do you think?"

Cyclops nodded. "Seems like a good theory to me. Only Trentham or Mirnov could have made it move."

"And since no break-in has been reported at the toyshop, it must be Trentham."

But the others weren't convinced. "Nash says magic isn't faulty," Brockwell pointed out. "It either works or doesn't."

"I'm not suggesting the magic was faulty, just that it didn't work the way Trentham intended."

Duke seemed to be warming to my theory. "The slim person dressed in the coat who was seen leaving the toyshop on the night of the murder could be the automaton in disguise."

The notion was so absurd that I almost laughed again, despite the seriousness of the situation. And then I remembered something. "It was missing from the shop when we first inspected the scene of the crime after the murder. It was found the following day, in an alley, and we all thought it was stolen then dumped. But what if it ran away and that's as far as it got before the magic ran out?"

"But who let it out of the toyshop?" Matt asked. "It's mindless. It can't open locks without direction and it can't murder, either. Someone manipulated it."

"Unless Nash is wrong," I said. "Perhaps the magic in it *is* faulty. It moved of its own accord on several occasions, according to Mrs. Trentham."

"I agree, but only to a point. Tonight's behavior certainly seems like a fault in the magic controlling it. But the murder and subsequent escape are a different matter. That's intentional."

Cyclops made a shape with his hands as if strangling someone's throat. "I reckon you're right, and it is the murder weapon. That explains why Trentham was strangled instead of having his head bashed in with one of the tools nearby."

I was glad Aunt Letitia wasn't near to hear that. "Thank you for your vivid description."

He lowered his hands. "Sorry, India. But do you understand? Matt assumes the magician was in the room with the automaton. Right?"

Matt nodded.

"But he didn't have to be. When you made the carpet fly, how did you do it?"

"I pictured it flying in my mind as I spoke the spell."

Cyclops pointed a finger at me. "Aye, you pictured it in your mind. You didn't have to *see* it. You didn't have to be in the same area as the carpet."

"So the magician didn't have to be in the same room as the automaton or Trentham," Matt finished, nodding along. "He simply had to picture the automaton's hands around Trentham's neck as he spoke the moving spell."

"It would have been more difficult to picture the right tool that happens to be nearby," Brockwell agreed. "The murderer would have had to guess."

It fit together too neatly for it to be any other way. It meant the stolen spell had indeed been used on the automaton to kill Trentham. I shuddered. What an awful way to die.

Matt rubbed my hand. "Are you all right?"

I nodded. And then it struck me why he was looking at me so intently with such concern in his eyes. The spell that had been used was my spell. I'd created it. I'd created the murder weapon.

A lump swelled in my throat. I tried to swallow it down, but it remained there, lodged. If I needed another reason to stop creating new spells, I had it. The potential for them to be misused was too great. I felt sick to my stomach at my role in Trentham's murder.

"You're going to make an excellent detective," Brockwell said to Cyclops.

Cyclops smiled shyly. "If I ever stay awake long enough through training."

"I remember those lectures. I'll see what I can do about getting you on active duty soon."

Cyclops straightened. "Thank you."

Duke clicked his fingers. He was the only one who didn't seem to be listening to the exchange between Brockwell and Cyclops. "It must be Mirnov then. He's the only one who can manipulate the automaton with India's moving spell. Besides India, I mean. Nash said no tin magician could move the automaton, only a toy magician."

"Agreed," Matt said. "Mirnov didn't have to see Trentham to kill him, he just had to visualize the automaton doing it. But how do you explain the automaton getting out of the toyshop?"

"He pictured the lock in his mind?"

"It's possible, but the automaton would have needed to use a key. It didn't look as though it could operate a key with its metal fingers, let alone find it in the first place."

Duke deflated a little. "Mirnov would have needed to be

inside to find the key and turn it. That means he had to be inside before Mrs. Trentham locked up for the night."

I looked around at each of their faces. If they were thinking the same thing as me, none showed it. They all looked quite stumped by the conundrum. "He *could* have been inside before Mrs. Trentham locked up," I said. "She could have let him in if they're lovers."

That got all eyes looking at me. I smiled in triumph. The more I considered it, the more I liked my theory. Just because they said they'd never met didn't mean they were telling the truth. We'd seen them together at the Rose and Crown, an unlikely place to have a business meeting but not an unusual place for two lovers to enjoy one another's company.

"It explains everything," Cyclops said, nodding.

"It also gives him a strong motive to murder Trentham," Brockwell added. "He removes his rival in business and love."

"And the subsequent erratic behavior of the automaton?"

"A fault, after all," I said with a shrug. "Professor Nash can't know everything there is to know about newly created spells. His sources may not have first-hand knowledge. We still have much to learn when it comes to new spells. Not that we will learn by creating any more. I am definitely *not* going down that path again." I rubbed my arms against a sudden chill. "The risks are too great."

Matt circled his arm around me and kissed the top of my head. His warmth and love helped stave off my melancholia.

"We need to find solid evidence of a connection between them," Brockwell said. "I'll take them both in for further questioning."

"With due respect," Matt said, "we've tried questioning them and we got nowhere. We need a more covert solution to this problem. I propose we go to the shop tomorrow under the guise of helping Mrs. Trentham tidy up, and search her personal belongings when she's not looking."

Brockwell shook his head. "It's too risky. She could be Mirnov's accomplice. If she suspects what you're doing, she might retaliate. I can't send anyone into danger."

"You won't be. I've made the decision without you. I'll go."

I pulled away from him. "No. I will. You're staying home."

"We've been through this, India."

"It's for one day, Matt. It won't kill you to stay here and spend some time with your aunt."

"It might," he muttered.

"Your presence tomorrow isn't required. Mrs. Trentham won't suspect me whereas she might suspect you." He opened his mouth to protest only to close it again when I put up a finger to silence him. "Cyclops, Duke and Willie can't continue to follow you around as your bodyguard. Cyclops has police training."

"I'm not stopping him from attending."

I tilted my head to the side. "Just one day, Matt."

He sighed. "Very well. One day. But you're taking Duke and Willie."

"One of them should stay here with you."

"Willie," Duke said quickly before Matt could respond.

Matt sighed again. "It's going to be a long day."

* * *

THE TOYSHOP WAS in a similar state to how we left it the evening before. Mrs. Trentham was grateful for the help, particularly having someone as strong as Duke to lift the heavier objects. He taught me how to use a screwdriver to put the shelf back up, but there was nothing we could do about the broken table.

"It made quite a mess," I said, surveying the work still to be done.

"Where is it now?" Mrs. Trentham asked.

"In a storage facility in Scotland Yard's basement."

"Good. That creature needs to be locked away until the magic fades."

I picked up a doll and returned it to the table with the others. I needed to think of a way to search Mrs. Trentham's rooms soon or we'd be finished here and the opportunity would be lost. But I'd already discovered the privy was located in an outhouse in the rear courtyard, not upstairs. Unfortunately I'd intended for it to be featured prominently in my ruse.

Duke stood with hands on hips beside a broken rocking horse. "I can fix this with a hammer. May I look through the workshop, Mrs. Trentham?"

"Don't you have one in your toolbox?" she asked.

He shut the toolbox lid with his foot. "No."

She indicated the door that led to the workshop. "Then be my guest."

Duke gave me a speaking look before he picked up the rocking horse. Mrs. Trentham held the door open for him and looked as though she was about to follow him.

"Would you mind helping me locate the rest of these marbles?" I asked her.

Together we searched for the marbles, finding them underneath tables, other toys, and even behind the counter. I kept up a conversation the entire time so she could not find a spare moment to make her excuses and follow Duke. Not unless she wanted to be rude. As a well brought up middle class woman, I guessed Mrs. Trentham wouldn't want to be considered impolite.

Duke returned after twenty minutes and placed the rocking horse near the front of the shop where it could be seen through the window. He dusted off his hands as he admired his handiwork.

"You did a good job," I told him.

"Thanks. Now, I'm starved. Anyone else want something to eat?" He winked at me. With his back to Mrs. Trentham, she wouldn't have seen.

At his encouraging look, I said, "Shall I make some sandwiches?" Upon his smile, I added, "Your kitchen is upstairs, Mrs. Trentham?"

"I couldn't ask you to work in the kitchen, Mrs. Glass. Not after everything you're already doing here."

"It's quite all right. I don't have the opportunity to potter about in the kitchen at home. Our cook doesn't like it. I rather miss it." I headed toward the door before she could get ahead of me.

"But I don't have any bread," she said.

Even better. "Is there a bakery nearby?"

"In the next block."

I dug some coins out of my reticule where I'd left it on the counter. "Would you mind purchasing a loaf? And anything else you require to fill a good sandwich." I gave her more money, more than she'd need. "Something hearty for my friend." I leaned closer and whispered, "He eats a lot."

She smiled an innocent, trusting smile. She didn't have a clue what I was about to do. "Of course. And thank you again for your help, Mrs. Glass. "

After she left, Duke joined me at the counter. "I didn't get long upstairs. I didn't want to make her suspicious and I still had to fix the rocking horse. You go and I'll keep watch. I'll whistle when I see her approaching."

"Where did you look?"

"The sitting room. I left the bedroom for you."

"You're very clever to think of this, Duke. Well done."

I raced off through the workshop and up the stairs. The landing opened up to the sitting room which contained a sofa, some small occasional tables, and a writing desk. Duke would have searched it, so I continued on to the bedchamber. If there was no correspondence in the writing desk between Mrs.

Trentham and Mr. Mirnov, then the dressing table was the next obvious place.

I searched high and low, including looking for hidden compartments and false bottoms. There were none. There was so little personal correspondence that I realized Mrs. Trentham had very few friends and no family. I felt a little sorry for her, even though she could be a conspirator in her husband's murder.

I shook an appointment diary but the only thing to fall out was a doctor's card. I turned my attention to the bed. There was nothing under it except dust and a pair of old shoes. The wardrobe contained men's and women's clothing, but all pockets were empty and it didn't feel like anything had been slipped into the lining. The top of the wardrobe revealed nothing of use either, just an empty hat box, small traveling trunk filled with musty blankets, and some books.

I put everything back and surveyed the room again, hands on hips. If there had ever been secret correspondence between lovers, it had been destroyed.

I picked up the diary again and flipped through the pages. Most days were empty. Wives of shopkeepers usually attended meetings for a particular society or interest, but Mrs. Trentham seemed to belong to none. She met with a woman named Edith for afternoon tea once a month and she and Mr. Trentham attended the theater in June and a dinner at the guild hall in September. The only name that appeared more than once was the doctor's. She saw him twice several months ago.

I picked up the card. *Doctor Shelby*, it read in bold lettering. In smaller type underneath it listed his specialties as *Women's Complaints, Hysteria, and Fertility.*

I pocketed the card and was about to look through the dressing table again when Duke whistled. I picked up my skirts and raced downstairs. I pushed open the workshop door just as Mrs. Trentham entered through the front door. Hopefully she assumed I'd just paid a visit to the outhouse.

"I'll take those upstairs for you," I said, accepting a paper bag from her.

Mrs. Trentham insisted on coming with me and together we made sandwiches in the kitchen. I didn't want to look suspicious so we stayed for another hour after lunch then left. I directed Woodall to drive to Scotland Yard instead of home, however.

"But we have nothing to report to Brockwell," Duke said as we drove off.

"I'm not so certain." I showed him the card and told him about the appointments.

"How is this relevant?"

"It might not be, but I want to speak to the doctor and to do that, we need Brockwell. A doctor won't talk about a patient to us but he might to the police. If nothing else, it gives us a clearer picture of Mrs. Trentham's state. If she has a terminal illness, it might explain why she killed the man she didn't love to be with the man she does."

Duke didn't look convinced. Nor did the inspector when I explained my theory to him.

"We have nothing else to go on at this point," I said, my exasperation coming through in my tone. "Shouldn't we at least learn why she had two appointments with this doctor?"

"They were months before her husband's murder," Duke pointed out.

Brockwell pushed back his chair, scraping the legs on the floor. "I don't think it will help, but I'll talk to him."

"*We'll* talk to him," I said. "Your presence will make the interview official and mine will ease his mind when you insist he hand over all her records."

"How will it ease his mind?"

"He's a doctor of women's complaints and I am a woman."

Brockwell and Duke exchanged glances.

I plucked my reticule off the desk and stood. "I'm joining you in that interview whether you like it or not, Inspector. Come along."

* * *

DOCTOR SHELBY'S clinic was located in a row house in an upper class neighborhood. The bronze plaque on the wall beside the door merely stated his name. It did not mention his specialty as the card had. His patients wanted discretion and privacy.

The patient in the waiting room turned scarlet upon seeing the inspector then dipped her head low.

"May I help you?" asked the female assistant sitting behind a desk.

"I'm Detective Inspector Brockwell and this is Mrs. Glass, my associate. We need to speak with Doctor Shelby."

She pointed at the chairs. "You'll have to wait."

We waited and when the adjoining door opened and a woman emerged, we stood. I apologized to the waiting patient and assured her we wouldn't be long, then followed Brockwell through. The room was sparsely furnished with a metal framed bed to one side, a desk and two chairs. Aside from a filing cabinet and a shelf of books, the room was empty. There weren't even pictures on the white walls, and the lack of a fireplace meant the air was cold. I shivered and clutched my coat closed at my throat.

Doctor Shelby was a small man of late middle age with thin hair on his head and wiry gray hair on his chin. He peered closely at the inspector through his spectacles.

Brockwell introduced us and stated our business in his direct, matter-of-fact way.

Doctor Shelby flatly refused to comply with his request. "I

can't hand over patient records to the police! I must maintain my integrity."

"I'm ordering you," Brockwell said.

Doctor Shelby squared his shoulders. "Don't you need paperwork for that sort of thing?"

"And I will get it if you continue to resist, but time is of the essence. Our murder investigation hinges on what's contained in Mrs. Trentham's file."

Doctor Shelby was unmoved. "I'm sorry but my files are confidential. Unless a judge orders me to hand over her records, I'm going to respectfully refuse."

Brockwell scratched his sideburns. He looked at a loss. I suspected identifying himself as a policeman and mentioning murder usually got results. Doctor Shelby was an ethical fellow and I felt somewhat awful for what I was about to say to force his hand. But it was necessary.

"Obtaining permission will mean your assistant and waiting patients will learn that their information has been rifled through by the detective and a number of constables. Unfortunately, everyone knows constables aren't all that discreet. If we do it now, it will just be the two of us. As a woman, I would find that less intrusive. Having constables know my intimate business would be humiliating and make me less likely to return here."

Doctor Shelby paled. "Would constables need to be involved?"

"Not if you let us view Mrs. Trentham's file now."

"That's blackmail."

"I prefer to call it common sense."

He removed his spectacles and pinched the bridge of his nose. After a heavy sigh and a shake of his head, he returned them. "If she is a murderess, I suppose it's my duty to let you look at her file."

"Not a murderess, merely an accomplice," Brockwell said. "Do you remember her?"

"A little. I saw her husband's name in the papers, but her appointments were some time ago and I don't recall the particulars of her situation." He opened a cabinet and flipped through the files. "Here it is." Now that he'd decided to help, he no longer seemed angry. He opened the file and started reading. "Good lord, now I remember. She asked me a rather odd question. It was easy enough to answer, but unusual."

He handed the file to Brockwell. We read it together. Mrs. Trentham had come to Doctor Shelby's clinic looking for a treatment for infertility. She had asked if there was a medical reason why she had not conceived after years of marriage. The doctor had inspected her and declared he could not find one. He had informed her that it's not unusual to never discover a reason, and that she and her husband should keep trying.

"How was she after the first consultation?" I asked.

"Deeply upset," he said. "No woman likes to hear there is no cure for infertility. I discussed the, er, process with her to make sure she and Mr. Trentham were doing it correctly. You would be surprised at how often ignorance is the cause. But there were no issues there."

Brockwell, who'd continued to read, tapped his finger on a sentence in the report. "It says here she asked about consanguinity and its effect on infertility. What's that?"

"Blood relations. In essence, she was asking me if the kinship between her and Mr. Trentham could be a cause of their inability to conceive."

"Kinship?" I echoed. "You mean they're related?"

"Yes, but I can't recall how distantly. It wasn't close."

I tried to think back to my conversations with Mr. Trentham about his magic and whether he'd inherited it from his mother or father. "Can you recall on which side they're related?"

"I didn't ask."

Brockwell and I exchanged glances. He closed the file, but

I'd caught sight of something further down the page.

I took it off him and read the doctor's report of the second appointment. Mrs. Trentham had returned to ask Doctor Shelby if her husband could be the reason they hadn't conceived, not her. The notes said that she informed him that Mr. Trentham had been married before and since there was no child born from the marriage, could *he* be the infertile one.

"Tell me about the second appointment," I said, handing the file back to Brockwell to read.

"I didn't expect to see her again, so I was surprised when she returned," Doctor Shelby said. "She informed me of her husband's previous marriage and lack of children, and asked if that meant he was infertile, not her. I told her that was most likely the case. She got very irate with me for not telling her that could have been the reason during her first consultation, but I pointed out that she hadn't asked me about her husband, just herself."

"So you let her believe the problem lay with her?" I bit off. Too often, men let women take the blame for things that were not their fault. In the case of childlessness, the woman always bore the brunt of blame, from society as well as their own families. A doctor ought to know better and give a full explanation for peace of mind, if nothing else.

Doctor Shelby snatched the file off Brockwell. "I suggested they should keep trying and if that doesn't bear fruit there's adoption. She didn't appear to be listening, however."

"Probably because she was still reeling from discovering her husband was infertile." Or perhaps she was already plotting his murder.

I exchanged a glance with Brockwell. He gave me a small nod. He was thinking the same thing—Mrs. Trentham had motive. Considering she could also be a toymaker magician, she also had the means to manipulate the automaton.

Forget Mirnov—Mrs. Trentham had just become our primary suspect.

CHAPTER 11

"We can't arrest her yet," Brockwell said as we sat in the carriage outside the doctor's clinic.

We were debating where to go next. Duke agreed with me that we should at least question Mrs. Trentham about what we'd learned, but Brockwell wanted more evidence.

"We need to find out if she is a toymaker magician," Brockwell said. "Then our case against her will be tighter, and we'll have more leverage to get a confession from her. You think Trentham's magic came from his father, India?"

"I recall him saying as much at his lecture."

"Then we just need to prove she is related to him on his father's side. May I give your coachman instructions?"

"Go ahead."

He opened the window and directed Woodall to the General Register Office in Somerset House on the Strand. I felt a little guilty for continuing this far into the investigation without Matt. We always did this sort of thing together. But I comforted myself with the knowledge that he was safely at home with Willie protecting him.

I was very glad to be undertaking this part of the investigation with Brockwell, however. The presence of a Scotland

178

Yard detective had been invaluable with Doctor Shelby and proved to be again at the Register Office. Requests to look at birth, death or marriage certificates were usually added to a long queue, but the administrative staff fetched Mrs. Trentham's records immediately.

The marriage certificate told us everything we needed to know. Her maiden name was the same as her married name, which meant husband and wife were indeed related on the magical paternal side. An amendment had been attached to the certificate with details of their kinship. According to the family tree, they shared the same great grandparents.

Mrs. Trentham was most likely a toymaker magician too.

That meant *she* could manipulate the automaton from afar by using my new moving spell. She could have made it strangle her husband.

"Do you think they married just so they could have magician children?" Duke asked.

"I'm almost certain of it," I murmured as my eye settled on something on the marriage certificate. I gasped, not quite believing it. "My god. Look at this."

Duke and Brockwell leaned in. "Coyle!" Duke cried.

Brockwell took the certificate from me. "Why was Lord Coyle at their wedding?"

"He didn't just attend the Trenthams' wedding, he was the witness." I smiled to myself. He'd made a rare mistake. This was proof that he'd lied about knowing Mrs. Trentham.

"But why?" Brockwell asked again. "Did he arrange it?"

"Possibly," Duke said.

"I think it's very likely," I said. "He probably introduced them in the hope they'd marry and have toymaker magician children." My heart beat faster as another thought occurred to me. "Inspector, can you ask the staff to fetch the marriage certificate for Mr. Trentham's first marriage?"

Brockwell rose. "You think Coyle organized that one too?"

"I'm not sure, but I also want to see the first Mrs. Trentham's death certificate."

"Ah." He buttoned up his jacket. "Now I follow."

Duke watched him approach the desk where the clerk was busily filling out forms. "Do you think Brockwell has the power to arrest Coyle if we prove he murdered the first Mrs. Trentham?"

"Probably not, but I don't think we'll find proof, anyway. It'll only be conjecture. Coyle certainly won't admit to it, even if we confront him. But it might be enough to let him know that we know, and perhaps that'll make him think twice about doing it again in the future."

Duke dragged a hand over his mouth and chin. "India," he said quietly. He sat forward, but his gaze didn't lift to mine. "If he's capable of murdering a woman to clear the path for her husband to marry a magician and have magician children, then he could be behind the shooting of Matt for the same reason." His gaze locked with mine. "To make you a widow."

The blood rushed to my toes. I felt light-headed, unbalanced. I clutched the edge of the desk to steady myself and Duke, realizing, clasped my elbow.

"I'm sorry," he mumbled. "I shouldn't have said anything."

I breathed deeply to suppress the well of emotions filling me. "I'm glad you did. If we're going to keep Matt safe, we need to know what we're up against. *Who* we're up against." I took his hand and squeezed. "He won't succeed, Duke. I promise you. I won't let him."

It was some time before the clerk brought us the two new documents. Lord Coyle's name was not on the marriage certificate.

"This is interesting." Brockwell showed us the death certificate. "The first Mrs. Trentham died just a few months before her husband remarried. That's not a very long period of mourning."

"What did she die of?" Duke asked.

"It says 'Unknown'. Unfortunately it's very common for the doctor to have no idea what caused a death. It makes murder investigations somewhat difficult."

The picture was becoming clearer. Mrs. Trentham or Coyle —or both—had killed Mr. Trentham's first wife so that he would be free to marry a toymaker magician and beget magician children. But when there were no offspring forthcoming, they struck again, this time killing *Mr.* Trentham so that his widow would be free to marry Mirnov, another toymaker magician and also recently widowed.

It was getting worse and worse. "I suspect the Shaws are partly right," I murmured. "Albina's death was suspicious, but she wasn't killed by her husband. She was killed by Mrs. Trentham or Coyle so that Mrs. Trentham could marry Mr. Mirnov."

Brockwell sat up straight and gave a small pump of his fist. It was the most animated I'd ever seen him. "We need to see Albina Mirnov's death certificate."

"Why?" Duke asked. "We know she died of heart failure."

"Because *if* Mrs. Mirnov's death occurred around the same time the current Mrs. Trentham discovered her husband was infertile, it points to the likelihood that Mrs. Trentham murdered her because she wanted to marry Mr. Mirnov and bear his children."

We'd gone from one death to three in a matter of hours, and all for the sake of bearing magician children.

It seemed to take an age for the clerk to fetch the death certificate. My mind was reeling now, joining all the pieces of the puzzle together. Matt was going to be shocked at our progress. He would be pleased that we had found evidence of Coyle's involvement, but he would insist on confronting the earl.

Coyle should be confronted, but I wasn't so sure if Matt was the right person to do it.

"I wonder if Mr. Trentham knew he was being manipulated by his second wife and Coyle," Brockwell said as we waited for the clerk to fetch the document.

"He didn't seem like he knew," I pointed out. "He spoke to Coyle after the lecture at Louisa's house, and I didn't detect any animosity."

The clerk arrived with the death certificate and our theory gathered momentum. Mrs. Mirnov died two days after Mrs. Trentham's second appointment with Doctor Shelby; two days after she discovered her husband was infertile and couldn't give her the magician children she desired.

Or was it a case of the magician children *Lord Coyle* desired her to have?

* * *

WITH DUKE there to assist him, Brockwell decided to arrest Mrs. Trentham immediately rather than return to the Yard to fetch constables. Duke was very pleased with the idea, and so was I. The longer we delayed, the more opportunity she had to leave the city.

We found her at home above the toyshop. When she smiled at me, a pang of guilt twisted my gut. I'd liked her. Even when I thought her an accomplice of Mirnov's, I'd liked her.

But she was not the woman I thought she was, manipulated by a man she was in love with. She was a cold-hearted killer. Whether she'd killed three people or Coyle had arranged it, it didn't matter. She was complicit and just as guilty.

"Thank you again for your help clearing up the mess," Mrs. Trentham said. "It's much appreciated and, as you can see, the shop is back as it was now. I can reopen tomorrow."

Brockwell cleared his throat. "Mrs. Trentham, you are under arrest for the murders of Mrs. Clara Trentham, Mr. Trentham, and Mrs. Mirnov."

Her face paled. She blinked rapidly at Brockwell then turned to me. "Wh—what is this? What's going on? I haven't murdered anybody."

"I'll take you to Scotland Yard shortly, but I'd like to ask you some questions first." Brockwell was doing this here for my benefit.

I would have smiled my thanks but he wasn't looking at me, and I didn't have the heart to smile.

"Mrs. Glass, I don't understand! Why does the inspector think I murdered my husband and those other people?"

"We know about your husband's infertility," I said.

She swallowed. "How?"

"We know that you're a toymaker magician—a relative of Mr. Trentham's, in fact."

Her jaw firmed. At least she didn't try to deny it.

"We know your marriage to him was arranged by Lord Coyle," I went on. "We know you killed the first Mrs. Trentham so that her husband could be free to marry you. And when you learned he was infertile, you killed Mrs. Mirnov. Then, after a suitable length of time, you murdered Mr. Trentham using the spell you stole from Fabian Charbonneau on the automaton."

She clutched her throat. It wasn't the first time she'd done it, but it was the first time I'd realized she did it whenever the strangulation of her husband was mentioned. Again, she didn't try to deny it. That surprised me. I thought she'd blame Coyle. Indeed, she looked as though she were thinking.

"You killed two innocent women simply because they happened to be married to the men you wanted for yourself."

The hand clutching her throat shook as it dropped to her side. "This is absurd. I haven't killed anyone." The hysteria in

183

her voice was replaced with steeliness. "What evidence do you have?"

Brockwell didn't answer. Instead, he asked a question of his own. "You initially told us that you saw Lord Coyle mere days before your husband's death then changed it to weeks. Why?"

The sudden focus on Coyle made her blink in surprise. "I made a mistake."

"Or were you trying to implicate him in the murder at the beginning of our investigation?"

A look of dread came over her. "No!"

"Is it not the case of one murderer turning on the other?"

"No," she whispered through white lips.

Brockwell pressed on. "We know Coyle witnessed your marriage to Trentham. Did he arrange it?"

She turned huge eyes onto me. "Mrs. Glass, please."

"Just answer him," I snapped. I was tired of being lied to. She had manipulated me, just as she had manipulated her late husband.

She backed up to a table and gripped its edge. She gave a small nod. "I've known Lord Coyle for years. He approached my parents when I was fifteen with the suggestion that he arrange my marriage to another toymaker magician. He told them it was for the benefit of magic, strengthening the lineage and ensuring we had magician children. My parents refused, saying I was too young. I never forgot him or his offer, however. So when I was ready to marry, I sought him out. My parents had died by that time, and as their only child, I wanted to continue my father's lineage."

When she fell into silence, I filled it. "So you found Lord Coyle and asked him to arrange your marriage, only to learn that the man—your distant cousin—had married in the meantime."

She nodded. "I was disappointed. The more I thought

about it, the more I wanted magician children. Lord Coyle told me to be patient."

"Why?" Brockwell asked. "Did he promise Mr. Trentham would become available for you?"

"He promised nothing of the sort. It was a simple letter with a simple message; be patient. So I waited. Then a year later, Coyle wrote to me again saying that Mr. Trentham's wife had died and would I like to meet him."

"He killed Mrs. Trentham?"

"I don't know. But I assure you, I didn't."

Brockwell and I exchanged glances. "Go on."

"We married in a small ceremony with Lord Coyle present."

"Did your husband know you are a magician?" I asked.

"Of course. I told him why I was marrying him, and he thought it was as good a reason as any to marry again. We both hoped for children. When they didn't arrive, I went to see a specialist. At first he let me think I was to blame. It didn't occur to me that my husband could be the reason until I thought on it some more. When the doctor confirmed that my husband was most likely the infertile one, since he didn't have children by his first wife, I became upset."

"By this time you'd learned of another toymaker magician, right here in London," Brockwell said.

"Yes, I knew of Mr. Mirnov, but I didn't kill my husband so that I could marry his business rival."

Brockwell was having none of it. "You went to Coyle and suggested you should be married to Mirnov instead of Trentham, and asked him to remove your husband to free you to marry Mirnov."

"No. Lord Coyle wasn't even aware of Mr. Mirnov's existence until very recently. Let me assure you, Inspector, I didn't approach Coyle to kill my husband."

Why wasn't she implicating Coyle? We were leading her to do so, and yet she did not, even though it could save her.

"What about Mrs. Mirnov?" Brockwell asked. "Did you kill her?"

She focused on the floor. "No."

"I suggest you killed Mrs. Mirnov, so that her husband would be widowed, then you waited for an appropriate time and killed your husband."

"After stealing my moving spell and using it on the automaton," I added.

Her chin wobbled, but she managed to shake her head.

"You flirted with Mirnov in the meantime so he would be open to a marriage between you when the time came," I went on. "You were desperate for magician children, so you committed murder for your dream to come true."

"Please, you must believe me, I didn't kill anyone!"

"Did Coyle ask you to steal the spell for him?" Brockwell asked.

She squeezed her eyes shut and shook her head.

"But he told you about it, didn't he?"

Her eyes sprang open. They were filled with tears. "Yes. He told me when I touched the carpet for him. The fake carpet you sold him, Mrs. Glass. There was no magic in it." She gave me a small but triumphant smile. It vanished as quickly as it had appeared.

"It was *you* we saw leaving Coyle's house." I recalled the woman driving away in a cab, her face hidden from view. It must have been Mrs. Trentham, leaving after testing the fake carpet for Coyle.

"How did you break into Fabian's house unnoticed?"

"The window latch was loose and snapped off without much effort. I climbed through the window easily enough. The desk drawer presented more of a problem, but I have some experience opening that type of lock without a key. I learned to pick the locks on my father's desk when I was growing up, for something to do."

"Where is the spell now?"

She hesitated before placing her fingers down her bodice. Duke stepped forward to grab her wrist if necessary, but she merely pulled out a piece of paper and passed it to me. The handwriting was neither mine nor Fabian's.

"This is a copy," I said. "Where's the original?"

"I lost it."

"Did you give it to Coyle?"

"No."

"I don't believe you."

"That is hardly my problem, is it?" she spat.

I rubbed my temple. This was going nowhere. She wasn't going to implicate Coyle, no matter how much we pressed. Nor had she confessed to the murders.

That was because *she* hadn't done them. The automaton's hands had wrapped around Mr. Trentham's throat, not hers. It was a distinction that didn't matter to me.

"Your magic was stronger than your husband's, wasn't it?" I asked.

"Yes."

"Tell us about using the stolen spell on the automaton," I said.

Her gaze met mine. Her eyes were swimming with unshed tears, but her jaw was set hard. "I wanted to see if Lord Coyle was correct and the spell would work for a magician using it on their own craft, so I spoke it into the automaton. It proved to be very strong and unpredictable."

"In what way?"

"I tried to direct it with my mind, but I couldn't. It would turn around and around, or move without reason. It smashed some toys. I couldn't control it." Her voice grew louder in her desperation for us to believe her innocent. "I could sense that my magic wasn't strong enough to direct it. It was like it was pulling me in a direction I didn't want to go. I tried to rein it in, Mrs. Glass. I truly did. But it took over from me altogether. It strangled my husband. The automaton killed him, not me."

"Are you saying it strangled him of its own accord?" Brockwell asked.

I glanced sharply at him. He sounded like he believed her —or wanted to. I did not.

"That's right," she said on a rush of breath. "I tried to stop it, but couldn't. It ran off after my husband stopped breathing."

"How did it get out of the shop when the door was locked?"

"The door wasn't locked. It simply turned the handle and ran outside. It must have finally run out of magic in the laneway where it was found the next day."

"Why didn't you tell us any of this earlier?" Brockwell asked.

"Would you have believed me?" She folded her arms. "You would have thought I directed it to murder him. Mrs. Glass thinks that now."

I lifted my chin.

"But it's all true," she said. "You saw how the automaton acts without warning. It scared your friend. And do you think I would have directed it to smash up the shop?" She indicated the toys on the tables. "It almost destroyed everything."

"What about Coyle?" Duke asked.

She seemed surprised that he had anything to say at all. "What about him?"

"Did he kill Mrs. Trentham and Mrs. Mirnov?"

"Do you think a man like that confides in me?"

"Did he tell you how to kill your husband with the stolen spell so that you would appear innocent?"

"I stole the spell of my accord then lost it after making a copy. It was my idea to use it on the automaton, and mine alone. I didn't direct the automaton to kill my husband. The magic was too strong for me to control it properly. If you want to blame me for something, blame me for that. But aside from telling me about the spell, Lord Coyle had nothing to do with my husband's death."

"Damn it, Mrs. Trentham. We're giving you an opportunity to pin all of this on someone else."

"Duke," the inspector snapped.

Duke rounded on him, his hands curled into fists at his sides. "Tell her a judge will be lenient on her if she implicates Coyle. Tell her, Brockwell!"

"A judge?" Mrs. Trentham wailed. "But I'm innocent. You can't arrest me."

Brockwell sighed. "I have to take you to the Yard for further questioning."

"Will I be charged with my husband's murder?"

Brockwell looked uncertain how to answer. I suspected he couldn't yet give one. Whether Mrs. Trentham was charged with murder or not might be a decision for Brockwell's superiors. The idea of a murderous magical automaton might be less palatable to the authorities than the hanging of a widow.

"Just come with me to the Yard."

"But I didn't do it! The automaton did."

When she didn't move, Duke grabbed her arm. "Are you keeping Coyle's name out of this because you're afraid of him?" he asked.

"Duke," Brockwell growled. "That's enough. Take her to the carriage. India, may I use it to transport Mrs. Trentham to Scotland Yard?"

"Yes, of course," I said as Duke marched her out of the toyshop. "Send Woodall and Duke home when she's safely locked away."

"You won't stay? It shouldn't be a long wait."

"No."

He eyed me carefully. "You are going straight home, aren't you?"

"Where else would I go, Inspector?"

* * *

BROCKWELL SEEMED to have made up his mind that Mrs. Trentham was innocent. Even Duke assumed she had done it under the direction of Coyle. I was in two minds. I wasn't convinced she couldn't control the automaton using my spell. But I also suspected Coyle had more to do with it than she let on.

I doubted Brockwell would get her to confess to directing the automaton to murder Mr. Trentham using my spell. I also doubted he would confront Coyle. He wouldn't see the point, considering Coyle would simply deny it then speak to Brockwell's superiors and have the investigation stopped.

So I would have to confront him myself.

I sat with Hope in the drawing room while the footman fetched Lord Coyle. The footman returned without him, however, and asked me to call on his lordship in his study. It was an unusual request considering I was an unaccompanied woman.

Hope bristled. "Why?"

The footman said nothing. Indeed, he pretended not to have heard her.

I followed him out, glancing over my shoulder as I exited the drawing room. Hope sat in the middle of the sofa, her slender frame erect, her chin lifted. She looked very much like someone trying to hold herself together. But whether she was trying to suppress anger or hurt, I wasn't sure.

Lord Coyle did not look up upon my entry. "Sit, Mrs. Glass."

I sat and waited for him to finish writing. It gave me a moment to gather my wits, although I'd had the entire hansom cab journey from the toyshop to think about what I wanted to say to this man. I watched him writing, his head bent to the task, his bulk hulking over the desk. I should be afraid of him. I was in his house, surrounded by people who would do his bidding, and I hadn't informed anyone where I was going.

But I wasn't afraid. Lord Coyle might want to kill Matt, but Matt wasn't here. It was just me, and Lord Coyle liked having me alive. I was the most powerful magician of his acquaintance, and that would keep me safe until a more powerful one appeared.

I had to believe that or I would be a trembling mess.

He finally put down his pen. "Have you come to sell me another fake magical object?"

"I've just come from Trentham's toyshop. Detective Inspector Brockwell has taken Mrs. Trentham in for questioning over the murder of her husband."

The chair creaked as he sat back. "Is that so? And what does that have to do with you being here?"

"She admitted that you told her about my spell."

"So?"

"We know that you killed Mr. Trentham's first wife so that he could remarry."

"Is that what she told you?" When I didn't answer, he added, "I didn't kill her. I don't know who did, but it sounds like the inspector has the murderer in custody."

"You introduced the Trenthams and even witnessed their marriage."

"That part is true. But I can assure you, I've killed nobody for her. It's most likely she acted alone. I've long thought her mad." He reached for his pipe and a box of matches. "She was desperate for children. Not just any children—magical ones. I suspected she killed the first Mrs. Trentham, of course, but the police never came knocking on my door, so I didn't offer my help."

"What about Mrs. Mirnov?"

"I've never met her or her husband."

"You were seen at his place of residence."

He puffed three times on the pipe. Smoke billowed then

191

thinned and drifted away. "Mrs. Trentham's a liar. She sent me to Mirnov's house so I'd be seen there, making a false connection between us to fool the police. She also lied to the police about seeing me at the toyshop days before her husband's death."

"She later changed her statement about the timing. Why?"

He removed the pipe from his mouth and pointed it at me. "You would have to ask her that, Mrs. Glass." He plugged the pipe back into the corner of his mouth. "The fact is, I am a convenient scapegoat for her."

"Except she's not using you as a scapegoat." I leaned forward. "What have you said to her? What have you threatened her with if she talks?"

He merely continued to puff on the pipe.

"Clearly she tried to implicate you early in the investigation," I pushed on. "When we told you that, did you send her a message saying she must retract her statement? Did you threaten her if she dragged your name into it?"

"You're seeing things that aren't there, Mrs. Glass."

I steeled myself against his insults. This conversation would not be over until I wanted it to be.

Deep creases formed at the corners of his eyes. "You're lost in these interrogations without your husband, aren't you?"

"Pardon?"

"He would have worked it out by now."

"Worked what out?"

"Why I had nothing to do with the deaths of Mr. Trentham, his first wife, or Mrs. Mirnov. Let me help you, since I don't want to wait for you to discover it yourself." He removed the pipe, licked his lips, and plugged it back in. I wanted to shove it down his throat. "While there's no doubt I am interested in the future of magic, I am more interested in its present. Specifically, the power my magical collection, contacts and knowledge gives me now. That has always been the case, and I think you know that. What happens in the next generation is not much of a concern to me, although I do hate to see a good magical lineage die out. That's why I initially approached Mrs. Trentham's family when she was young. It was a disappointment that they refused to marry her off, but that's all. Just a disappointment."

"What about Mr. Hendry?"

"What about him?"

"You helped him avoid conviction when he was accused of murder so that he'd owe you, and now he is married. Mr. Hendry was not interested in marriage. You forced him."

"Perhaps he changed and decided it was a good idea. Some men like him do, you know. A wife is a convenience to avoid suspicion."

I knew from Willie that a man of Mr. Hendry's inclination did not simply change, although having a wife would certainly make him more respectable in the eyes of the world. "You forced him so that he would have magician children. I assume his wife is also a magician."

He tapped the end of the pipe on the table to loosen the tobacco before putting it back in his mouth. "If I were so greatly concerned with the continuation of magical lines, to the point of committing murder to make sure two magicians married one another, wouldn't I have killed more artless spouses of magicians before now? I know dozens upon dozens of magicians, many of them married to artless." He pointed the pipe at me. "Including you, Mrs. Glass."

This was my opening. This was my moment to accuse him of shooting Matt.

But I was no longer sure. Coyle made a good point. He did know many magicians married to artless. Why kill for Mrs. Trentham but not the others?

Even so, if there was any chance at all that he was guilty of shooting Matt, I had to let him know that I suspected him. It probably wouldn't make him stop—but on the other hand, it might, and it was worth it if it worked.

"Someone shot at my husband," I said. "Twice."

"I'm very sorry to hear that."

"You don't seem sorry. Nor do you seem surprised."

"Are you accusing *me* of shooting him?" He huffed around the pipe, either in derision or genuine amusement, I couldn't tell. "Mrs. Glass, for the same reason I just explained that I didn't kill Trentham, I wouldn't go to the trouble of killing your husband. I have no particular interest in making you a widow so you can remarry. The continuation of your line doesn't matter to me. Besides, not even I can force someone down the aisle, and I doubt you would choose your second husband because he's a magician. I suspect you're one of those people for whom affection in marriage is important. Now, is that all? I have work to do." He picked up his pen and dipped it in the inkwell.

I rose and pressed my palms to the desk. I felt a little out of control, like the automaton operated by a magician from afar. Confronting such a powerful man was not in my nature —but in this moment, I was not quite myself. I might not know precisely what words would come out of my mouth, but I did know I couldn't stop them.

"Let me make one thing clear, my lord. If Matt dies of unnatural causes, I *will* assume you are responsible, and I will do everything in my power to turn magicians against you. The influence you now enjoy because of your magical acquaintances and knowledge will vanish. I'll see to it."

Something flickered in his eyes. It was the only sign that I'd got through to him and perhaps even worried him. I straightened as a sense of satisfaction coursed through me, as vivid as any magic.

He bent over the papers to write. "Good day, Mrs. Glass. See yourself out."

I marched out of his office only to pause when I saw

Hope. Had she been listening? I closed the office door and headed for the stairs. She followed a few steps behind and caught up to me on the next landing.

"Is Matt all right?" she asked.

So she had been listening. "Yes." I went to walk off but she grabbed my arm.

"What happened?"

I glanced up the stairs. "Ask your husband." I wrenched free.

Her hand curled into a claw, clutching at the air. She stared at me with those lovely, big eyes of hers. I turned away, hating that I felt sorry for her for marrying Coyle. Although we'd warned her, and she knew he wasn't a good man, I suspected she'd come to realize the power she coveted in a husband wasn't worth the price.

CHAPTER 12

"*W*ell it's about time you came home." Willie's greeting upon my return was said with one hand on her out-thrust hip.

I handed Bristow my coat and hat. "Why? What's happened?"

"Matt's been watching for you through the window for an age and complaining that you weren't back."

Matt must have heard my voice because he emerged from the library, tie askew and hair messy as if he'd been running his hands through it. He came to me, planted his hands on my shoulders and a kiss on my lips. It lasted until Willie cleared her throat.

Matt took my hand and drew me into the library. "Thank goodness you're back."

"Why?"

"Willie and Aunt Letitia are maddening."

Willie followed us inside and shut the door. "You're the maddening one. You've been pacing back and forth, up and down, all day. You can't settle."

"It's difficult to concentrate on other things when there's an investigation happening without me."

She turned to me. "He tried working, playing cards, and even helped Letty with some embroidery. That was a mistake. He ain't got no patience for it. Finally I banished him in here to give us some peace. I never thought I'd say this, but Matt, you're irritating when you're bored."

"*I'm* irritating? You don't close your mouth when you chew."

Willie ignored him. "I forgot to mention he's in a bad mood. Now that you're back, he's your responsibility."

Matt raked his hand through his hair. When it fell away, he gave me an impish look that made me want to draw him into a hug. "I just need to get out. I've felt more alive since I used my watch after the shooting, and I've got more energy than ever. Yet I'm holed up in here, unable to expend it." He shook out his hands, as if trying to shake off the excess energy. "Willie's right. I need to get out, even if just for a walk."

"I'm not sure that's wise," I said gently. "Someone still wants to kill you." I almost told him about my visit to Lord Coyle, but decided against it. He wouldn't like that I'd called on him alone.

"I've thought about that. I can go out disguised as one of the footman."

Willie burst out laughing.

"Or I can go for a drive, dressed as Woodall. With a hat, coat and scarf, only my eyes will be visible. From a distance, no one will know it's me."

It was actually a good idea. Although I preferred he remain inside, I had to concede it wouldn't work for long periods of time. "You will always have someone who knows about your watch with you, Matt. Is that clear?"

"Yes ma'am." He grasped my hips and drew me closer for another kiss.

Willie clicked her tongue. "If you go out in disguise, make sure it ain't in a dress. Nothing good comes from wearing dresses as a disguise. Trust me, I know. So does Farnsworth." She went to walk off, but I called after her.

"Don't you want to hear how today went? There were a number of developments."

"Is that why you were gone for so long?" Matt asked.

I glanced at the clock on the mantel. "It's only two."

I tugged on the bell pull to summon Bristow and asked him to bring sandwiches. Ten minutes later, he returned with a platter of cucumber and ham sandwiches cut into triangles. Duke followed him.

"I was just about to tell them what happened today," I told him after Bristow departed.

He pulled out a chair from the central table. "Then you all better sit down. We've got a mighty interesting tale to tell."

We told them how we progressed from assuming Mrs. Trentham was Mirnov's unwitting accomplice in the murder of her husband, to the murderess responsible for three deaths. I also explained why we suspected Coyle was involved, but given Mrs. Trentham's reluctance to implicate him, it would be impossible to convict him.

"Brockwell confirmed it just before we parted at the Yard," Duke added. "The authorities won't touch Coyle unless there's no doubt of his guilt."

"Then what do we need?" Willie asked. "We'll find the evidence."

"A good start would be Mrs. Trentham's statement accusing him of orchestrating the murders. Brockwell said he'll continue to pressure her."

I wasn't hopeful of success on that score. The threat from Coyle would be greater than any threat from the inspector.

Willie blew out a breath and reached for a sandwich.

Duke slapped her hand away. "You already ate lunch. These are for India and me."

"But I'm still hungry," she whined.

"Go ahead," I said. "Have mine."

She poked her tongue out at Duke and picked up a sandwich. "Will Jasper tell Mirnov or the Shaws that Albina was murdered by Mrs. Trentham?"

Duke shrugged as he chewed.

Matt had been very quiet up until now. He'd not asked a single question throughout the retelling and he seemed to be lost in thought.

I touched his arm. "Are you all right?"

"Of course," he said, sounding distracted.

I watched him from beneath lowered lashes. He was not all right. Something about the case bothered him. I was about to ask when Willie spoke with her mouth full of sandwich.

"All this for children."

"Not just ordinary children," Duke pointed out. "Magic ones."

"Seems to me like there's lots of people thinking about magician children lately. Mrs. Trentham, Louisa, Coyle."

"I'm not sure about Coyle," I said. "He wants power, but why would he care about the future of magic? He won't be around to take advantage of the next generation of magicians."

Willie dusted crumbs off her chest, then slumped in her chair, legs outstretched. She looked like she was settling in for a lazy afternoon in front of the fire. "Well, that was an easy investigation."

"For you," Duke said. "India, Brockwell and I did all the work today."

"I'm glad we don't have to go back to the gypsy camp. I don't trust them Romany."

Duke pushed his chair back from the table and assumed a similar pose to Willie. "I wanted to find out if the curse Albina put on Trentham was real or not. Guess we'll never know for sure now."

"The professor said they were real and that's good enough for me."

I studied Matt as they talked. He didn't seem to be listening. When he rose and excused himself, I followed him out of the library.

"Matt?" I caught up to him at the base of the stairs. "Matt, what's wrong?"

"Nothing."

"You've gone quiet all of a sudden."

"I'm just thinking." He gave me a smile. It didn't convince me that all was well.

"What about?"

"About you and me."

I narrowed my gaze. "All this talk about Trentham's infertility... Has it brought up thoughts about us not having conceived yet?"

"No! No." He skimmed his knuckles down my cheek to my chin. He grasped it gently. "India, I don't care if we don't conceive. I'm more than happy to adopt. You know that."

I couldn't help feeling relieved all over again. We'd already discussed it and decided on adoption if we couldn't have our own children, but his silence in the library had brought the old doubts to the surface.

"Then what's wrong?"

He smiled, a genuinely sweet smile. "Nothing, my love. Nothing." He kissed me on the lips and would have continued if Aunt Letitia hadn't interrupted.

I spent the remainder of the afternoon in her company. The others didn't join us until five o'clock when Duke entered the drawing room, whistling.

"Where are Matt and Willie?" I asked.

He stopped whistling and gazed longingly at the door as if he wished he'd never entered.

"Duke?" I pressed.

"They've gone out." He gave a pointed glance at Aunt Letitia who'd just set aside her embroidery due to the poor light.

If we must have this conversation while keeping the truth from her, then so be it. But we *were* having it. "Where?" I asked oh-so-sweetly.

"Driving."

Aunt Letitia clicked her tongue. "Honestly. We have Woodall for that. Matt shouldn't be seen on the coachman's seat. It's unseemly. What if an acquaintance recognizes him?"

What if that acquaintance wanted to kill him? I clutched my book tighter to steady my jangling nerves.

"No one will recognize him," Duke went on. "Anyway, don't blame the messenger. It ain't my fault he feels like a caged animal at home all day. Nor Willie's. She tried to stop him, but when he said he'd go alone, she gave in and went with him."

That was something, at least. She knew where he hid his magic watch. Of course if a bullet killed him instantly...

I swallowed and tried to put the thought from my mind.

Cyclops suddenly burst into the drawing room brandishing a newspaper. He was a little out of breath as he handed it to Duke. "Read that article." He stabbed the front page. "It's about Trentham's workshop."

"You mean the murder?" I asked, rising.

He shook his head. "The automaton."

Duke swore under his breath only to apologize when he remembered Aunt Letitia. "The headline says all we need to know. OUT OF CONTROL AUTOMATON RUNS AMOK IN SHOP OF MURDERED MAKER. IS MAGIC TO BLAME?"

I groaned as I read the opening paragraph. "How did the newspaper learn about the automaton, let alone that it was magical?"

"That is a ridiculously sensationalist headline," Aunt Letitia piped up. "I don't trust those kinds of newspapers. I only believe it if it's printed in *The Times*."

"It doesn't *say* it's magical," Cyclops said. "It only suggests."

"That's enough to have everyone believing it is," I said. The article mentioned how the automaton had been found in a lane the morning after Trentham was murdered in his toyshop. It also told how it was rumored to have run amok in the shop yesterday.

"I reckon it was the constables that informed the journalist," Duke said with a shake of his head. "Brockwell needs to have a word with them."

"It might not have been them," I said. "Several people walked past the window, and some might have peered in. If they saw the mess and the suit of armor in handcuffs, they would put two and two together."

"But what about magic?" Duke pointed to a paragraph on the newspaper. "How did the journalist find out Trentham was a magician and the automaton had magic in it?"

"A good guess?" Cyclops suggested. "Mirnov? Maybe he's the journalist's source."

"It's more likely to be an artless toymaker who wants to stir up trouble," I said. "Perhaps someone knew, or suspected, that Trentham was a magician and decided this was a good opportunity to discredit him and other magicians too. The journalist has certainly made it look as though magic is to blame for the automaton's behavior."

The article didn't claim the automaton was responsible for murdering Trentham, but it was implied. The journalist must have written it before knowing about Mrs. Trentham's arrest as it wasn't mentioned.

"This will cause a sensation," I said. "It does not bode well at all."

"Oh dear," Aunt Letitia murmured from the sofa. "Oh dear, oh dear."

I sat beside her. "What is it, Aunt?"

"Oh, Veronica, it's you. Thank goodness you've come. My brother Harry seems to have forgotten all about me. He was supposed to meet me here before we go for a walk. Have you seen him?"

I gently took her hands and guided her to stand. "Let's look for him together."

She allowed me to lead her out of the drawing room and up the stairs. At least when her mind wandered, she was amenable to suggestions that she rest. When I saw her settled in her room, I returned to the drawing room.

Matt and Willie had returned. Matt looked up from the newspaper while Willie read on.

"Is she all right?" he asked.

"I think so. She thought I was her former maid again. She must have been listening to us discuss the automaton and murder and it upset her. I'm sorry, I wasn't thinking."

"Usually talk of our investigations doesn't bring on one of her episodes. Perhaps it was the idea of the automaton being out of control." He returned to the paper and finished reading. "Bloody hell," he muttered when he reached the end. "This is a disaster."

I sat beside him with a sigh. "What can we do?"

"Write another article discrediting it," Duke suggested.

"It's too late," Willie said. "The bull's out of the lasso, and it ain't going to get caught again, no matter how hard we try."

She was right. There was nothing we could do except hope the public's reaction wouldn't be as unfavorable as we assumed. Perhaps no one would believe the newspaper's claims.

Matt wasn't giving up so easily, however. He spent the evening penning a response that included the detail that Mrs. Trentham was taken in for questioning by Scotland Yard over her husband's murder. He made copies and sent it to all the major dailies first thing in the morning.

Just after he sat down to breakfast with Willie, Duke and me, we had a visit from Brockwell. The inspector looked more crumpled and disheveled than usual, and tired too.

"You get any sleep last night?" Willie asked him.

He helped himself to coffee at the sideboard without being invited. Not that we minded. He was almost part of the household. "I was woken at one this morning by a constable who informed me that Mrs. Trentham escaped from her cell."

"Escaped!" we all cried.

"How?" I asked.

He drained his cup and refilled it from the coffee pot. He placed it on the table and returned to the sideboard to make up a plate of sausages and toast. Matt drummed his fingers on the table as he watched the inspector with a tight-lipped frown.

Willie cracked first, however. "Jasper! How did she escape?"

Brockwell unfolded a napkin and tucked it into his collar. "She used her magic on the automaton. She called it to her, for want of a better way of putting it."

"Called it to her?" I echoed. "How far away from her cell was the automaton?"

"Both the evidence room and holding cells are located in the basement, but at different ends of the building."

It was too far, surely. While I hadn't tried making the carpet fly while standing in a different room, I doubted my moving spell would work from such a distance.

Brockwell must have guessed the direction of my thoughts. "Several witnesses saw the automaton break open the lock on her cell door."

"But did they see it break out of the evidence room?"

"You may be onto something there."

I waited for him to continue, but he took a bite of a sausage and chewed slowly. After he swallowed and took a sip of coffee, he dabbed at his mouth with the napkin then finally continued.

"The constable on duty in the evidence room has disappeared."

"How can he just disappear?" Willie asked. "Have you gone to his home?"

"He didn't return there, nor did he clock off at the Yard. We searched everywhere. He has vanished."

"Are you treating him as a suspect or victim?" Matt asked.

"I'm keeping an open mind. He might have come to harm or he might have conspired with Mrs. Trentham to set the automaton free. I have men looking for evidence of a connection between them."

"Is a constable usually assigned to staff the evidence room?" Matt asked.

Brockwell sliced through the sausage and was about to put it into his mouth when Willie reached over and caught his arm. With a sigh, Brockwell lowered his fork to the plate. "There's a sergeant on duty during the day and evenings, but most nights it's a constable."

Like Brockwell, I wasn't sure whether to think of the constable as a victim or accomplice. I was still trying to understand what had happened—and how. Either Mrs. Trentham was a more powerful magician than we'd thought, or she'd had help in freeing the automaton from the evidence room.

"I assume you've read the newspaper article," Matt said.

Brockwell nodded. "My superiors brought it to my attention late yesterday afternoon. I explained that Mrs. Trentham had most likely controlled the automaton and that it had not acted of its own accord."

"What did they think about that?"

"They don't confide in me, Glass. You might learn more from the Commissioner, since you two are better acquainted and you don't work directly for him." He sliced through the sausage. "But if I had to guess, I would say they don't like to have magic mentioned at all in a matter as grave as murder. Whether Mrs. Trentham directed the automaton or it somehow broke free of her control is irrelevant. The fact is, magic was put into that automaton and the automaton killed a man."

It sounded to me like he wasn't merely guessing at his superiors' thoughts but voicing his own. He wouldn't be alone in his reasoning either. The artless public would be just as critical and place the blame on magic. Even magicians would blame magic.

I did.

I rubbed my temples where a headache was starting to bloom. We were in precisely the position we never wanted to find ourselves in. One where magic was openly acknowledged and caused fear among the general populace.

I felt sick.

"Someone needs to put out a statement denying the existence of magic," Duke said. "It's the only way."

Matt rubbed his forehead. "No one will believe it. Not enough people, anyway. After months of rumors and suggestion that began with Barratt's article, this will confirm it for many."

Willie swore under her breath. "What're you going to do, Jasper?"

"My job." Brockwell finished his cup of coffee and wiped his mouth with a napkin. "I've been tasked with finding Mrs. Trentham and bringing her to trial. She'll be charged with her husband's murder."

"She'll mention the out of control magic as part of her defense," Matt said. "Is that what the authorities want?"

"That is for people with more power than me to decide." Brockwell folded up the napkin and placed it beside his empty plate. "I want to question Coyle. That's why I'm here. I want you to come with me, Glass. You too, India. Yesterday I didn't want to confront him over his involvement when there wasn't enough evidence and Mrs. Trentham wouldn't accuse him. But that's all changed with her disappearance."

Matt agreed to join him. "He might have helped her escape. Shall we go now?"

"That's an excellent plan." Brockwell rose, as did Matt, Duke and Willie.

I looked down at my plate. I'd hardly eaten a thing.

"India?" Matt asked. "Is something wrong?"

"I have a confession to make." I rose too and met his gaze. "I spoke to Lord Coyle yesterday after parting with Duke and the Inspector."

Matt frowned. "You went alone?"

"You confronted him without me?" Brockwell asked. "India, this is police business. You could have jeopardized the investigation."

"Nonsense," I snapped. "I'm quite capable of asking him questions. He denied any involvement with Mrs. Trentham and blamed her entirely for the murders. I suspect his answers would have been the same no matter who asked him." I turned to Matt. "As to going alone, yes, I did. Do you think harm would have come to me in his own house with his wife and staff present?"

He looked taken aback by my outburst. He was certainly lost for words.

"I told him if he shot at you again, I'd call on London's magicians to shun him."

I strode out of the dining room. I wasn't going to apologize for confronting Coyle. I'd left Coyle's house with a sense of relief that he would not try to kill Matt again, if he had indeed been the one to shoot him. I'd also left with a sense of pride. Coyle had taken my threat seriously. I'd made him wary of *me*, of *my* influence among the magician community. And I'd done it on my own. It was a very satisfying feeling.

Willie caught up to me and slapped my shoulder. "Good for you, India. You're finally living up to your maiden name." When I didn't respond, she added. "Steele by name, steel by nature."

"I understand, Willie."

She squeezed my shoulder and raced up the stairs ahead of me.

Matt took her place. "You're cross with me," he said.

"No. I know you're just worried."

"Then why do I feel like you're cross?"

"I wouldn't knowingly place myself in danger, Matt. I was perfectly safe speaking to Coyle in his home and you know it."

"I still wish I'd been with you," he muttered.

I stopped and faced him. "It would have undermined what I wanted to say. My threat wouldn't have been as effective if I needed my husband there to chaperone me." I took his hands in mine. "He needs to know that I'm capable of being strong and vengeful, even if something happened to you and I found myself grieving. Otherwise my threat would have fallen on deaf ears."

He sighed. "You're right. It's just that I feel utterly useless right now. The investigation has moved on without me, and you no longer need me."

I grasped his face. "Of course I need you. I want you by my side, always. But that one time, my point had to be made on my own." I planted a brisk kiss on his mouth. "Now, stop feeling sorry for yourself and let's get ready to pay a visit on Coyle."

"Oh-ho! So you're letting me come with you today?"

"I suspect asking you to spend another day at home will be doomed to failure."

He touched my fingers as we headed up the stairs together. "True. There is only so much embroidery and idle chatter a man can stand."

* * *

BROCKWELL BEGAN the interrogation by asking the same questions of Lord Coyle that I had asked yesterday. His lordship gave the same answers. He confirmed that he introduced Mr. Trentham to his second wife, and was present for their marriage, but he did not murder Mr. Trentham, his first wife, or Albina Mirnov.

"Mrs. Trentham worked alone," he said. "And I'm growing tired of these accusations."

This time Hope was present, and the interview was conducted in the drawing room. She sat on the sofa with me, while her husband sat in his usual wingback chair, a cigar in hand. The smell of smoke, both stale and fresh, clung to the furniture and hung in the air. The smell had briefly disappeared after they married, but now that Lord Coyle was smoking again, it had returned.

So far, Hope had remained quiet and still. I constantly expected her to interject with her own opinion, but she did not. She simply played hostess by pouring tea nobody drank and sitting quietly while Brockwell fired questions at her husband.

"Then I have a new accusation for you," the inspector said. "Overnight, Mrs. Trentham escaped from her cell."

Lord Coyle had been puffing on his cigar, but stopped. He removed it. "And you think I helped her?" A deep chuckle welled up from his chest along with a thick cough. Once the cough subsided, he plugged the cigar back in. "Don't be absurd. You think me more influential than I am if you assume I can do that. What do you think, my dear?" he asked Hope. "Am I powerful enough to set a prisoner free from one of Scotland Yard's holding cells?"

Hope's nostrils flared. "I wouldn't know."

He chuckled again.

"So you are not harboring Mrs. Trentham?" Brockwell asked.

"No."

"You did not help her escape or have one of your men assist her?"

"No."

"Yet you benefit from her escape," Matt pointed out.

"Why? I still have you three coming here and bothering me, as well as your two bodyguards." He waved a hand at Duke and Willie, standing quietly by the door.

"If she hadn't escaped, you ran the risk of her exposing your involvement in the murder of her husband, and perhaps that of his first wife and Mrs. Mirnov."

Coyle removed his cigar. "I wasn't involved."

Matt pressed on. "Her disappearance means there'll be no trial. You're safe, as long as she doesn't appear in court where you can't control what she says."

"Can't I?" Coyle snarled.

Beside me, Hope flinched.

Coyle held up his cigar and studied the smoldering tip. "You're too narrow-minded. All of you. Think about who else benefits from her escape. It's not just me." When none of us answered, his lips spread in a smile. "You've seen the newspaper article?"

"What has that to do with it?" Brockwell asked.

"He's suggesting the government had just as much reason for wanting Mrs. Trentham to disappear," Matt said. "They wouldn't want her mentioning magic at her trial. A trial which would have been watched very closely by the public and journalists."

Coyle pointed his cigar at Matt. "I knew you'd catch on, Glass. So you see, Inspector, Mrs. Trentham had to disappear. She's probably dead. Alive, she's too much of a risk to the authorities who want to keep magic suppressed."

"*You* want to keep magic suppressed," I pointed out.

"I do, but I'm not the only one. Indeed, your husband has motive, too. I've heard him say on numerous occasions that he doesn't want magic exposed."

"You're being petty and ridiculous," Hope hissed.

Lord Coyle stroked his moustache. "Come, my dear, don't be upset. I know Glass is your beloved cousin, but I am merely pointing out that Mrs. Trentham's disappearance benefits more than you and I. I wouldn't be surprised if the good inspector is told to note in his report that Mrs. Trentham was deemed guilty of her husband's murder, and that the automaton had nothing to do with it." He turned to Brockwell. "Perhaps you'll be encouraged to write that she stated as much in her interrogation. Wouldn't it be of great benefit to so many if that report was then leaked to the press?"

Brockwell didn't deny it. He knew better than anyone that a manipulation of the facts by his superiors was a distinct possibility. If they did choose that path, there was nothing he could do about it. I wasn't sure I wanted him to do anything, anyway. Coyle was right. The scenario he painted was best for us.

Except that it meant the death of Mrs. Trentham, or her permanent disappearance at the very least. A chill rippled down my spine.

Brockwell rose and placed his hat on his head. "Thank you for your time, my lord. We'll see ourselves out."

"Hope will escort you." Coyle smiled at his wife but it didn't reach his eyes. "She enjoys the few rare moments with her cousin. Don't you, my dear?"

Hope's chest rose and fell with her deep breaths. She led the way out of the drawing room, striding ahead of us down the stairs. When we caught up to her at the front door, Matt touched her elbow to get her attention.

"I know it's none of my business, but...are you all right?" he asked quietly.

She lifted her chin. "Yes."

"Does he hurt you?"

"He doesn't lay a finger on me."

I suspected Coyle hurt her in other ways, however. As

someone who'd suffered at the hands of Eddie Hardacre, my former fiancé, I knew that some men who held power over women didn't always use violence as a means of control.

"Call on us if you require anything," Matt urged her.

Hope clung to his arm and pecked his cheek. She whispered something in his ear before he moved away and joined us at the door.

We drove Brockwell to Scotland Yard then returned home. The inspector promised to keep us informed of any developments, but otherwise, there was nothing more to do. The investigation was complete. It just didn't feel as though it was.

We spent a listless afternoon indoors. Despite his frustrations at being cooped up, Matt didn't leave. The arrival of Lord Farnsworth after dinner was a welcome distraction. Even Matt greeted him with enthusiasm. He clapped his lordship on the back and invited him to join us in the drawing room for a game of poker.

Aunt Letitia insisted on a word with him first, however. She patted the seat beside her on the sofa and whispered something to him. Lord Farnsworth's lips quirked with his smile and his gaze lifted to Willie.

Willie's eyes widened. "India. Go and find out what she's saying."

"No."

She clicked her tongue and watched them from beneath lowered lashes. They'd stopped sharing secrets, and Aunt Letitia's voice returned to its usual volume.

"Any luck finding a new candidate for marriage?" she asked him.

"Alas, not yet, but I haven't given up."

"Good to hear, Davide. Make sure she's a robust kind of girl and not prone to flights of fancy." She directed a speaking glance at Willie.

Willie gasped and frowned with all her might at Aunt Letitia.

Lord Farnsworth didn't notice. "A little bit of fantasy is all right in a wife." He chuckled. "Not madness, of course. There's enough of that already in my blood." When Aunt Letitia gave him a blank look, he tapped his temple. "My mother. She's do-lally."

Aunt Letitia's lips formed an O.

"But I agree that the girl should be robust," he said. "Don't want one easily scared off."

"Precisely. And don't look for girls, either. You need a more mature woman, not a debutante."

"Quite right. Maturity is a must."

"And it doesn't particularly matter if she hasn't got the right breeding or upbringing."

He looked at her aghast. "Steady on, Letty. You've been around Americans too long."

I smiled beneath my hand. Beside me, Willie snorted.

Matt invited Lord Farnsworth to join him, Cyclops and Duke at the card table. Willie protested that she wasn't included, and Cyclops told her to draw up another chair.

I declined altogether and joined Aunt Letitia on the sofa. "What did you whisper to Lord Farnsworth earlier?"

She smiled and leaned closer. "I told him Willie's been talking about him a lot since his last visit."

"But she hasn't."

"He seemed rather pleased."

"Of course he did. He likes being the center of attention. That doesn't mean he wants a relationship with her, or she with him. Aunt Letitia, you have to stop trying to match them. It won't work."

She waved off my doubts. "Tosh. It could. They're well suited."

"As friends, not as anything more. She told me she doesn't desire him."

"What has desire got to do with marriage?"

I sighed. This was going nowhere. "He won't marry someone so far beneath him. You heard him. And you of all people should understand that."

She sniffed. "I used to be prejudiced, but I'm not anymore."

"Not in this instance, because he's not family." My words didn't seem to be getting through to her if the small smile on her lips was anything to go by. "Aunt Letitia, this has to stop. No more matchmaking. Not for Willie, anyway. If you do want to find someone for Lord Farnsworth, look among the relations of your friends. Surely someone has a niece or daughter who's neither mad nor..." I waved at Willie, not quite sure how to describe her in a single word.

Aunt Letitia gave me her promise, although I wasn't sure I believed it. I took comfort in the fact that a match between Willie and Lord Farnsworth was something neither of them wanted, so her plan would be thwarted sooner or later if she persisted with it.

They played poker into the evening, and I joined them when Aunt Letitia retired. When the clock struck midnight, it was as if its chime triggered something inside Lord Farnsworth. He suddenly threw down his cards, face up, and made a declaration.

"I almost forgot why I came here tonight. I've learned something that might interest you. Whittaker and the home secretary are meeting tonight." He tapped his finger against the side of his nose. "In secret."

"How do you know?" Matt asked with a large dose of skepticism in his voice.

"I've paid the staff at the club to tell me if they overheard conversations between the two men."

"Why didn't I think of bribing the staff?" Matt muttered.

Lord Farnsworth picked up his cards again, a smug smile

on his face. "They wouldn't have spied for you. You're not a long time member, like me. They trust me."

"What are they meeting about?" Duke asked.

Lord Farnsworth placed two matchsticks into the middle. "I don't know, but it's worth finding out, don't you think? So who's coming with me?"

"You're going to spy on them?" I asked. "Tonight?"

They all blinked at me. "Of course," Willie said. "Want to come?"

I glanced at Matt. He pressed his lips together and pretended to study his cards. "I'll stay home," I said. "As will Matt."

He suddenly looked up.

"I say, India, you can't keep a good man out of his own fight," Lord Farnsworth said.

"Somebody shot at him the other day. He almost died. He is a walking target, Davide. Not to mention that Sir Charles could be the gunman."

Lord Farnsworth's eyes widened as he regarded Matt. "You look remarkably well for someone who almost died."

Matt tossed his cards into the middle of the table. "I'm strong."

"The four of you go," I said. "We'll stay here and await your report."

Lord Farnsworth suggested they leave immediately to get to the meeting place before Whittaker and the home secretary so they could hide. Fortunately it was going to take place at the southern end of the Broad Walk in Regent's Park. Lined with trees, they shouldn't have any trouble remaining hidden from view in the dark.

After they left, I curled up beside Matt on the sofa. He didn't place his arms around me, however. He was still disappointed at being left out of his own adventure.

"Stop pouting," I scolded. "This is for the best."

"But it's not fair."

"You're behaving like a child."

He stopped pouting and finally put his arms around me.

I caressed his jaw then planted a trail of light kisses from his throat to his ear. "The servants and Aunt Letitia have gone to bed and we're alone. Put some more coal on the fire."

His gaze heated and a wicked smile curved his lips. "That'll make it hot in here."

"Yes, it will." I unbuttoned his waistcoat. "You'd better take off some clothes to cool down."

CHAPTER 13

*C*yclops arrived home alone almost two hours later. Duke, Willie and Lord Farnsworth had decided to go on to one of their favorite gambling dens after leaving Regent's Park and had left it to Cyclops to deliver their report.

The report was very brief. They'd overheard nothing. "Whittaker and the home secretary met at the southern end of the Broad Walk and we were hidden behind nearby trees. Unfortunately, they walked as they talked and if we tried to follow, they would've seen us."

"Damn," Matt muttered.

"At least we know they're up to something. Nobody meets in the middle of a January night in a public park unless they don't want others to overhear."

It certainly pointed to a suspicious connection, and the only connection I could think was that Whittaker was a spy for the government. One so secretive that they couldn't meet in the home secretary's office.

The following morning, Matt declared he was going to confront Sir Charles Whittaker. "There's no other way to get answers," he told me as he dressed.

"He's hardly going to give direct answers if he is spying for England," I said.

"He might let something slip." He finished knotting his tie and fastened his waistcoat buttons. "Get dressed if you want to come with me."

I yawned as I climbed out of bed. "Go and wake one of the others. You need a guard."

"Let them sleep. Nobody will shoot me this early in the day."

I eyed him dubiously. "And how did you reach that conclusion?"

"Nobody will expect me to be out before breakfast on a Sunday."

It was not a theory that held much water in my opinion, but Matt didn't want to hear my protests. He left, as I dressed, to send word to Woodall to bring the carriage around.

Once we were seated safely inside the cabin, I asked for one of the pistols that were stored in the compartment under the seat. Matt didn't utter a word as he produced it and checked it was loaded. He handed it to me and I tucked it into my muff along with only one of my hands. The other wouldn't fit now.

"Feel better?" he asked.

"Not particularly. I doubt I can shoot someone before they shoot you, particularly if they catch us by surprise."

He leaned forward and planted a hand on the seat on either side of me. His face was very near mine. "You're beautiful and brave."

"Compliments won't work, Matt. We shouldn't be doing this alone. We should have roused one of the others."

He kissed me briskly then sat back. He wisely remained silent until we reached Sir Charles's residence.

The landlady fetched him, leaving us standing on the porch, exposed. I scanned the street but it was quiet. Nobody was out this early on a cold Sunday morning. When Sir

Charles opened the door, he at least had the decency to invite us into the hall where it was warmer. The smell of bacon made my stomach grumble in hunger.

"Come to accuse me of shooting your husband again, Mrs. Glass?" he asked.

"We know that wasn't you," Matt said.

I would have told him we knew no such thing, but we'd agreed on the way over that we must let him think we didn't suspect him anymore. We didn't want this visit to be diverted off-course.

Sir Charles gave a shallow bow. "I'm pleased to be exonerated. But now I'm intrigued as to the nature of this visit."

Matt got straight to the point. "You were seen last night talking with the home secretary."

Sir Charles went very still. He stared at Matt and, after a moment, he checked over his shoulder and indicated we should enter the adjoining parlor. He closed the door. "What is this about?"

"We want to know why you're spying on us for the home secretary."

"What makes you think I am?"

"We're not fools, Whittaker, so don't treat us as though we are. You are a spy for the government and you're spying on us. On my wife."

Whittaker scoffed. "This is absurd."

"Then why did you bring us in here and close the door?"

Whittaker's throat moved with his swallow. "What do you want, Glass?"

"I want to know if you are spying on India specifically or all magicians."

"I'm not answering that. Please leave."

Matt pressed on. "You were part of the collector's club before they were even aware of her, so I suspect the latter. I'm going to assume the British government wants to know who all the magicians are and to keep an eye on them. That's what

I'd do in their position. I suspect you've been instrumental in building a file on India."

"I didn't think you'd be prone to storytelling, Glass."

"You might as well admit it," Matt went on. "There's nothing I can do about it. Indeed, there's nothing I want to do. As it happens, we are on the same side. The government want magic kept quiet, to exist only in the shadows, the way it has done for centuries. So do we."

Sir Charles moved further into the room. "I'm not the only one who knows Mrs. Glass has been working on creating new spells with Mr. Charbonneau. That is not a secret."

"I've given up. Truly," I added when he gave me a skeptical look. "The thing is, I've come to realize that my spells can be misused by magicians who don't have the best interests of others at heart. New spells can be dangerous. Some could even be used as weapons. I don't want that."

"And nor does the government, does it?" Matt said.

Sir Charles didn't deny it. It was confirmation enough for me that he was indeed working as a spy for the home secretary. "What about Mr. Charbonneau? Has he decided to give up?"

"He has to. He can't do it alone."

"And there is no one else aside from yourself capable of creating new spells with him?"

"No one." I adjusted my grip on the pistol inside the muff. "And you can be assured that I no longer want to do it. The problem with Mr. Trentham's automaton has proved to me how dangerous it can be when a spell is stolen and falls into the wrong hands."

He tilted his head to the side. "Stolen? Are you talking about the new spell you created with Charbonneau?"

I nodded.

"I read about the automaton in the newspaper, of course, but...was the stolen spell retrieved when Mrs. Trentham was arrested?"

"Unfortunately not."

"We suspect Coyle was behind the theft of the spell from Charbonneau's residence," Matt said. "We think he urged her to do it."

Sir Charles tapped a finger against his thigh as he considered this. It was the only outward sign that it troubled him. The cool, debonair gentleman looked as unruffled as ever.

"What will be the official stance about the incident, specifically, and about magic, in general?" Matt asked. "I assume that's what you were discussing last night with the Home Secretary."

Sir Charles continued to tap his thigh. "You can read it for yourself. I have this morning's editions upstairs. Apparently Mrs. Trentham killed her husband. It had nothing to do with the automaton. She simply blamed it to escape justice. Scotland Yard got her to confess in the end."

Matt nodded, not at all surprised. "It'll require more than a few statements to quell the public's interest in magic."

"I agree."

"So what will the home secretary do next?"

Sir Charles barked a laugh. "He doesn't tell me his plans, Glass." He glanced at the door. "Have we finished?"

"One more question," Matt said. "Does Coyle also work for the home secretary?"

Sir Charles leveled his gaze with Matt. "Coyle only has his own self-interests at heart."

"Do you also work for him?"

"No."

"Then why have you met him in secret and talked about India with him?"

"You're mistaken. Now, if you don't mind, my breakfast smells ready." He rested his hand on the doorknob, but before opening it, he turned to me. "Tell me, Mrs. Glass, *is* it possible for that automaton to work without a toymaker magician operating it?"

C.J. ARCHER

"No. I suspect every time it did work seemingly without anyone controlling it, Mrs. Trentham was in fact whispering the spell. There is no such thing as faulty magic. She lied when she told us it was acting of its own accord so she could later blame her husband's murder entirely on the automaton. I'm sure it was all her doing."

"She was an accomplished liar," Matt murmured.

Sir Charles gave me a shallow bow. "Thank you. That is indeed something useful."

Once Matt and I were safely inside the carriage, I finally felt as though I could breathe normally again. My chest had been tight during that entire encounter. "Do you think we achieved anything?" I asked.

"He knows we're on the same side, that we want the same thing. Perhaps now the government will focus their resources on dampening these latest rumors and the resulting fear rather than worrying about what you're going to do next."

It was something of a comfort to have called a truce with Sir Charles, for that's precisely how it felt. We *were* on the same side now that I'd given up spell casting. We all wanted to keep Britain safe from those who would use magic for ill purposes.

Now all we had to do was find all copies of the stolen moving spell and destroy them. The task would not be easy, but at least Sir Charles and the home secretary now knew where to begin their search—with Coyle.

* * *

THE NEWSPAPERS DID INDEED HAVE further articles on the topic of magic and, more specifically, the Trentham murder and the automaton. While all reported that the police stated Mrs. Trentham confessed to being solely responsible for the murder of her husband, and that magic had nothing to do with it, opinion pieces were divided. Most believed the official police statement—but not all.

Tellingly, her escape from Scotland Yard's holding cell wasn't mentioned. Officially, she was awaiting trial.

"They can't keep her escape secret forever," Cyclops said, turning the page of the newspaper he read at the breakfast table. We'd arrived home from Sir Charles's to find most of the household just getting out of bed. Only Aunt Letitia was missing, preferring to have her breakfast in her room.

Willie, sitting beside him at the table, clicked her tongue. "I ain't finished."

Duke walked past on his way to the sideboard and Willie thrust out her empty coffee cup, blocking his path. "Another one," she said without looking up from the paper.

Duke rolled his eyes. "Yes, ma'am."

Cyclops picked up his empty cup and handed it to Duke too with a smile. "Thanks, Duke."

"I'm only doing it for you because you're a working man now and a man's entitled to have a Sunday off."

"Then why are you doing it for Willie?"

"She would've punched me in the arm if I didn't."

Willie looked up. "I've been working all week too. So've you, Duke."

"It ain't the same and you know it," Duke said.

I folded up the newspaper I was reading and reached for another. "We're all going to church today and we're going to mingle with the other parishioners. I want to gauge the reactions of the general public to these articles."

"I think we should split up," Matt said. "You and I will attend our usual church with Aunt Letitia, and the three of them should go to other areas. That way we'll learn the opinions of different types of people."

"Good idea," Willie said. "Not everyone in the city thinks the same as Lord and Lady Tosspot from Mayfair."

"You are not going anywhere, Matt," I told him. "You can stay home. Aunt Letitia and I will go without you."

He grumbled but accepted my decision when I refused to back down.

It turned out that people from the same part of the city didn't all think the same. At our church alone, opinions varied. Some believed the official statement that Mrs. Trentham murdered her husband and simply used magic and the automaton as a scapegoat. Others were skeptical and suspected the government was covering up the existence of magic. Of those who stated they believed in magic, not all thought the automaton responsible for the murder. The reactions were just as varied at the other churches.

What became clear, however, was that magic was utmost on people's minds. As Willie had put it, the bull was out of the lasso and couldn't be caught again.

Brockwell arrived after lunch. It was unusual for him to miss a meal if he could help it, but he told us he'd just come from Scotland Yard where he'd been all morning. I could tell he wanted to talk to us about something but was reluctant in front of Aunt Letitia. When she finally made her excuses, he closed the door behind her himself.

"Out with it, Jasper," Willie said. "You been acting like you're sitting on a hornet's nest ever since you arrived."

"This won't come as a surprise, I suspect," he said, moving to stand in front of the fireplace. "Mrs. Trentham was found dead overnight."

I was the only one who gasped. Not that I was surprised. I'd expected it. But it was still a shocking thing to happen. I'd been talking to her mere days ago. I'd helped her clean up the toyshop after she'd directed the automaton to make a mess.

"How did she die?" Matt asked.

"A gunshot through the head," Brockwell said.

"An execution," Cyclops muttered. "They didn't even try

to make it look like an accident. Only someone who thinks they're above the law does that."

"Or someone who is the law," Matt said.

We all looked to Brockwell, who was scratching his sideburns. When he realized, he lowered his hand. "There's more. The constable who was on duty in the evidence room hasn't been found."

"Do you think he's dead too?" Willie asked.

"I don't know, but I don't think he's innocent. He hadn't lived at the address he gave very long. He also volunteered to do duty in the evidence room that night. That in itself is unusual. No constable would rather be on duty inside when he can be out. Particularly constables who are new recruits that come highly recommended."

Cyclops lifted his head. "How recently did he complete his training?"

"Three weeks ago. Interestingly, he wasn't a young man."

"Most trainees are barely out of the schoolroom," Cyclops told us. "They call me Pa."

"Any chance you can find out more about him from your supervisors?" Matt asked him.

Cyclops nodded. "I'll try tomorrow."

"Have you read the papers?" Willie asked Brockwell. "They say Mrs. Trentham confessed to murdering her husband. Your superiors don't want magic blamed."

"They told me as much this morning when they questioned me."

"Questioned you about what?" I asked.

"Magic, my experiences with it, and with investigating alongside you. They asked me a lot of questions about you, India."

The planes of Matt's face hardened. "What did you say?"

Brockwell resumed his seat. "They're already aware of the existence of magic. You know that, Glass. Trying to deny it will do no good." He turned to me. "All I told them was that you were a law-abiding citizen who wanted to do no harm. I assured them you don't even practice magic anymore since you no longer own a business."

"Did they ask about my spells with Fabian?"

He nodded. "I told them you'd stopped after seeing what harm the spells can do. I did not tell them the spell was stolen and was what Mrs. Trentham used on the automaton."

"They'll soon find out," Matt said. He told Brockwell about our meeting with Sir Charles, and Sir Charles's meeting with the home secretary. "He's a spy for the British government, and he infiltrated the collector's club to spy on magicians and collectors."

Brockwell scrubbed absently at his sideburns. "Interesting. It means they've believed in magic all this time, from before I even met you, despite some trying to deny it to me."

"Maybe they've known for a while," I said. "Perhaps even centuries."

That statement left a hefty silence in its wake. It didn't break until Aunt Letitia returned.

Brockwell stayed with us for the rest of the day and seemed to appreciate the distraction from his work. The weather cleared just before the sun set but we did not leave the house. It didn't seem fair to go for a walk when I wanted Matt to remain indoors. For his part, he no longer seemed agitated by being made to stay home. He didn't complain, although I did catch him gazing longingly at the sky at one point.

We received two letters during the afternoon. One was from Louisa, who wanted to know more about the Trentham case, and the second was from Mrs. Delancey, who suggested we needed a collectors club meeting to discuss recent developments.

"She seems to have forgotten we're not members," I said.

"Will you go to a meeting if you're invited?" Matt asked.

I shook my head. I didn't want to discuss magic with

anyone. At least, not with those who took it upon themselves to be the curators of magical objects.

The following day was uneventful as we waited for Cyclops to return from work. I went shopping in the morning with Aunt Letitia and listened in on conversations. Magic was on many lips but opinion was divided about whether it existed or not. A popular theory was that it was a hoax the newspapers were playing on the public to sell more copies. Considering the newspaper that had first implied the automaton murdered Trentham was of the gutter variety, that theory could gain momentum.

I hoped so. It would help our cause.

Matt greeted us with enthusiasm when we returned. I quickly realized it wasn't because he had something to report, but because he needed the distraction. He was bored at home with only Duke and Willie for company. They went out after lunch while Matt spent some time with Aunt Letitia until she left to rest in her room.

Shortly after that, Cyclops arrived home with Brockwell, even though it was too early for them to have finished work. Going by their solemn expressions, they had news.

I poured tea from the warm pot and invited them to sit.

Cyclops accepted the cup and cradled it in his big hand. "I asked my supervisors if they remembered the constable from his training days, the one who disappeared on the night of Mrs. Trentham's escape. None did."

I almost dropped the teapot. It wasn't the answer I'd expected. "But he was a trainee mere weeks ago."

"He wasn't a trainee at all," Cyclops went on. "Brockwell had them check their records. The constable was never there."

Matt sat forward. "So how did he come to be assigned to Scotland Yard?"

"His papers and letter of recommendation from the academy are on file," Brockwell said. "I saw them myself just this morning. Everything was in order. The signatures looked authentic, the letterhead and forms all correct."

"Good forgeries," Cyclops said.

"This was not a simple, amateur operation. It was planned weeks in advance and meticulously carried out." Brockwell sounded impressed. "The person or persons behind it knew what they were doing."

"Coyle," Matt growled.

"Or the government," I said. "They gained just as much as he did from Mrs. Trentham's disappearance."

"I'm not so certain. They would probably prefer it if she blamed Coyle in the trial rather than disappear altogether and leave the public wondering. Her sudden death means the journalists will ask awkward questions, just like we are. But if she went to trial, those questions could have been answered in the government's favor. They could convince her to say whatever they wanted by offering her a lenient sentence."

I must have gone a little pale because Matt approached and crouched before me. He gently clasped my hands and rested them on my knees.

"You would prefer it if the government were to blame for her murder?" he asked.

"I...I don't know. Just thinking about Coyle being that ruthless gives me chills."

"We've known for some time that he's not a good man."

"It feels different now."

"Yes." His thumbs rubbed my knuckles. "I need to warn Hope. We'll visit her now."

"That's not wise," Brockwell said. "Coyle might be there."

Matt rose. "Hope is my cousin. I might not like her, but I have a duty to protect her if I can. If Coyle is there then good. I want him to know that we're aware of what he's doing. You don't have to come, Inspector."

Brockwell slowly sipped his tea until the cup was empty

then he placed it gently on the saucer. "Is it all right if I stay here until Willie returns home?"

"Be our guest," I said.

Matt and Cyclops exited the room but I remained behind to have a word with the inspector. "How are things between you and Willie?" I asked.

"Well." He exhaled heavily and settled back into the armchair. "She does her own thing and I do mine. Sometimes our paths coincide." It sounded like a business transaction.

"But are your affections engaged?"

"Yes, as are hers."

That was a relief to hear. If he'd answered in the negative, I could never trust my instincts again.

"I know we're unconventional," he went on, "but we like it this way, for now."

"For now? So you see a future where that might change? Perhaps you'll want something more…secure?"

"You mean marriage?" He chuckled. "I don't believe in gypsy fortunes. I believe in human nature, and that is not predictable."

I couldn't argue with that.

"Perhaps we'll marry one day, and perhaps we won't. That's the beauty of life, India. We never know what's going to happen in the next chapter."

CHAPTER 14

ord Coyle was indeed at home, and Hope too. While we waited for the footman to fetch his lordship, we were able to speak with Hope alone. Cyclops remained by the door to keep watch while Matt took a seat beside her on the sofa. She looked delicate next to him with her lithe, slender frame and fragile beauty. It was easy to think her weak and in need of saving, but I knew better. I thought Matt did too, but now I wasn't so sure.

"We don't have long," he said. "So please listen to what I have to say without interruption. You're about to learn some truths about Coyle and his endeavors."

"I know what he is, Matt." At least she didn't *pretend* to be the damsel in distress.

"You told us he doesn't physically harm you, but there are other forms of harm. Is he cruel to you?"

She touched the large diamond ring on her finger. "He can be generous."

"But kind?"

Her gaze slid away. It fell on me. "Our relationship is not like yours, if that's what you mean. We cannot all be so fortunate."

Matt clicked his tongue in frustration at her vague response. "I meant it when I said I can help you. If you ever need anything, please come to me. As your cousin and the Rycroft heir, it's my duty—"

"*Don't* talk to me about duty," she snapped.

Matt sat back as if she'd pushed him. He wasn't used to having such an offer flung in his face. Usually women readily accepted his assistance.

"He's trying to help you," I said. "This is not his fault."

Her lips thinned. "This marriage is no one's *fault*, India, and I am not a helpless victim. I get something from this marriage. More than Coyle, I can assure you."

"And does he remind you of that?"

She blinked hard.

Cyclops cleared his throat and moved away from the door. A few moments later, Lord Coyle entered. He paused in the middle of the room and surveyed our faces. He knew something had transpired in his absence. No doubt he would try to find out from Hope later.

Instead of occupying his usual seat in the armchair, he moved to stand behind her. He settled a hand on her shoulder. It was the hand that held his cigar. She touched her nose then turned her face away. The smoke drifted into her hair and a sprinkle of ash fell on her sleeve.

"Another visit from my favorite magician," Lord Coyle said jovially. "To what do I owe the pleasure this time, Mrs. Glass?"

While I'd assumed Matt would do most of the talking, since Coyle addressed me, I had to answer. I met his gaze. "We wanted to tell you that we're aware of your involvement in the Trentham murder."

"I told you, that was nothing to do with me."

"We know you placed one of your men in Scotland Yard. He made it look like Mrs. Trentham used magic on the automaton to aid her escape but, in truth, it was all his doing."

"What makes you think he works for me?"

"No one else could be behind the escape. The government wanted her alive to testify. Only the real killer benefits from her death."

"Death?" Hope echoed. "She's dead?"

Lord Coyle's thumb stroked her throat. She stilled. "There, there. Don't upset yourself, my dear."

The column of her throat moved with her swallow, but she otherwise remained utterly still.

"Mrs. Trentham died from a gunshot wound to the head," Matt said. "There's no doubt in our minds that she was shot to stop her from admitting who was behind the murders of her husband, his first wife, and Mrs. Mirnov. If Mrs. Trentham was allowed to testify, she would implicate the person who orchestrated the murders to save herself."

Coyle grunted. "Perhaps she escaped of her own accord. Perhaps the constable who helped her escape was her lover or a paid accomplice."

"I did not say he was a constable," I pointed out.

Coyle lifted the cigar to his lips. "A guess."

Hope took the opportunity of being released to shift along the sofa. She stared straight ahead, her face white, her breathing shaky. She turned slowly to face her husband. "Did you do it?" she whispered. "Did you assist in her escape then have her killed to silence her?"

Lord Coyle puffed on his cigar. Smoke billowed from his nose and mouth like a dragon. "You never used to believe everything you're told. That's what I liked about you. You questioned everything. You considered things from all angles before making a decision. Have you forgotten how to do that, my dear? Has marriage to me made you too comfortable?" He removed his cigar from between his lips and studied the tip. "Shame."

Hope pressed a hand to her stomach and turned her back to him. She stared down at the rug.

"Can I expect a visit from that idiotic policeman?" Coyle asked.

"We have no proof," Matt said. "Not without the constable."

Coyle grunted. "I read the newspapers. How convenient for the government that Mrs. Trentham is blamed instead of magic."

"Convenient for many."

Coyle pointed his cigar at Matt. "In that, we agree. But I assure you, Glass, I didn't murder anyone, nor did I orchestrate the murders. It must have been all Mrs. Trentham. She planned the murders and carried them out in the hope Mirnov would marry her and have children with her. It was a gamble, if you ask me, considering he had no children by his first wife." He tugged on the bell pull. "But some people do enjoy playing a risky game to get what they want, in my experience. Isn't that right, my dear?"

The butler entered and we rose to leave.

Hope did too. "I'll see you out."

Coyle grasped her arm. "Stay. Keep me company."

She slowly sank onto the sofa again. With the cigar wedged between his lips, Coyle rested his hand on her shoulder again. Hope winced.

Matt hesitated. He wanted to rescue Hope, but he knew there was nothing he could do unless she requested his assistance. Hope wasn't willing to seek his help.

Not yet.

* * *

IT WAS my idea to visit Mr. Mirnov next. If Coyle was right, and Mrs. Trentham murdered her husband and Albina to

233

marry Mirnov, he must have had some notion. Now that she was dead, I hoped he would admit it.

Cyclops sat beside Woodall on the driver's seat to better see our surroundings, while Matt kept his gaze glued to the view through the rear window. When we arrived at Brick Lane, both declared that we had not been followed. Even so, my nerves stretched thin as we walked briskly through the market.

A hawker stepped out in front of me, shouting, "Get your chestnuts here!" It was enough to send my heart crashing against my ribs.

We found Mr. Mirnov occupying his usual place at the end of the market. He stood by his cart, his back to us, rearranging a row of toy soldiers. A small boy hovered nearby. He gazed longingly at the soldiers and took a step forward, only to stop and glance warily at Mr. Mirnov.

"Come closer," Mr. Mirnov said. "You can play with them."

The boy hesitated.

"Don't be afraid of this. I won't hurt you."

I couldn't see what he pointed to when he referred to "this."

"Mr. Mirnov," Matt said.

Both Mirnov and the child turned to us. The child took one look at Cyclops, gasped, and fled. But Cyclops was too stunned by the gruesome sight of Mirnov's face to care. We all were.

Mr. Mirnov touched the skin near the long cut on his cheek. The sutures made him look like the monster from the Mary Shelley novel. "You're as bad as the children," he said wryly.

"Shouldn't that be covered with a bandage?" Cyclops asked.

"It doesn't stay on. You, of all people, shouldn't stare like that."

Cyclops fingered his eye patch and looked away.

"What happened?" Matt asked.

"My wife's family decided it was time that I pay for murdering my wife." He spat the words out as if they were bitter. "It's better than losing a limb, I suppose. Or my life."

I gasped. "You think they'll try to kill you?"

"I'm surprised they haven't already. Romany law says an eye for an eye." He went to touch the wound, but stopped himself. "This injury means they're not sure of my guilt. If they were, I wouldn't be here now."

"We know you didn't kill your wife, and we can inform them, if you like."

He stared at me, his mouth ajar. "Yes! Please, inform them! But how do you know it wasn't me? Did someone else confess?"

"We need you to confirm something first," Matt said. "Tell us about your acquaintance with Mrs. Trentham."

Mirnov leaned back against the cart. "I read about her arrest." He heaved a sigh. "I suppose it's only right that I confess now. I've met her on several occasions. The last time was when you saw us at the Rose and Crown. As you've probably guessed, we weren't discussing business."

"Were you discussing marriage?" I asked.

"No! Her husband had just died. Now that I know she killed him, I suppose it wouldn't have been a surprise if she had suggested it, but at the time, I would have been shocked. I had no idea she murdered him. No idea." He rubbed his chin but got too close to the wound and winced. "Good lord, she could have killed me next if we'd married."

Matt told him that she'd killed Mr. Trentham because of his infertility, and that she'd probably planned his murder for some time. "She wanted magician children. She was a toymaker magician too. Did you know that?"

He nodded. "She told me but said it was a secret. Only her

husband knew. She even told me of her desire to have children one day."

"Magician children?" I asked.

"She just said children." He shook his head. "I cannot believe *she* killed him because of his infertility." He frowned. "Wait, you say she wanted magician children. Are you implying she killed my wife too? So that she could then marry me after she became a widow?"

"We believe so," I said gently. "She committed the murders several months apart to avoid suspicion. I'm so sorry."

He leaned more heavily against the cart, his shoulders stooped. The realization of how he'd been unwittingly involved in murder had begun to sink in. "My God."

It was quite a lot to take in and we let him digest it before we continued. What we said next was going to be another shock.

"We have another suspect, however," Matt went on after a few moments. "Someone who may have either committed the murders himself or coerced Mrs. Trentham. Someone who wanted to see the toymaker lineage continue."

Mr. Mirnov straightened. "Who?"

"You don't need to concern yourself with that. But to get a clearer picture, we need one answer from you."

"Go on."

"You say Mrs. Trentham never mentioned marriage to you in all your acquaintance, but did she flirt with you?"

His face flushed. He cleared his throat. "Yes. Quite strongly, in fact."

Matt, Cyclops and I exchanged glances.

"Why? What does that mean?" Mr. Mirnov asked.

"It means Mrs. Trentham did indeed kill your wife," Matt said. "I'm sorry."

Mr. Mirnov squeezed his eyes shut and dug his fingers into the sockets. His chin wobbled and his breathing became ragged. We gave him a moment to gather himself then said our goodbyes.

"Wait," he called as we walked off. "You said you'd inform the Shaws for me. Is that a promise?" He indicated his wound. "I don't feel like doing it myself."

"Of course," Matt said.

"Thank you. Be careful of the dog. This isn't my only injury, it's just the one you can see."

Dear lord.

Matt placed a hand to my lower back and steered me between the market stalls.

"So it wasn't Coyle," I said when we reached our waiting carriage. "Mrs. Trentham acted on her own and tried to implicate him, just as he claimed, otherwise she wouldn't have flirted with Mirnov."

"Coyle and Mrs. Trentham could have acted together," Matt pointed out. "I have no doubt she wanted to marry Mirnov and bear his children, but I think Coyle helped her to realize her dream, just like he helped her marry Trentham years ago."

"But her plan failed this time," Cyclops added. "She got caught."

"And so he had to get rid of her or risk her implicating him," I finished.

We drove to Mitcham Common in silence. The more I thought about it, the more I suspected Matt was right. Both Mrs. Trentham and Lord Coyle were to blame for the murders of Mr. Trentham, his first wife, and Mrs. Mirnov.

But only Coyle was to blame for the final murder of Mrs. Trentham. He'd killed her to protect himself because he couldn't trust her not to implicate him in a trial.

I blinked up at the ominously dark clouds and pulled my cloak tighter at my throat against the chill. I'd always known he was a ruthlessly powerful man, but I was just beginning to realize the lengths he was willing to go to for magic.

I closed my hand around Matt's. If anything happened to him, I knew who to blame.

Coyle would discover just how far I'd go to take away the thing he loved too.

* * *

THE SHAWS' camp was deserted. There was no one about, not even the dog. The fire had been extinguished, although the ash was still warm, and there were no belongings left out. No chairs, cooking utensils, tent, and no sign of life. If it hadn't been for the presence of the caravan and horses, we'd have assumed they'd left.

"They're about to depart," Cyclops said.

Matt turned over a burned log in the fire with the toe of his boot. The coals glowed. "They were here recently."

Where did they go? And why did they leave?

It started to rain fat icy drops. I'd foolishly left the umbrella in the carriage and my coat didn't have a hood.

"Let's go," Matt said. He called out to Cyclops who'd been about to peer into one of the caravan windows.

Cyclops turned away from it.

The door to the caravan burst open. The man named Lancelot stood in the doorway and pointed a shotgun at Cyclops's head. "Don't move or I kill your friend."

Cyclops slowly put up his hands. Matt and I followed suit. Matt took a step back to be closer to me.

"I said don't move!" Lancelot stepped slowly down the ladder to the ground.

Behind him, Mrs. Shaw emerged. She ordered someone to stay inside—the children?—and she too stepped down the ladder. She scanned Cyclops from head to toe then turned to us. "This is the second time you've come poking your noses around our property."

"We mean you no harm, Mrs. Shaw," Matt said. "I'd appreciate it if Lancelot lowered his weapon."

Mrs. Shaw approached, hand on hip. "The first visit's free. You have to pay for the second. Hand over your valuables." She put out her palm to me. "Your ring, missus. And your watches."

The only ring I wore was my wedding band. I could part with that. Matt would buy another. But my watch had taken months of tinkering and spell speaking before it had truly become my own. After the one my parents had given me was broken beyond repair, Matt purchased another for me. At first, I'd thought it would never behave like my original one, chiming when I faced danger and saving my life. But it eventually proved itself.

If she took it, I would have to start all over again.

Matt gave her his watch. Not his magical one, the regular one he kept for simply telling the time. The other was well hidden. "India, do as she says."

But I wasn't giving in so easily. "We're not here because we missed your company, Mrs. Shaw. We came to tell you something about Albina and her death. But you'll never learn what if you rob us."

Mrs. Shaw's lips parted in her silent gasp. "Albina?" she said weakly.

Lancelot pressed the end of the shotgun into Cyclops's temple. "Don't believe them, Ma!"

Cyclops closed his eye and swallowed.

"Don't shoot!" I cried. "Please, lower the gun."

Mrs. Shaw took a step forward. In that moment, the rain came down harder. It was as if the sky parted and a sea plunged through. I was drenched in an instant. Ice-cold water slid past my collar, down my back, and formed puddles in the already soaked ground.

Mrs. Shaw didn't seem to notice. Her midnight-dark eyes

drilled into me. She grabbed my arms. "I want to know about my Albina. Tell me about Albina!"

Matt caught her wrist. "Let my wife go!"

Lancelot swung around and pointed the gun at Matt. "Don't touch my mother!"

As if his shouts were a signal, a dog ran out of the nearby copse of trees. The snarling, growling creature raced toward us. Saliva dripped from jagged teeth. Mud flung behind it, dug up by sharp claws.

My watch chimed an ominous warning inside my reticule. The high-pitched sound was barely audible over the splattering rain and barking dog. I removed it with trembling fingers. If the dog attacked me, my watch would save me.

The dog kept coming and coming. But not for me.

For Matt. My watch wouldn't save him.

"India!" he shouted. "Get back!"

I didn't move.

Out of the corner of my eye, I saw Cyclops lunge at Lancelot and try to wrestle the shotgun off him.

The gun went off.

But the dog kept coming.

CHAPTER 15

The rain didn't slow the dog. It kept coming, straight for Matt, its razor-sharp teeth bared with each ferocious bark. The muscular body propelled it forward at an alarming rate.

Cyclops shouted for the dog to be called off. There were other voices too, all shouting over the top of each other, but they seemed muted all of a sudden, like they were under water, or I was. My focus centered on the dog, blocking out everything else. Even the freezing rain ceased to affect me.

I spoke the spell.

I'd learned it by heart and it came to me easily. I pictured the speed and direction I wanted my watch to take, and in that moment, with the dog a mere three feet from Matt, my watch flew off my outstretched palm. The chain wrapped around the dog's snout. The creature halted, sliding in the mud to come to a standstill at Matt's feet. It pawed at the watch chain but to no avail. The chain remained firmly in place, muzzling the dog. I spoke the spell again, and the watch itself tapped the dog on the nose. It quieted in surprise.

A man raced out of the woods, but he was not armed, and

two women burst from the caravan. All three talked at once, loudly, then Mrs. Shaw and Lancelot joined in.

"Quiet!" Cyclops shouted. He pointed the gun at Lancelot's head. "Be quiet or I shoot."

His threat silenced all but one of the Shaws. "Release my dog!" snapped the man who'd come from the woods. He looked remarkably like Lancelot and had the same dark eyes as their mother.

Matt grabbed the dog by its collar and walked it to the caravan. He ordered the women and children to leave and they obeyed without question. They must have been watching the events unfold through the windows. Matt released the dog inside and shut the door. He nodded at me.

I pictured the watch unwinding itself from the dog's snout and spoke the moving spell again. A tapping sound came from inside the caravan and Matt opened the door just enough for the watch to slip through. The dog tried to catch it, but missed. It barked in frustration. Matt closed the door again and picked up the watch. He jumped down to the ground and handed it to me with a small smile.

I smiled back and drew in a fortifying breath. Thank God that had worked. I hadn't been entirely sure I had the focus to do it under pressure. It seemed I did.

The Shaws had stopped talking and now stared at me with a mixture of wonder and uncertainty. Even the formidable matriarch was lost for words.

Matt put out his gloved hand. "My watch and my wife's ring, if you please."

Mrs. Shaw handed back our belongings.

Matt pocketed his watch. "I'm wet through to my skin. I have nearly been eaten by a dog. My wife and friend are just as soaked. I have a good mind to walk off and not tell you what we know about Albina's death."

"No!" Mrs. Shaw cried. "Come into the caravan out of the rain." She tried to usher us to the van, but I refused.

"I'm already wet and I'm not going near that dog," I said.

The rain had eased a little but still fell steadily. At least I no longer had to blink away the drops from my eyes.

"Who killed my daughter?" Mrs. Shaw prompted. "Was it him? Was it that cur of a husband?" She spat into the ground. Her daughters-in-law did too.

"No," Matt said.

Mrs. Shaw glanced at me for clarification.

"It wasn't Mirnov," I said. "It was Mrs. Trentham."

The brothers exchanged glances. Mrs. Shaw stared at Matt.

"The wife of the rival toymaker," Matt reminded her. "Her husband was a magician too, and so was she, although few knew it. She wanted to have magical children, but discovered her husband was incapable. To fulfill her dream, she turned to your daughter's husband in the hope he could provide her with the children she wanted. She killed Albina and then, some months later, killed her own husband."

Lancelot surged forward only to stop upon Cyclops's order. "Where is she?"

"Dead," Matt said. "You can read about it in the newspapers if you don't believe me."

Lancelot swore loudly. His brother lowered his head. Their mother, however, met Matt's gaze. There were no deep breaths or hard swallows, no wobble of her chin or tears, only resignation in the stoop of her back.

"So it is over," she said.

"It's over," I repeated. "You should apologize to Mr. Mirnov. You've left him with terrible injuries."

She grunted. "He was not a good husband to my Albina. He deserves what he got."

Lancelot leaned back against the caravan and squinted up at the sky. Rain washed over his face. It dripped off his hair and fell into his mouth as he opened it to let out an anguished cry. One of the women went to him, but he shook her off.

"She did it to herself," he cried. "Albina brought about her own death."

The woman frowned and glanced at her sister-in-law. But Mrs. Shaw and the other man seemed to understand. Mrs. Shaw finally lowered her chin. She plodded with heavy steps to her other son, as if the mud weighed down her boots. He put his arm around her. She had never looked so small or frail, just like any other grieving elderly woman who'd lost her beloved daughter.

"What do you mean?" Matt asked.

"She cursed her husband's magic rival many years ago," Lancelot said. "When he was married to another woman."

"Yes, to diminish the strength of his magic. We know."

Lancelot shook his head. "The curse didn't affect his magic. It made him infertile. Albina wanted her own children by Mirnov to be the only magician toymakers of the next generation. Without rivals, they would be the best in London."

Good lord. I could hardly believe it. She'd been as ruthless as Mrs. Trentham. To curse a man like that was almost as horrid as committing murder. She had stopped him from having children and in doing so had sown the seeds for her own life to be cut violently short.

Mr. Trentham had once claimed that his magic had been strong before the curse. But that could not have been the case. It was never strong. The description he'd given of how it used to work must have been how his wife's stronger magic behaved. He'd lied to make himself more powerful in my eyes. Or perhaps he'd come to believe it after repeating the lie so many times.

"Did Mirnov know?" Matt asked.

"He knew about the curse but not what it did. He assumed it affected the other magician's magic, and Albina never told him otherwise." Lancelot went to his mother and brother and placed a hand on Mrs. Shaw's shoulder.

She clasped it. "Albina always wanted more than what she had," she said sadly. "If only she was happy with this life, she would still be here. She might even have children by another husband. That Mirnov's seed is as weak as his cursed rival's." She and her daughters-in-law all spat into the ground again.

Matt signaled to Cyclops, and Cyclops emptied the shotgun of bullets. He pocketed them and leaned the gun against the caravan. Matt placed a hand to my lower back and steered me away.

"May I tell your fortune?" Mrs. Shaw called out. "I owe you for what you've told us. Would you like to know your future, Mrs. Glass?"

"Certainly not," I said.

"India." Cyclops jerked his head at Matt. "Don't you want to know what'll happen so you can avoid something bad?"

"The future cannot be changed," Mrs. Shaw said. "Only foretold so you can prepare."

Cyclops doffed his hat at her. "Then India's right. We don't want to know."

We traversed back across the common through the mud, avoiding the deepest puddles. We were thoroughly soaked, and the journey home was wretchedly cold, despite Matt wrapping me in the blanket and his arms.

The journey was also a silent one. He checked for anyone following us, but none did. I, however, was lost in my own thoughts. Matt had been right when he said everywhere we turned of late, the stakes were pegged to a magician's lineage. Louisa was marrying Oscar for his magic. Coyle had helped Mrs. Trentham marry another toymaker magician. She, or both of them, had killed so that she could be rid of her infertile husband and marry another. Albina had ruined a couple's life so she could bear London's only toymaker magician children.

No wonder Matt felt his artlessness keenly of late.

I snuggled into him and closed my eyes. "I love you," I murmured.

His arms tightened and he kissed the top of my head. "I love you too."

* * *

A WARM BATH was just what I needed. I soaked in it until the water cooled and headed downstairs. After a quick word with Mrs. Bristow about some housekeeping, I joined the others in the drawing room. Everyone was there. Spread out on their laps, tables and even the floor were dozens of newspapers. They must have purchased a copy of every daily.

They looked up on my entry and their grave faces told me everything I needed to know. The news was not good.

Matt folded up the paper he'd been reading and tucked it under another on the table beside him. "Feeling better?" he asked.

"Much."

"You should not have gone out in such weather," Aunt Letitia said in her snippiest tone. "You could catch your death."

"It's just rain, Aunt," Matt said.

"*Cold* rain."

Wisely, he didn't continue. He looked handsome with his semi-dry hair and fresh face, and when he smiled at me, my heart fluttered. Something was wrong, however. The smile he gave was the one he used when trying to distract me.

Instead of settling beside him, I picked up a newspaper and scanned the page. It had been left open at an opinion piece on magic.

"Just ignore it," Duke said before I'd read very far. "It's written by someone who doesn't know anything about magic."

"That journalist is an idiot." Willie threw her newspaper

on the floor and picked up another. After a moment, she threw it down too. "Another idiot. Why are there so many in the newspaper business?"

"Barratt ain't an idiot," Duke pointed out.

"He also doesn't work for the papers no more. He lost his job because they didn't want to see things from the magicians' side. They just wanted to sell more copies with this bull..." She glanced at Aunt Letitia. "Bull patty."

I smirked. Willie usually didn't care if her words offended anyone, even Aunt Letitia. Perhaps she was maturing. Now there was a promising notion, particularly for Brockwell.

I read to the end of the article and set it aside; I picked up another newspaper. It was the same, however, with another opinion piece on magicians and magic. The editor of the third newspaper had written a similar piece. The articles weren't questioning whether magic existed anymore. The argument had moved on to questions of ethics. Should magicians be allowed to practice their craft and sell magical wares? Should there be a limit placed on the sale of their goods? Guild masters were quoted, as were members of the public, but no magicians. It was as if they'd gone into hiding. More likely they'd just never been sought out and asked.

This third article included a suggestion. "The writer proposes that each guild keep a list of magicians skilled in their particular craft," I said. "That way if something goes wrong again, like with the automaton, it will be easy to find the culprit."

"That's absurd," Aunt Letitia said.

I bit my tongue. I didn't think it was a terrible idea, but it required more thought before I could give a considered opinion.

"I'm sure a list already exists," Matt said. "But it won't be the guilds that have it."

I lifted my gaze to his. He was referring to the government.

"Coyle's got one." Cyclops tapped his forehead. "Even if it's kept up here."

Aunt Letitia lowered her newspaper. "India, I think you ought to invite the Coyles to dine with us. Perhaps you can have some of your other friends too. Lady Louisa Hollingbroke, Lord Farnsworth…" She stared into the distance, no doubt searching for more names from the nobility to add to the list. Thankfully she didn't mention the Rycrofts.

"No," Matt said before I could. "Hope is welcome, but Coyle is not."

"But he's your cousin, Matthew."

"*She* is my cousin. He's a leech. He won't be invited to dinner."

"She's hardly going to come without him."

"Good," Willie said emphatically. "We don't want her here. She's a spiteful b—"

"Willie!" I cried.

She gave me a smug smile. "I was going to say bride."

Duke snorted. "You were not."

I wandered around the room, picking up newspapers, reading a few paragraphs then putting them down again. When I finally came to the table near Matt, I quickly picked up both newspapers, only to discard the one sitting on top. He didn't try to stop me reading the one he'd tried to hide, but I could feel his intense gaze on me as I read.

The article was a little different to the others. It took an uncompromising angle that suggested the dangerous magicians should be locked away in asylums for the safety of the public. It mentioned the danger posed if the magic was faulty, or if the magician was of a criminal nature.

"There's a lot of misinformation in that article," Matt pointed out. "For one thing, we know Mrs. Trentham used your spell, not her own magic, and no other magicians have access to it."

"Except we don't know that. My spell is missing. We never recovered the original."

He went on, undeterred. "There's no such thing as faulty magic. Everything the automaton did, it did because Mrs. Trentham made it."

"That gives fuel to the second part of the argument— when the magician has a criminal nature." I folded up the newspaper and returned it to the table. "No one will lock us away simply for being magicians. By that logic, they'd have to lock up anyone who carries a gun or knife. Or even people who keep rat poison in the house! Just because someone has access to a potential weapon doesn't mean they want to commit murder."

He pushed to his feet and strode to the mantelpiece where he faced the fire. "You have greater faith in the authorities than I do."

"If the worst happens, we'll go to America. Gabriel can come with us, since he'll have to flee England too or risk being imprisoned." I touched his shoulder until he looked at me. The hollowness in his eyes worried me. "But it won't come to that, because I'm going to strike a bargain with the government."

He frowned. "What kind of bargain?"

"I'm going to offer to make a list of all known magicians. If something ever goes wrong of a magical nature, then the list can be consulted and the appropriate magician brought to justice."

"Or they could use that list to round up every magician and imprison them."

"That's why they're not going to keep the list. We are."

Matt's smile started out slowly, tentatively, and finished as a grin. "That might be a solution everyone can work with."

* * *

MATT and I spent the next two days starting our list and writing a document on its aims, benefits, and the rules surrounding its use and storage. We wanted it all in order before we approached Sir Charles Whittaker and the home secretary.

During that time, the public's interest in magic didn't wane. If anything, it grew. Newspaper articles continued to print opinion pieces, although few were from the point of view of magicians. Not all the articles were against magicians. Indeed, some suggested they didn't deserve to be vilified for something that was not their fault. There were calls for magicians to be allowed to belong to craft guilds and freely trade, to allow the commercial marketplace to decide what to pay for their products and those of their artless competitors.

Those pieces were few and far between, however. Oscar's journalistic voice was conspicuous by its absence. He'd not been commissioned by any newspapers to write an article, despite his experience. The reason was revealed the following morning.

He'd been too busy getting his book published.

A stack of copies first caught my eye as Aunt Letitia and I passed a bookshop window. The bright orange and black cover with the elaborate gilded border was striking enough, but the title would see the book fly off the shelves.

THE BOOK OF MAGIC it said in large type. The subtitle stated it was a book about "The facts, myths, histories and rites of sorcery in England and around the world as written by a modern magician."

I purchased a copy and started reading on the way home. Upon arrival, I raced up to Matt's office where Bristow said he was working. I deposited the book on his desk.

"We need to visit Oscar," I announced.

He read the cover then flipped to the first page and began reading. "This will create even more of a sensation."

I perched on the edge of the desk. "I suppose that's the

whole point. He decided to rush through its publication to take advantage of the current press."

Matt continued to read. "Nash's chapter on magical history is written in a rather dry style, although the content is fascinating. I hope he doesn't suffer for his contribution. I'd hate for him to lose his position at the university."

"If anyone suffers, it will be the book's author. I hope Oscar is ready for the backlash."

Matt turned the page. "He's mad to put his name on it."

"It would be cowardly of him not to, and no matter what you think of him, he's no coward. Nor is Louisa. I doubt she would let Oscar publish it under a pseudonym."

"That's because she doesn't have to bear the brunt of the reaction. He will. They're not married yet, and I'm beginning to think they may never be." He placed the book on the desk and tapped the cover. "He should have secured her before this was published. Now she has no reason to go through with the marriage."

"You think she'd break off the engagement? Why?"

He indicated the book. "That's what she wanted. By being engaged to him, she has been able to be at his side, ensuring he finished it quickly. She has also funded it, I expect, and supported him after he lost his job at the *Gazette*. But now, what else is in the marriage for her?"

I shrugged. "The hope that her children by him will be magical? Isn't that what we've always supposed she wanted from him?"

"Let's find out, shall we?" He rose and strode past me to the door, only to turn back and grab the book off the desk.

I had to walk quickly to keep up with his pace. His keen-ness to leave probably wasn't so much because he wanted to see Oscar, but more because he was desperate to get out of the house again.

I insisted he dress like a coachman and sneak out to the coach house where he could instruct Woodall to take the day off. Fifteen minutes later, he drove the carriage around to the front where I climbed in alone. I was pleased to see Willie seated on one side of him and Duke on the other. Willie had a blanket over her lap and I wondered if she clutched her gun beneath it.

The drive to Louisa's house was uneventful, thankfully. Duke and Willie remained with the horses and carriage while Matt and I entered the house. As we expected, we found Oscar there too. They were all smiles as they shared a bottle of Bollinger Champagne.

Oscar indicated Matt's clothes. "Slumming it, Glass?" He didn't wait for Matt to answer, but instead tapped the rim of the crystal flute clutched in his ink-stained fingers. "Care for a glass?"

"It's a little early in the day for me," I said.

Matt simply said, "No. Congratulations, by the way."

Oscar eyed him carefully. "Is this the point where you berate me? Tell me what a fool I am for endangering the lives of all magicians?"

"You seem to have worked that out on your own."

Oscar chuckled. I suspected he was already a little drunk. "No, I was merely saying what you are thinking. I know you've never been in favor of the book."

Matt's scowl darkened. Perhaps I shouldn't have brought him after all. He'd been cooped up in the house so long, I was beginning to worry that he'd gone a little mad.

Louisa flitted from the drinks trolley, where she refilled her glass, to the sofa. "Come now, let's set aside our differences. Today is a unique day, whatever you may think of the book." She raised her glass.

Oscar touched his glass to hers and they both sipped.

Matt continued to scowl. I was worried he might not be able to contain his anger much longer. Perhaps we ought to get this meeting over with quickly and leave.

"Did you decide to bring forward the book's release to

coincide with all the recent press surrounding magic?" I asked.

Oscar grinned, looking very pleased with himself. "Since the book was finished, I asked the printer and he agreed. The good thing about being an ink magician is I can write rather fast. As fast as my thoughts form. And I make very few mistakes."

Louisa bestowed a somewhat condescending smile on him, like a teacher would a child who'd finally accomplished something he'd been struggling to achieve. "Oscar has been working like a demon since his dismissal from *The Weekly Gazette*. It was scheduled to be printed next week, but everything changed when we saw the reports in the newspapers. Thank goodness for that Trentham woman. If it weren't for her magical automaton murdering her husband then we would have needed to find a way to get the bookshops to stock it, but as it turned out, they want more copies than we have."

"You do realize Mrs. Trentham died," Matt growled. "And *she* murdered her husband with the automaton. It did not act of its own accord."

Louisa waved the hand holding the glass. A little Champagne sloshed over the sides. "The point is, we don't need to do any publicity for the book. It will sell itself."

"Thank goodness for losing one's job so I could finish the thing!" Oscar clinked his glass to Louisa's again. "Now that it's all over, I think I'll ask for my job back. I miss it."

"Oh, don't do that," she said.

"Why not? You always said you don't mind if I continue to work."

"Yes, but not there."

He blinked at her. "What's wrong with the *Gazette*?"

"They dismissed you. They don't want you working there anymore."

"That was before. Now that magic is being talked about

C.J. ARCHER

openly, they'll want me back to write from a unique perspective. I'll speak to the editor tomorrow."

"No!" Her vehemence seemed to surprise even her. She pressed a hand to her chest. "Don't do that, Oscar."

He frowned. "Why don't you want me working at the *Gazette*?"

She turned to him and took his hand. He snatched it away and she sighed. "Stop acting like a child. All I'm saying is there's a lot of water under the bridge between you and the *Gazette*'s editors. Don't you wish to start afresh? Somewhere nobody knows you?"

"No. And one or two people aside, the rest of the *Gazette* staff are magnificent, dedicated, intelligent individuals. I think they'd be happy to have me back to write about magic from my perspective as a magician."

Louisa's smile became strained. "Let me speak to some people. My father was friends with a publisher of a magazine. I'm sure he'll do a favor for me and hire you."

Oscar turned away from her. "I'd rather find my own work, and I wish to return to the *Gazette*, if they'll have me."

"Well they won't, will they? They dismissed you. Save yourself the bother and don't speak to them."

"You don't know they won't rehire me. You can't know." His jaw hardened. "Can you?"

She sipped.

"Louisa! Why can't I go back to the *Gazette*?"

She swallowed. "You were dismissed and nobody likes a groveler."

Oscar's nostrils flared "Why are you avoiding looking at me?"

She looked up and held his gaze.

"Did you have me dismissed?" he snapped.

She swallowed.

"DID YOU?"

She jumped, sloshing Champagne over the sides of her

254

glass. She switched it to her other hand and shook the spilled droplets from her fingers. She did not take her gaze off him. "It would have taken you an age to finish the book if you continued to work there. The newspaper was taking up too much of your time. This way you could concentrate on it fully, without distraction."

"Without distraction," he bit off. "You've kept me holed up here, working my fingers to the bone, with hardly any sleep. And now I discover *you* had me dismissed!"

"I'll get you other employment, Oscar. Stop being silly. The book is all that matters."

"It is not all that matters! Not to me. And don't try to find me other employment. I can find something without you and your bloody self-important connections looking down on me."

"Nobody looks down on you." She plucked the flute from his hand. "Perhaps you've had enough to drink."

For a moment, I thought he'd snatch it back, but instead he seemed to recall they weren't alone. He adjusted his tie and tugged on his cuffs. "We don't usually fight like this. It's just the surprise of learning that my fiancée has been manipulating my life without my knowledge. We do love one another, don't we, darling."

Louisa sat with a smile plastered to her face. The moment stretched and awkward silence filled it.

Oscar cleared his throat. "Perhaps not love but we're fond of one another. Deeply fond. And, of course, there are mutual benefits to our union. We both want it."

The more he spoke, the more he sounded like he was trying to convince himself. Or was he trying to convince her?

"We look forward to the wedding." As soon as I said it, I wished I could take it back. I was no longer sure there would be a wedding.

Matt, however, didn't seem to see the problem with my

question. "Now that the book is released, you'll want to focus on the happy occasion next."

"Certainly," Oscar said with a great deal of enthusiasm. "We're looking forward to it, aren't we, my dear?" He took Louisa's hand in his. She grimaced.

Matt rose and buttoned up his jacket.

"Going already?" Oscar asked, also rising. "Please stay. We enjoy your company."

"Yes, tell us about Fabian," Louisa said, turning to me. "How is he? Have you seen him recently? Is he well?"

Oscar huffed out a harsh laugh. "Do you care about me as much as you do about him?"

"Don't be so childish," she spat.

"Me? Childish? You're the one who's in love with another man who doesn't want you. That's the height of silliness."

Louisa drained her glass, stood and headed for the drinks trolley.

Matt signaled that we should leave. I gladly followed him out. Their relationship was not a healthy one, and I worried for their future if they went through with the wedding.

Oscar's angry voice traveled down the stairs with us. "*Do you love him? Or do you prefer him because his magic is stronger than mine? Is it because you wish to have children with iron magic instead of useless ink magic?*"

It was a relief to leave their bickering behind, but as the front door closed behind us, a thought occurred to me. "Coachman!" I called out as Matt settled on the driver's seat. "I'd like to make a stop on the way home."

"Certainly, Mrs. Glass," he said with mock seriousness. "Do you wish to stop at Lowell and Son to buy your husband a gift? They make fine gloves and Mr. Glass is a fine fellow. He deserves it."

"You shouldn't listen to idle gossip. There'll be no shopping for my husband today. I'd like to stop at Mr. Charbonneau's residence."

Matt touched the brim of his hat. "Right you are, Mrs. Glass. And might I say how lovely you look today."

Willie, standing beside me with her hand on the open door, rolled her eyes. "Sometimes you two make me sick."

So much for her maturing.

CHAPTER 16

Fabian deserved to be kept informed of the final developments in the Trentham investigation, and I also wanted to discuss Oscar's book and the newspaper articles with him. As the most knowledgeable magician of my acquaintance, his opinion was important to me. His first question upon seeing me, however, was about the stolen spell.

"Has the original been recovered?" he asked after he got over his surprise at seeing Matt dressed in a coachman's great coat.

"Unfortunately not," I said as I led the way into the drawing room. I stood by the fire and removed my gloves. The heat thawed my frozen fingers in an instant.

"Are you sure you didn't make another copy before it was stolen?" Matt asked.

"Of course I am sure!" Fabian drew in a deep breath and put up a hand in apology. "I am sorry. I should not have shouted. I am upset."

"Of course you are," I said gently. "I am too."

"What is the inspector doing about it? Has he searched Coyle's residence?"

"No."

"Why not?"

"Because he doesn't have enough evidence," Matt cut in. He sounded a little irritated with Fabian, most likely because he didn't like me being hounded with questions. "Even if he did, the spell is probably somewhere no one will find it. Not to mention Coyle would have made copies by now."

"So we just give up? We do not confront Coyle?"

Matt squared up to Fabian. Next to the immaculately tailored suit Fabian wore and his perfectly combed hair, Matt ought to look subservient in his coachman's outfit, but it was the opposite. His height and manner gave him an air of superiority that Fabian did not possess in that moment. Indeed, Fabian seemed quite distressed.

"I know it's not what you want to hear," I said gently. "But we can't pursue the spell. We must accept that others are in possession of it."

"Coyle," he bit off.

I sat down, a signal for Fabian and Matt to sit too. "We have to hope he's content to possess it and not try to find someone to use it in a way that will prove detrimental to the reputations of magicians."

"Like the Trentham woman."

"Like poor Mrs. Trentham."

"She was not 'poor,' India. She brought trouble on herself when she fell in with Coyle. She must take some of the blame."

He was right, and I couldn't entirely lay the blame at Coyle's feet. Mrs. Trentham had been greedy. Twice she'd coveted a husband who already belonged to another; not because she loved either of them but because they might be able to give her magician children. But how much of her situation had been her own fault and how much was Albina's curse on Mr. Trentham to blame for Mrs. Trentham's madness?

"One thing to have come out of this was a certainty that

we're doing the right thing in stopping our experiments," I said. "I know you want to continue to make new spells, Fabian, but we can't."

Fabian rested his elbows on the chair arms and steepled his fingers. "You are right. I agree. It is too dangerous." He smiled a satisfied smile. "Coyle will be disappointed that there will be no more spells for him to steal."

"What will you do now?" I asked.

"My brother has tasked me with making business contacts here in London." He pulled a face. "I do not like the iron business, but if I wish for my allowance to continue, I must pull my weight, as you English say." He winked. "I will also continue with magic research. According to Professor Nash, there are some excellent libraries with some very old books on the subject, but as many are in private hands, he has not been granted access. He hopes with my money and contacts, that will change. We will research together."

I rose and put out my hand. "I'm glad you've got something to do. I was worried about you being idle."

He took my hand and kissed it instead of shaking it. We walked out together, Matt behind us. "Have you read Mr. Barratt's book?" Fabian asked.

"Parts of it. Have you?"

"Yes. It is very good but aimed at the reader with no knowledge of magic. I do not mingle very much in public, but my staff tell me there is a lot of talk about magic among the people now. They are hungry for knowledge. Some are against magicians, of course, but many are curious and in favor. It is an exciting time to be in London."

I stayed silent. I didn't want to dampen his enthusiasm and remind him what could happen if those against magic had the loudest voices. He was right in that this could very well be an exciting time. But it was also worrying.

The butler opened the door and Matt strode ahead, down the front steps to the carriage.

Fabian touched my hand to halt me. "Why is he dressed like that? Is it a game you like to play?"

I laughed. "Something like that."

He kissed the back of my hand. "You are very tolerant of his strange American ways."

That only made me laugh more.

* * *

I CALLED on Catherine the following day, but Ronnie told me she wasn't at work. Their eldest brother was ill so she'd gone to help her father in the family shop. I found her there with both her parents and the youngest brother, Gareth.

Mr. and Mrs. Mason greeted me cordially, if a little stiffly. Catherine enveloped me in a warm hug, and Gareth flashed me a grin that no doubt melted the girls' hearts. Of the four siblings, he was the rogue, the one with the handsome face and easy manner, but the least discipline. His parents and older siblings despaired of him. I was surprised to see him in the shop. Usually he was out with the local troublemakers, in between running the occasional errand for his father. He appeared to be working, although he could have just been filling in time until something more interesting came along.

"How wonderful to see you, India," Catherine said. "How is everyone at home?"

"In excellent health, thank you. Is Orwell all right?"

"He has a head cold," Mrs. Mason said.

"It's just a little cough," Gareth told me. He grinned again, but this time it was more playful. "So how's the big pirate, India?"

Catherine glared at him. Mr. and Mrs. Mason pretended not to be listening.

"Nate is well," I said, using Cyclops's real name. "He's almost finished his police training. He was able to skip a lot of it on account of his experience. The rest has come easily to him, particularly memorizing all the laws." I decided to end it there. Any more and my enthusiasm might come across as forced.

I hoped for some guidance from Catherine as to how she wanted to proceed. Continue talking about Cyclops or leave the subject altogether? She had told us she had a plan that would see her parents accepting him, but if that plan was in motion, she didn't have the opportunity to tell me.

It was her father who broke the silence. "Go on, Gareth. You've dawdled long enough. That clock won't deliver itself."

The youth scooped up a box from the counter and tucked it under his arm. As he passed me, he winked. He opened the door but had to step aside as a man pushed past him as if he weren't even there. With his head bowed and hat pulled low, perhaps he hadn't seen Gareth.

Gareth made a rude hand gesture behind the man's back then left.

"Come in out of the cold, sir," said Mr. Mason. "How may I help you?"

The man looked up and my heart sank to my toes. It wasn't a customer. It was Mr. Abercrombie.

I tried to think of a polite way to excuse myself before he saw me, but it was too late. His sleek moustache twitched with dislike upon seeing me. Beneath it, his lips stretched with an unconvincing smile.

"I didn't know you were still friends with the Masons," he said.

"Why would you think that?" Catherine asked before anyone could respond. "Some may think me silly, but I can assure you, I am not fickle. India is my best friend and always will be." She hooked her arm through mine. "Good day, Mr. Abercrombie. We were just leaving."

"Wait." He removed Oscar's book from his coat pocket. "I assume you've read it, Mrs. Glass?"

"Yes," I said carefully. What was he getting at?

He tucked it back into his pocket and removed his pince-nez. He placed it on the end of his nose, wrinkling it so that it stayed on. With his slicked hair and sharp features, he looked like a rat that had just crawled out of the sewer. "You should tell your kind to be careful."

I bristled.

"Why?" Catherine asked.

"Honest, hard-working craftsmen are angry. We won't stand by and see our livelihoods suffer because of the likes of you, Mrs. Glass."

I took a step closer to him. Despite my rapidly beating heart and pounding blood, I smiled as serenely as possible. "Mr. Abercrombie, I do sympathize with all honest, hard-working men, but you are not one of them. You rode on the coattails of your name until your wealthy and titled connections learned that the quality of your timepieces had diminished since you took over the family business."

The muscles in his face moved all at once as if in a battle with each other. "Your father cheated! Your grandfather too!"

"Magic isn't cheating. It's a gift some are born with, just like beauty or intelligence."

He scoffed.

I walked off. "If I were you, I'd concentrate more on regaining your lost reputation than worrying about me. This obsession you have with me will ruin you."

"Obsession? Ha! And it will be *you* who are ruined. You're a witch. Do you know what they did to witches in the past?"

Despite every fiber of my being screaming at me to turn away, to ignore him, I stopped near the door. "Thankfully we live in a more enlightened era."

"Do we? Or are we a mere step away from locking witches up and throwing away the key?"

My bones chilled. I knew from his slick smile that my face

showed that his words rattled me. As much as I wanted to appear calm and unfazed, I could not hide my apprehension. He could very well be right.

"Get out!" Mrs. Mason snapped. "Get out of our shop!" At first I thought she was speaking to me, but her cold gaze bored into Mr. Abercrombie. She flapped her hands at him, shooing him.

"Pardon?" he spluttered.

"You heard my wife." Mr. Mason came around from behind the counter. "Leave this instant. You are not welcome here anymore."

Catherine opened the door and smiled at him.

Mr. Abercrombie sniffed. With a final glare for me, he scuttled past us and hurried along the pavement with short but brisk strides.

Catherine slammed the door closed. "Good riddance." She dusted off her hands as if she'd personally thrown him out.

Mrs. Mason drew me into a hug as warm as her daughter's had been. "Be careful, India. You must promise me you'll watch out for people like him."

I hugged her back, more fiercely than I ever thought I could hug her again. Despite her fear that I would bring danger to her door because of my magic, she was a long-time family friend. She would always look out for me, for my parents' sakes.

* * *

I TOOK great delight in telling the others after dinner how the Masons threw Mr. Abercrombie out of their shop. "It was extremely satisfying to see the shock on his face."

"Wish I'd been there," Cyclops said without looking up from his cards. We'd retired to the drawing room after dinner. Willie, Cyclops, Duke and I played poker, while Matt, Chronos and Aunt Letitia read.

"Seems you don't have much to worry about with the Masons no more," Duke said to Cyclops.

Cyclops dealt more cards to Duke after he discarded two. "What does throwing Abercrombie out have to do with them accepting me?"

"It means they're good folk."

"I know they're good folk."

"But they haven't accepted you yet."

"Don't mean they're not good folk. They're just thinking about Catherine's future and how hard it will be for her if she's with me."

Duke sighed. "You're too nice all the time. It's getting real irritating."

Willie threw down her entire hand, giving up. "Aye."

Both Duke and Cyclops pulled out of the round too, which meant I won. I raked in my winnings and added the matchsticks to my pile.

I looked to Matt, seated beside his aunt on the sofa. He was reading a newspaper while she dozed off, a book open on her lap.

Chronos sat on another chair by the fire, also reading. His book kept him wide awake. "This isn't a bad read. The chapter written by Nash lacks something, however. The fellow sounds like a lecturer of history." He chuckled. "But Barratt's chapters are engaging. He's a good writer with a style that appeals to the masses. It's no wonder the book is flying off the shelves."

"I hear it's going to have another print run," Cyclops said.

My grandfather was clearly pleased to see magic being openly debated. When it came to magic, he was keen for its possibilities to be explored, for the ancient wonders of it to be brought to life once again. If he had his way, not only would magicians live freely, we'd be creating new and spectacular spells every day, consequences be damned. Sometimes I admired him for his childlike wonder, but mostly I worried what he would do next.

I abandoned the game and took a turn about the room to stretch my legs. "Have you stopped selling the extension spell to other magicians?" I asked him.

"I have," he said.

"Can you look at me when you say that?"

He sighed and set down the book. "You're more overbearing than your grandmother, sometimes."

"I'm proud to be like her," I shot back, just to irritate him.

"I have stopped selling the extension spell to other magicians. Happy now?"

"Yes."

He returned to the book. "How is Charbonneau?"

"He's well, although the theft of our spell from his house upsets him still."

"I wouldn't worry if I were him. He would have made copies."

"He claims he didn't. Anyway, that's not what worries him, or us. We're worried about others using the spell for nefarious purposes."

"None can. No magician is strong enough to use it except on their own craft, which is very limiting." He smiled up at me. "None are as strong as you, India. You have Steele blood flowing through your veins."

I smiled. Praising my abilities as a magician was the closest he ever came to showing he was proud of me. Hoping it were otherwise would only lead to disappointment on my part. I'd learned that months ago.

"Coyle must hate this book," Chronos said, turning the page. "That's reason enough to hope it sells well. He must be worried his collection's value will drop."

Matt joined us and leaned against the mantelpiece. "If anything, it will increase. The more people who desire magical objects, the higher the price he can demand for the items in his collection."

"But he doesn't want to sell them," Chronos said. "He simply wants to covet them, and show them off to a select few friends."

I nestled into Matt's side and rested a hand on his chest over his heart. "I think Coyle covets information more than his collection. Now that information about magic is more readily available, he loses a little more of his power."

I wondered yet again about the connection between Lord Coyle and Sir Charles Whittaker. Although Sir Charles denied it, he had certainly shared information about me with Coyle. We'd heard him.

Matt kissed my temple. I tilted my head up and he kissed me on the mouth.

Duke made a sound of disgust in his throat. "You two make a man want to go out and get drunk."

Willie clapped him on the back as she passed him, heading for the sideboard. "Sounds good to me. What about you, Cyclops?"

Cyclops looked like he was about to decline but changed his mind. "All right."

Willie let out a whoop. "It'll be almost like old times. Matt, you want to make it four?"

"No thanks," he said. "Why not invite Brockwell?"

She shook her head so vigorously it was in danger of rolling off her shoulders. "No lovers allowed."

"What about Farnsworth?" Duke asked.

She stamped a hand on her hip. "Didn't you just hear what I said?" She tossed her head and marched out of the drawing room.

We all stared after her, jaws dropped. She and Farnsworth were lovers?

Aunt Letitia's eyes suddenly opened and she smiled. "I knew it."

Available from 7th September 2021:
THE SPY MASTER'S SCHEME
The 12th Glass and Steele novel

GET A FREE SHORT STORY

I wrote a short story for the Glass and Steele series that is set before THE WATCHMAKER'S DAUGHTER. Titled THE TRAITOR'S GAMBLE it features Matt and his friends in the Wild West town of Broken Creek. It contains spoilers from THE WATCHMAKER'S DAUGHTER, so you must read that first. The best part is, the short story is FREE, but only to my newsletter subscribers. So subscribe now via my website if you haven't already.

A MESSAGE FROM THE AUTHOR

I hope you enjoyed reading THE TOYMAKER'S CURSE as much as I enjoyed writing it. As an independent author, getting the word out about my book is vital to its success, so if you liked this book please consider telling your friends and writing a review at the store where you purchased it. If you would like to be contacted when I release a new book, subscribe to my newsletter at http://cjarcher.com/contact-cj/newsletter/. You will only be contacted when I have a new book out.

ALSO BY C.J. ARCHER

SERIES WITH 2 OR MORE BOOKS

Cleopatra Fox Mysteries

After The Rift

Glass and Steele

The Ministry of Curiosities Series

The Emily Chambers Spirit Medium Trilogy

The 1st Freak House Trilogy

The 2nd Freak House Trilogy

The 3rd Freak House Trilogy

The Assassins Guild Series

Lord Hawkesbury's Players Series

Witch Born

SINGLE TITLES NOT IN A SERIES

Courting His Countess

Surrender

Redemption

The Mercenary's Price

ABOUT THE AUTHOR

C.J. Archer has loved history and books for as long as she can remember and feels fortunate that she found a way to combine the two. She spent her early childhood in the dramatic beauty of outback Queensland, Australia, but now lives in suburban Melbourne with her husband, two children and a mischievous black & white cat named Coco.

Subscribe to C.J.'s newsletter through her website to be notified when she releases a new book, as well as get access to exclusive content and subscriber-only giveaways. Her website also contains up to date details on all her books: http://cjarcher.com She loves to hear from readers. You can contact her through email cj@cjarcher.com or follow her on social media to get the latest updates on her books:

Made in the USA
Monee, IL
20 June 2023

36429500R00163